SELECTED SHORT STORIES

DOVER THRIFT EDITIONS

Leo Tolstoy

DOVER PUBLICATIONS
GARDEN CITY, NEW YORK

DOVER THRIFT EDITIONS

GENERAL EDITOR: SUSAN L. RATTINER
EDITOR OF THIS VOLUME: JANET B. KOPITO

Bibliographical Note

This Dover edition, first published in 2017, is a republication of nine stories by Leo Tolstoy: "The Forged Coupon," "After the Dance," and "Alyosha the Pot" are reprinted from *The Forged Coupon and Other Stories,* Dodd, Mead and Company, New York, 1911; "A Prisoner in the Caucasus," "The Bear Hunt," and "Two Old Men" are reprinted from *Twenty-Three Tales by Tolstoy,* translated by L. and A. Maude, Oxford University Press, London, 1906; and "The Snow-Storm," "The Raid," and "The Godson," reprinted from *Master and Man and Other Parables and Tales by Count Leo Tolstoi,* E. P. Dutton and Co., New York, 1911. A new Note has been prepared specially for this edition.

International Standard Book Number

ISBN-13: 978-0-486-81755-2
ISBN-10: 0-486-81755-5

Manufactured in the United States of America
81755505   2022
www.doverpublications.com

Note

Count Leo [Lev Nikolayevich] Tolstoy was born in 1828 at the family estate in Yasnaya Polyana, 120 miles south of Moscow. Brought up by relatives after the death of his parents, Tolstoy attended Kazan University but left without finishing his studies. He joined the Russian army with his brother during the Crimean War in his early twenties (his nonfiction work *Sevastopol Sketches* [1855] is an account of his experiences). His travels to Europe and his readings in political philosophy and education led to his founding a number of schools for the children of peasants in Yasnaya Polyana. In 1862, Tolstoy married Sophia Andreevna Behrs; they had thirteen children, many of whom did not survive childhood. The marriage deteriorated over the years, and Tolstoy's final separation from Sophia took place when he was eighty-two. He died of pneumonia in the Astapovo train station in 1910 after secretly departing Yasnaya Polyana.

His major writings, in addition to the masterworks *War and Peace* (1869) and *Anna Karenina* (1878), include the fiction works *Family Happiness* (1859), *The Cossacks* (1863), *The Death of Ivan Ilyich* (1886), *The Kreutzer Sonata* (1889), *Resurrection* (1899), and the philosophical/religious works *What Is to Be Done?* (1886) and *The Kingdom of God Is Within You* (1894).

The nine tales collected here range from the mid-nineteenth century to 1911. Their subjects include the nature of bravery ("The Raid"); the hazards of traveling during the Russian winter ("The Snow-Storm"); a terrifying encounter in the wild ("The Bear-Hunt"); an adventure story concerning kidnapped soldiers, drawing from the author's time in the military ("A Prisoner in the Caucasus"); a story contrasting two men of disparate fortunes who make a pilgrimage to Jerusalem ("Two Old Men"); a tale of miracles that evokes both fairy tales and biblical wisdom ("The Godson"); a novella concerning the effects of a schoolboy's deception ("The Forged Coupon"); the life-altering effects of a man's encounter with incomprehensible cruelty ("After the Dance"); and, finally, the brief account of a life simply lived, making hardly a footprint on Earth—the good soul Alyosha the Pot ("Alyosha the Pot").

Contents

THE RAID

Translated by Constance Garnett

I

On 12th July Captain Hlopov came in at the low door of my mud-hut, wearing his epaulettes and his sabre—a full uniform, in which I had not seen him since I had arrived in the Caucasus.

"I have come straight from the colonel," he said in reply to the look of inquiry with which I met him; "our battalion is marching to-morrow."

"Where to?" I asked.

"To N——. That's where the troops are to concentrate."

"From there they will advance into action, I suppose?"

"Most likely."

"Where? What do you think?"

"I don't think. I am telling you what I know. A Tatar galloped up last night with instructions from the general—the battalion to set off, taking two days' rations of biscuit. But where, and what for, and for how long—that, my dear sir, we don't ask; we're told to go and that's enough."

"If you're only taking biscuit for two days, though, the troops won't be detained longer than that."

"Oh, well, that doesn't prove anything. . . ."

"How's that?" I asked with surprise.

"Why, they marched to Dargi taking biscuit for a week and were nearly a month there."

"And can I go with you?" I asked after a short silence.

"You can, of course, but my advice is, better not go. Why should you run any risk?"

"No, you must allow me not to follow your advice; I have been a whole month here simply on the chance of seeing an action, and you want me to miss it."

"Go, if you will. Only, wouldn't it be better to stay here, really? You could wait here till we came back, you could have some shooting, while we would go, as God wills! And that would be first-rate!" he said in such a persuasive tone that I really did feel for the first minute that it would be first-rate. I answered firmly, however, that I would not stay behind for any consideration.

"And what is there you haven't seen in it?" the captain went on, trying to persuade me. "If you want to know what battles are like, read Mihailosky-Danilevsky's *Description of War*—it's a fine book. It's all described in detail there—where every corps was stationed and how the battles were fought."

"But that's just what doesn't interest me," I answered.

"What is it then? You simply want to see how men are killed, it seems? . . . In 1832 there was a civilian here too, a Spaniard, I think he was. He went on two expeditions with us, wearing a blue cloak of some sort . . . they did for him just the same. You can't astonish anybody here, my dear sir."

Though I felt sore at the captain's putting such a despicable construction on my intentions, I did not attempt to set him right.

"Was he a brave man?" I asked.

"How can I tell? He used to be always in the front; wherever there was firing, he was in it."

"Then he must have been brave," I said.

"No, it doesn't follow that a man's brave because he thrusts himself where he's not wanted."

"What do you call being brave then?"

"Brave? brave?" repeated the captain, with the air of a man to whom such a question is presented for the first time. "*He's a brave man who behaves as he ought,*" he said after a moment's reflection.

I recalled Plato's definition of bravery—*the knowledge of what one need and what one need not fear,* and in spite of the vagueness and looseness of expression in the captain's definition, I thought that the fundamental idea of both was not so different as might be supposed, and that the captain's definition was, indeed, more correct than the Greek philosopher's, because if he could have expressed himself like Plato, he would probably have said that the brave man is he who fears only *what he ought to fear,* and not *what he need not fear.*

I wanted to explain my idea to the captain.

"Yes," I said, "it seems to me that in every danger there is a choice, and the choice made, for instance, under the influence of a sense of duty is bravery, while the choice made under the influence of a low feeling is cowardice, because the man who risks his life from vanity, or curiosity, or greed of gain, can't be called brave; while, on the other hand, a man who refuses to face danger from an honourable feeling of duty to his family, or simply on conscientious grounds, can't be called a coward."

The captain looked at me with rather an odd expression while I was talking.

"Well, I'm not equal to proving that," he said, filling his pipe, "but we have an ensign who is fond of philosophising. You must talk to him. He writes verses even."

I had only met the captain in the Caucasus, though I knew a great deal about him in Russia. His mother, Marya Ivanovna Hlopov, was living on her small estate a mile and a half from my home. Before I set off for the Caucasus, I went to see her. The old lady was delighted that I was going to see her Pashenka, as she called the grey-headed elderly captain, and that I could, like a living letter, tell him how she was getting on, and take him a parcel from home. After regaling me with a capital pie and salted game, Marya Ivanovna went into her bedroom and fetched from there a rather large black amulet, with a black silk ribbon sewn on it.

"This is our Holy Guardian, Mother of the Burning Bush," she said, crossing herself, and kissing the image of the Mother of God, before putting it into my hand, "be so kind, sir, as to give it to him. When he went to the *Caucasus,* you know, I had a service sung for him, and made a vow that if he were alive and unhurt I would have that image made of the Holy Mother. Now it's eighteen years that our Guardian Lady and the holy saints have had mercy on him. He has not once been wounded, and yet what battles he has been in! . . . When Mihailo, who was with him, told me about it, would you believe it, it made my hair stand on end. If I hear anything about him, it's only from other people, though; he, dear boy, never writes a word to me about his campaigns—he's afraid of frightening me."

It was only in the Caucasus, and then not from the captain, that I learned that he had been four times severely wounded, and, I need hardly say, had written no more to his mother about his wounds than about his campaigns.

"So let him wear this holy figure now," she went on; "I send him my blessing with it. The Most Holy Guardian Mother will protect him! Let him always have it on him, especially in battles. Tell him, please, that his mother bids him."

I promised to carry out her instructions exactly.

"I am sure you will like my Pashenka," the old lady went on, "he's such a dear boy! Would you believe it, not a year goes by without his sending me money, and Annushka, my daughter, has had a great deal of help from him, too . . . and it's all out of nothing but his pay! I am ever truly thankful to God," she concluded, with tears in her eyes, "for giving me such a son."

"Does he often write to you?" I asked.

"Not often; usually only once a year; when he sends money, he'll send a word or two, but not else 'If I don't write, mother,' he says, 'it means that I'm alive and well; if anything, which God forbid, should happen, they'll write to you for me.'"

When I gave the captain his mother's present—it was in my hut—he asked for a piece of tissue-paper, wrapped it carefully up and put it away. I gave him a minute account of his mother's daily life; the captain did not speak. When I finished, he turned away and was rather a long time filling his pipe in the corner.

"Yes, she's a splendid old lady!" he said without turning, in a rather husky voice. "Will God send me back to see her again, I wonder?"

A very great deal of love and sadness was expressed in those simple words.

"Why do you serve here?" I said.

"I have to," he answered with conviction. "The double pay for active service means a great deal for a poor man like me."

The captain lived carefully; he did not play; seldom drank, and smoked a cheap tobacco, which for some unknown reason he used to call not shag, but *Sambrotalik*. I liked the captain from the first; he had one of those quiet, straightforward Russian faces, into whose eyes one finds it pleasant and easy to look straight. But after this conversation I felt a genuine respect for him.

II

At four o'clock next morning the captain came to fetch me. He was wearing a frayed old coat without epaulettes, full Caucasian breeches, a white astrakhan cap with the wool shabby and yellowish, and he had an inferior-looking Asiatic sabre slung over his shoulder. The white Caucasian pony, on which he was mounted, held its head down, moved with little ambling paces, and incessantly shook its thin tail. Though there was nothing martial nor fine-looking about the good captain's appearance, it showed such indifference to everything surrounding him that it inspired an involuntary feeling of respect.

I did not keep him waiting a minute, but got on my horse at once, and we rode out of the fortress gates together.

The battalion was already some six hundred yards ahead of us and looked like a dark, compact heavy mass. We could only tell that they were infantry because the bayonets were seen like a dense mass of long needles, and from time to time we caught snatches of the soldiers' song, the drum, and the exquisite tenor voice of the leading singer of the sixth company, which I had heard with delight more than once in the fortress. The road ran down the midst of a deep and wide ravine, along the bank of a little stream, which was at that time "in play," that is to say, overflowing its banks. Flocks of wild pigeons were hovering about it, settling on its stony bank and then wheeling in the air and flying up in swift circles out of sight. The sun was not yet visible, but the very top of the cliff on the right side began to show patches of sunlight. The grey and whitish stones, the yellow-green moss, the dense bushes of Christ's thorn, dog-berries and dwarf elm, stood out with extraordinary sharpness, in the limpid golden light of sunrise. But the hollow and the opposite side of the ravine were damp and dark with a thick mist that hung over them in rolling uneven masses like smoke, and through it dimly one caught an elusive medley of changing hues, pale lilac, almost black, dark green and white. Straight before us, against the dark blue of the horizon, rose with startling clearness the dazzling, dead-white of the snow mountains, with their fantastic shadows and outlines that were daintily beautiful to the minutest detail. Grasshoppers, crickets, and thousands of other insects were awake in the high grass and filling the air with their shrill, incessant sounds. An infinite multitude of tiny bells seemed to be ringing just in one's ears. The air was full of the smell of water and grass and mist, of the smell, in fact, of a fine morning in summer.

The captain struck a light and lit his pipe; the smell of the *Sambrotalik* tobacco and of the tinder were exceptionally pleasant to me.

We kept on the side of the road so as to overtake the infantry more quickly. The captain seemed more thoughtful than usual. He did not take his Daghestan pipe out of his mouth, and at every yard gave a shove with his feet to urge on his pony, who, swaying from side to side, left a scarcely visible dark green track in the wet, long grass. An old cock pheasant flew up from under its very hoofs, with the gurgling cry and the whir of wings that sets a sportsman's heart beating, and slowly rose in the air. The captain did not take the slightest notice of it.

We were almost overtaking the battalion when we heard the hoofs of a galloping horse behind us, and in the same instant a very pretty and boyish youth, in the uniform of an officer, and a high white astrakhan cap, galloped up. As he passed us, he smiled, nodded, and waved his whip. . . . I had only time to notice that he sat his horse and held his reins with a certain individual grace, and that he had beautiful black eyes, a delicate nose, and only the faintest trace of moustache. I was particularly charmed at his not being able to help smiling when he saw we were admiring him. From that smile alone one could have been sure that he was very young.

"And what is it he's galloping to?" the captain muttered with an air of vexation, not removing his pipe from his lips.

"Who is that?" I asked him.

"Ensign Alanin, a subaltern of my company. . . . It's only a month since he joined from the military school."

"I suppose it's the first time he's going into action," I said.

"That's just why he's so happy about it!" answered the captain, shaking his head with an air of profundity. "Ah, youth!"

"Well, how can he help being glad? I can understand that for a young officer it must be very interesting."

The captain did not speak for a couple of minutes.

"That's just what I say; it's youth!" he resumed in his bass voice. "What is there to be pleased about before one knows what it's like! When you have been out often, you're not pleased at it. We've now, let us say, twenty officers on the march; that somebody will be killed or wounded, that's certain. To-day it's my turn, to-morrow his, and next day another man's. So what is there to be happy about?"

III

The bright sun had scarcely risen from behind the mountains and begun to shine on the valley along which we were marching, when the billowy clouds of mist parted, and it became hot. The soldiers, with their guns and knapsacks on their backs, walked slowly along the dusty road; from time to time I heard snatches of Little Russian talk and laughter in the ranks. A few old soldiers in white canvas tunics—for the most part sergeants or corporals—marched along on the side of the road, smoking their pipes and talking soberly. The wagons, drawn by three horses and piled high with baggage, moved forward at a walking pace, stirring up a thick, immovable cloud of dust. The officers rode in front; some of them were jigiting, as they say in the Caucasus, that is, whipping up their horses till they made them prance some four times, and then sharply pulling them up with their heads on one side. Others entertained themselves with the singers, who, in spite of the stifling heat, untiringly kept up one song after another. About three hundred yards in front of the infantry, on a big white horse surrounded by Tatar cavalry, rode an officer famous in the regiment for his reckless daring, and for being a man who would tell the truth to anyone's face. He was a tall, handsome man, dressed in Asiatic style, in a black tunic with embroidered borders, leggings to match, new, richly-embroidered, closely-fitting shoes, a yellow Circassian coat and a tall astrakhan cap tilted backwards on his head. Over his chest and back he had bands of silver embroidery in which his powder-horn was thrust in front and his pistol behind. A second pistol and a dagger in a silver sheath hung at his belt. Over all this was girt a sabre in a red morocco case edged with embroidery, and over his shoulder was slung a rifle in a black case. His costume, his manner of riding and holding himself, and every movement he made showed that he was trying to look like a Tatar. He even spoke to the Tatars riding with him in a language I did not know. But from the puzzled and sarcastic looks the latter gave one another, I fancied that they did not understand him either. This was a young lieutenant, one of the so-called jigit-gallants who model themselves on Marlinsky and Lermontov. These men cannot see the Caucasus except through the prism of the "heroes of our times," of Mullah-Nur, etc., and in every gesture they are guided not by their own tastes but by the example of these paragons.

The lieutenant, for instance, was perhaps fond of the society of ladies and persons of importance—generals, colonels, adjutants—I feel sure, indeed, that he was very fond of such society because he was excessively vain. But he thought it his imperative duty to turn his rough side to all people of consequence, though his rudeness after all never amounted to very much. And whenever a lady made her appearance at the fortress he felt bound to pass by her window with his boon companions, wearing a red shirt and with nothing but slippers on his bare feet, and to shout and swear as loudly as possible. But all this was not so much from a desire to offend her as to show her what splendid white legs he had, and how easy it would be to fall in love with him, if he chose to wish it.

Often he would go out at night into the mountains with two or three peaceable Tatars to lie in ambush by the wayside so as to way-lay and kill hostile Tatars who might pass by, and though he felt more than once in his heart that there was nothing very daring in this, he felt bound to make men suffer because he affected to be disappointed in them for some reason and so affected to hate and despise them. Two objects he never removed from his person; a large ikon on his neck and a dagger which he wore over his shirt, even when he went to bed. He genuinely believed that he had enemies. To persuade himself that he must be avenged on someone and wipe out some insult with blood was his greatest enjoyment. He was convinced that the feelings of hatred, revenge and disdain for the human race were the loftiest and most poetical sentiments. But his mistress, a Circassian, of course, with whom I happened to become acquainted later on, told me that he was the kindest and gentlest of men, and that every evening after jotting down his gloomy reflections he made up his accounts on ruled paper and knelt down to say his prayers. And what sufferings he underwent simply to appear to himself what he wanted to be! For his comrades and the soldiers were unable to regard him as he wanted them to. On one of his night expeditions with his companions he chanced to wound one of the hostile tribesmen in the foot with a bullet and took him prisoner. This man lived for seven weeks after this in the lieutenant's quarters, and the latter tended him and looked after him as though he had been his dearest friend, and when his wound was healed let him go loaded with presents. Later on, when on one of his expeditions the lieutenant was retreat-ing in a line of scouts and firing to keep back the enemy, he heard one among them call him by his name and his wounded guest came forward and invited the lieutenant by signs to do the same. The lat-ter went forward to meet his visitor and shook hands with him. The mountaineers kept their distance and did not fire at him; but as soon as the lieutenant turned his horse several shot at him, and one bullet grazed him below the spine.

Another incident I saw myself. There was a fire in the fortress one night, and two companies of soldiers were engaged in putting it out. Suddenly the tall figure of a man on a coal-black horse appeared in the midst of the crowd, lighted up by the red glow of the fire. The figure pushed through the crowd and rode straight to the fire. Riding right up to it the lieutenant leaped off his horse and ran into the house, one side of which was in flames. Five minutes later he came out with his hair singed and a burn on his elbow, carrying in his coat two pigeons which he had rescued from the fire.

His surname was Rosenkranz; but he often talked of his origin, somehow tracing his descent from the Varengians, and proving unmistakably that he and his fathers before him were of the purest Russian blood.

IV

The sun had passed the zenith and was casting hot rays across the baked air upon the parched earth. The dark blue sky was perfectly clear; only at the foot of the snow mountains whitish lilac clouds were beginning to gather. The still air seemed to be filled with a sort of transparent dust. It had become unbearably hot. When we had come half-way we reached a little stream where the troops halted. The soldiers, stacking up their rifles, rushed to the stream; the officer in command of the battalion sat down on a drum in the shade, and expressing in every feature of his face the full dignity of his grade, disposed himself for a meal with his officers. The captain lay down on the grass under the company's baggage-wagon. Gallant Lieutenant Rosenkranz and a few other young officers, squatting on outspread cloaks, were preparing for a carouse, as might be seen from the bottles and flagons set out around them and from the peculiar animation of the singers, who stood in a semi-circle round them, playing and whistling a Caucasian dancing-song to the tune of the Lesginka:

> "Shamil plotted a rebellion
> In the years gone by
> Tri-ri, ra-ta-ti
> In the years gone by."

Among these officers was the youthful ensign who had overtaken us in the morning. He was very amusing; his eyes were shining, his tongue faltered a little from time to time; he was longing to kiss everyone and to tell them all how he loved them. . . . . Poor boy! He had not learned yet that he might seem ridiculous in feeling so, that his frankness and the affectionateness with which he approached everybody might set other people jeering at him instead of giving him the affection he longed for so much. Nor did he know either that when he flung himself down on his cloak, and leaning on his arm tossed back his thick black hair, he was exceedingly charming.

Two officers were sitting under a wagon playing "fools," with a barrel for a card-table.

I listened with curiosity to the talk of the soldiers and the officers, and watched the expression of their faces attentively. But not in a single one of them could I discover a trace of the uneasiness I was feeling myself. Jokes, laughter, stories—all expressed the general carelessness and indifference to the danger before them. It was as though no one could conceive that some of them were destined not to come back along that road.

V

At seven o'clock in the evening, dusty and weary, we entered the fortified gates of the fortress of N——. The sun was setting and casting a slanting pink light on the picturesque batteries of the fortress and its gardens full of tall poplars, on the tilled yellow fields, and on the white clouds, which, huddling about the snow mountains as though in mimicry, formed a chain as fantastic as beautiful. The new crescent moon looked like a transparent cloud on the horizon. In the Tatar village near the fortress, a Tatar on the roof of a hut was calling all the faithful to prayer. Our singers, with fresh energy and vigour, broke out again.

After resting and tidying myself up a little, I went to see an adjutant of my acquaintance to ask him to inform the general of my intentions. On the way from the outlying part of the town where I was staying I observed things I had not expected to find in the fortress of N——. An elegant victoria, in which I saw a fashionable hat and heard chatter in French, overtook me. From the open window of the commander's house floated the strains of some "Lizanka" or "Katenka" polka, played on a piano that was wretchedly out of tune. In the tavern by which I passed I saw several clerks sitting over glasses of beer with cigarettes in their hands, and I overheard one of them saying to the other: "Excuse me . . . but as regards politics, Marya Grigoryevna is our leading lady." A Jew, with bent figure and a sickly-looking face, wearing a shabby coat, was dragging along a squeaky, broken barrel-organ, and the whole suburb was echoing with the last bars of "Lucia." Two women with rustling skirts, silk kerchiefs on their heads, and bright-coloured parasols in their hands, swam by me on the wooden footpath. Before a low-pitched little house two girls, one in a pink and the other in a blue dress, stood with bare heads, going off into shrill artificial giggles, evidently in the hope of attracting the attention of officers as they walked by. Officers in new coats, white gloves and dazzling epaulettes swaggered jauntily about the streets and the boulevard.

I found my acquaintance on the ground-floor of the general's house. I had only just had time to explain what I wanted, and he to reply that it could easily be managed, when an elegant carriage, which I had noticed at the entrance, rolled past the window at which we were sitting. A tall, well-built man, in an infantry uniform with the epaulettes of a major, got out of the carriage and went towards the general's.

"Ah, excuse me, please," said the adjutant, getting up, "I must go to tell the general."

"Who has come?" I asked.

"The countess," he answered, and buttoning up his uniform he ran upstairs.

A few minutes later a short but very handsome man, in a coat without epaulettes, with a white cross at his button-hole, came out on to the steps. Behind him came the major, the adjutant and two other officers. In the carriage, in the voice and in every gesture of the general one could see that he was a man well aware of his own great consequence.

"Bon soir, madame la comtesse," he said, putting his hand in at the carriage window.

A hand in a kid glove pressed his hand, and a pretty, smiling little face under a yellow hat appeared at the carriage window.

Of the conversation, which lasted several minutes, I only heard, in passing, the general say with a smile :

"Vous savez que j'ai fait vœu de combattre les infidèles, prenez donc garde de le devenir."

There was laughter in the carriage.

"Adieu donc, cher général."

"Non, à revoir," said the general, as he mounted the steps, "n'oubliez pas que je m'invite pour la soirée de demain."

The carriage rolled away.

"Here, again, is a man," I mused as I went back home, "who has everything a Russian can desire; rank, wealth, distinction—and on the eve of a battle which will end, God only knows how, this man is jesting with a pretty woman and promising to drink tea with her next day, just as though he were meeting her at a ball!"

I met there, at the adjutant's, a man who amazed me even more. He was a lieutenant of the K. regiment, a young man of almost womanish timidity and gentleness. He had come to the adjutant to pour out his anger and indignation against the persons who had, he said, intrigued against his receiving a command in the coming action. He said it was disgusting to behave in such a way, that it was unworthy of comrades, that he should not forget it, etc. Intently as I watched the expression of his face and listened to the sound of his voice, I could not help believing that he was in earnest, that he was deeply hurt and disappointed at not being allowed to fire at Circassians and to expose himself to their fire. He was as sore as a child who has been unjustly whipped. . . . I was utterly unable to understand it all.

VI

The troops were to set off at ten o'clock in the evening. At half-past eight I mounted my horse and rode to the general's, but as I thought both he and the adjutant would be engaged, I waited in the street, tied my horse to the fence and sat down on a projecting part of the wall, meaning to overtake the general as soon as he rode out.

The heat and glare of the sun had by now given place to the coolness of the night and the dim light of the new moon, which was beginning to set in a pale half-circle of light against the dark blue of the starry sky. Lights had begun to shine in the windows of houses and through the chinks in the shutters of the mud huts. The graceful poplars in the garden looked taller and blacker than ever standing up on the horizon against the whitewashed huts with the moonlight on their thatched roofs. Long shadows of the houses, trees and fences lay picturesquely on the shining, light, dusty road. . . . By the river the frogs kept up an unceasing noise;* in the streets I could hear hurried footsteps and talk, and the tramp of a horse; from the suburb floated the sounds of a barrel-organ, first, "The Winds do Blow," then some "Aurora Waltz."

I will not describe my musings; in the first place, because I should be ashamed to confess the gloomy images which hovered in haunting succession before my heart, while I saw nothing but gaiety and cheerfulness around me; and secondly, because they do not come

---

* The frogs in the Caucasus make a noise that has no resemblance to the croaking of Russian frogs.

into my story. I was so absorbed in my thoughts that I did not even notice that the bell had struck eleven o'clock and that the general and his suite had ridden by me. The rearguard was already at the gates of the fortress. I had much ado to get over the bridge in the crush of cannon, caissons, baggage and officers loudly shouting instructions.

When I had ridden out of the gates, I trotted after the troops moving silently in the darkness and stretching over almost a verst of road, and overtook the general. Above the heavy artillery and horsemen drawn out in one long line, above, over the guns, the officers and men, like a jarring discord in a slow solemn harmony, rose a German voice, shouting:

"Antichrist, give me a linstock!" and a soldier hurriedly calling: "Shevchenko! the lieutenant's asking for a light!"

A great part of the sky was covered with long, dark grey clouds; stars shone dimly here and there between them. The moon had already sunk behind the near horizon of black mountains, visible on the right, and shed a faint tremulous twilight on their peaks in sharp contrast with the impenetrable darkness wrapped about their base. The air was warm and so still that it seemed as though not one blade of grass, not one cloud was stirring. It was so dark that one could not distinguish objects quite near at hand; at the sides of the road I seemed to see rocks, animals and strange figures of men, and I only knew they were bushes when I heard their rustling and felt the freshness of the dew with which they were covered. Before me I saw a compact heaving black mass followed by a few moving blurs; it was the vanguard of the cavalry with the general and his suite. A similar black mass was moving in the midst of us, but it was lower than the first; this was the infantry. So complete a silence reigned in the whole detachment that one could hear distinctly all the mingling sounds of the night, full of mysterious charm. The distant mournful howl of the jackals, sometimes like a wail of despair, sometimes like a chuckle, the shrill monotonous notes of the grasshopper, of the frog, of the quail, a vague approaching murmur, the cause of which I could not explain, and all those faintly audible night-movements of Nature, impossible to interpret or define, blended into one full melodious sound which we call the silence of the night. That silence was broken by, or rather mingled with, the dull thud of horses' hoofs and the rustle of the high grass under the slowly-moving detachment.

Only from time to time the rumble of a heavy gun, the jingling of bayonets, subdued talk, or the snort of a horse, was heard in the ranks.

All Nature seemed filled with peace-giving power and beauty.

Is there not room enough for men to live in peace in this fair world under this infinite starry sky? How is it that wrath, vengeance, or the lust to kill their fellow men, can persist in the soul of man in the midst of this entrancing Nature? Everything evil in the heart of man ought, one would think, to vanish in contact with Nature, in which beauty and goodness find their most direct expression.

VII

We had been marching more than two hours. I felt shivery and began to be sleepy. The same indistinct objects rose dimly in the darkness; at a little distance a wall of blackness with the same moving blurs; close beside me the haunches of a white horse which paced along switching its tail and straddling its hind legs; a black in a white Circassian coat against which a rifle in a black case and the white stock of a pistol in an embroidered cover showed up distinctly; the glow of a cigarette lighting up a flaxen moustache, a beaver collar and a hand in a wash-leather glove.

I was bending over my horse's neck, closing my eyes, and I kept losing myself for a few minutes, till suddenly the familiar rustle and thud would arouse me; I looked about me and it seemed as though I were standing still while the black wall facing me was moving upon me, or that that wall was standing still and I should ride against it in another moment. At one such instant of awakening that unaccountable continuous murmur, which seemed to come closer and closer, sounded more loudly than ever; it was the sound of water. We had entered a deep ravine and were close upon a mountain stream which was at that time overflowing its banks.* The murmur grew louder, the damp grass was thicker and higher, the bushes were closer, and the horizon narrower. Here and there, against the dark background of the mountains, bright fires flared up and died down again in an instant.

"Tell me, please, what are those lights?" I asked in a whisper of a Tatar riding beside me.

"Why, don't you know?" he answered.

"No, I don't."

---

* The rivers in the Caucasus overflow their banks in July.

"That's the mountaineer has tied straw to a stake and will wave the fire about," he said in broken Russian.

"What's that for?"

"That every man may know the Russian is coming. Now in the villages," he added, laughing, "aie, aie, there'll be a fine upset; everyone will be dragging his belongings into hiding."

"What! Do they know already in the mountains that the detachment is coming?" I asked.

"Aie! aie! To be sure he knows! He always knows! Our folks are like that."

"Is Shamil, too, preparing to fight then?" I asked.

"Nay," he answered, shaking his head. "Shamil is not going to come out to fight. Shamil will send his chiefs and look through a tube from up above."

"And does he live far away?"

"No, not far. Yonder to the left it will be ten versts."

"How do you know?" I asked him. "Have you been there?"

"I have. All of us have been in the mountains."

"And have you seen Shamil?"

"Pich! Shamil is not to be seen by us. A hundred, three hundred, a thousand guards are round him. Shamil will be in the middle!" he said with an expression of servile admiration.

Glancing upwards into the sky, which had grown clearer, one could already discern a light in the east, and the Pleiades were already sinking to the horizon; but in the ravine along which we were marching it was damp and dark.

Suddenly, a little in front of us, several little lights began to glimmer, and at the same instant bullets whizzed by us with a sharp ping, and in the stillness all around us we heard shots in the distance and a loud piercing shriek. It was the enemy's advance picket. The Tatars of whom it consisted halloed, fired at random, and scattered in all directions.

All was silent. The general summoned the interpreter. A Tatar in a white Circassian coat rode up to him and, gesticulating and whispering, talked to him about something for rather a long time.

"Colonel Hasanov, give the orders that the line of scouts move into more open formation," said the general, in a quiet, drawling, but very distinct voice.

The detachment had reached the river. The black mountains of the ravine were left behind; it began to grow light. The sky, upon which the pale, dim stars were hardly visible, seemed to be higher;

the red glow of dawn began gleaming in the east; a fresh penetrating breeze sprang up from the west, and a shimmering mist rose like steam over the noisy river.

VIII

The guide pointed out the ford; the vanguard of the cavalry and the general with his suite followed. The water rose breast-high about the horses and rushed with extraordinary force between the white stones, which, in some places, were visible at the surface, and formed swirling, foaming eddies round the horses' legs. The horses, startled by the noise of the water, threw up their heads and pricked up their ears, but stepped steadily and warily over the uneven bottom against the current. Their riders lifted up their legs and their guns. The infantry soldiers, wearing literally nothing but their shirts, held their muskets above the water with their clothes and their knapsacks slung upon them. The men linked themselves arm-in-arm in lines of twenty, and one could see, by the strained expression of their faces, the effort with which they withstood the current. The artillery riders, with a loud shout, urged their horses into the water at a trot. The cannon and the green caissons, over which the water splashed from time to time, rumbled over the stony bottom; but the sturdy Cossack horses, pulling all together, and churning the water into foam, with wet tails and manes struggled out on the other side.

As soon as the crossing was over the general's face suddenly showed a certain gravity and thoughtfulness. He turned his horse, and with the cavalry trotted across a wide glade, shut in by woods, which stretched before us. The Cossack cavalry scouts scattered along the edge of the wood. We caught sight of a man on foot, in the wood, wearing a Circassian coat and cap; then a second . . . and a third. One of the officers said: "There are the Tatars." Then there was a puff of smoke from behind a tree . . . a shot . . . and another. Our volleys drowned the sound of the enemy's firing. Only now and then a bullet whizzing by with a deliberate note like the sound of a bee showed that all the firing was not on our side. Then the infantry at a run, and the artillery at a quick trot, passed through the line of scouts. We heard the deep bass notes of the cannon, the metallic click of the ejected cartridges, the hissing of shells, the crack of the musketry. The cavalry, the infantry and artillery were to be seen on all sides of the glade. The smoke of the cannon, of the shells and of the muskets melted away in the greenness of the wood and mingled with the mist. Colonel Hasanov galloped up to the general and pulled his horse up sharply.

"Your Excellency," he said, raising his hand to his Circassian cap, "give the order for the cavalry to charge; there are the flags." And he pointed with his whip to some Tatars on horseback, before whom two men were riding with red and blue rags on sticks.

"Very well, Ivan Mihailovitch," said the general.

The colonel immediately wheeled his horse round, waved his sabre in the air and shouted:

"Hurrah!"

"Hurrah! Hurrah! Hurrah!" rang out in the ranks, and the cavalry flew after him.

Everybody watched eagerly; there was one flag, then another, a third, and a fourth. . . .

The enemy did not await the attack; they vanished into the wood and opened fire from there. Bullets flew more thickly.

"Quel charmant coup d'œil!" said the general, rising lightly in the saddle, in the English fashion, on his black slender-legged horse.

"Charmant," answered the major, rolling his rs, and flicking his horse with a whip he rode up to the general. "C'est un vrai plaisir que la guerre dans un aussi beau pays," he said.

"Et surtout en bonne compagnie," added the general with an affable smile.

The major bowed.

At that moment, with a rapid unpleasant hiss, one of the enemy's balls flew by, and something was hit; the moan of a wounded man was heard in the rear. This moan impressed me so strangely that all the charm of the picturesque battle scene was instantly lost for me; but no one but me apparently noticed it; the major seemed to be laughing with greater zest than ever; another officer finished a sentence he was uttering with perfect composure; the general looked in the opposite direction and said something in French with the serenest of smiles.

"Do you command us to answer their fire?" the officer in command of the artillery inquired, galloping up to the general.

"Yes, scare them a bit," the general assented carelessly, lighting a cigar.

The battery was drawn up and a cannonade began. The earth groaned at the sound; there was a continual flash of light, and the smoke, through which one could scarcely discern the moving figures of the gunners, blinded the eyes.

The Tatar village was shelled. Again Colonel Hasanov rode up, and at the command of the general dashed into the village. The battle-cry rang out again, and the cavalry disappeared in the cloud of dust which it raised.

The spectacle was truly magnificent. To me, taking no part in the action, and unaccustomed to such things, one thing spoilt the impression: the movement, the excitement and the shouting all seemed to me superfluous. I could not help thinking of a man swinging his axe and hewing at the empty air.

IX

The Tatar village had been taken by our troops, and not one of the enemy was left in it, when the general with his suite, to which I had attached myself, entered it.

The long clean huts, with their flat mud roofs and picturesque chimneys, were built upon uneven rocky crags, among which flowed a little stream. Upon one side lay green gardens lighted up by the brilliant sunshine and filled with huge pear trees and plum trees; on the other side loomed strange shadows—the tall, perpendicular stones of the graveyard, and tall wooden posts, adorned at the top with balls and different coloured flags. (These were the tombs of the *jigits*.)

The troops stood drawn up in order by the gate. A minute later the dragoons, Cossacks and the infantry, with evident delight, scattered among the crooked by-ways and the empty village was instantly full of life again. Here a roof was being broken down; we heard the ring of an axe against hard wood as a door was smashed in; in another place a haystack was blazing, a fence and a hut were on fire and the smoke rose in dense clouds into the clear air. Here a Cossack was hauling along a sack of flour and a rug. A soldier with a gleeful face was pulling a tin pan and a rag of some sort out of a hut; another was trying with outstretched arms to capture two hens which were cackling loudly and fluttering against a fence; a third had found somewhere a huge pot of milk; he drank from it, and then with a loud laugh flung it on the ground.

The battalion with which I had come from Fort N—— was also in the village. The captain was sitting on the roof of a hut and was puffing clouds of *Sambrotalik* tobacco smoke from a short pipe with such an unconcerned air that when I caught sight of him I forgot that I was in an enemy's village and felt as though I were quite at home.

"Ah, you are here, too!" he said, observing me.

The tall figure of Lieutenant Rosenkranz darted hither and thither about the village; he was incessantly shouting commands and had the air of a man extremely worried about something. I saw him come out of a hut with a triumphant air; two soldiers followed him out, leading an old Tatar with his hands bound. The old man, whose whole attire consisted of a torn parti-coloured tunic and ragged breeches, was so decrepit that his bony arms, bound tightly behind his back, seemed to be coming off his shoulders, and his bare bent legs were scarcely able to move. His face, and even part of his shaven head, was deeply furrowed with wrinkles! his misshapen, toothless mouth surrounded by close-cropped grey moustaches and beard moved incessantly as though he were chewing something; but his red lashless eyes still had a gleam of fire and clearly expressed an old man's contempt of life.

Rosenkranz, through the interpreter, asked him why he had not gone away with the others.

"Where was I to go?" he said, looking calmly round him.

"Where the rest have gone," answered somebody.

"The *jigits* have gone to fight the Russians, but I am an old man."

"Why, aren't you afraid of the Russians?"

"What will the Russians do to me? I am an old man," he said again, glancing carelessly at the ring which had formed around him.

On the way back I saw the same old man without a cap, with his arms bound, jolting behind the saddle of a Cossack of the Line, and with the same unconcerned expression gazing about him. He was needed for the exchange of prisoners.

I clambered on to the roof and settled myself beside the captain.

"It seems there were but few of the enemy," I said to him, anxious to learn his opinion of what had just taken place.

"Enemy?" he repeated in surprise, "why, there were none at all. Do you call these the enemy? Wait till the evening and see how we get away. You'll see how they'll escort us home; how they'll spring up!" he added, pointing with his pipe to the copse which we had passed through in the morning.

"What is this?" I asked, uneasily, interrupting the captain, pointing to a little group of Don Cossacks which had formed round something not far from us.

We heard in their midst something like a child's cry, and the words:

"Don't stab it! Stop . . . they'll see us. . . . Have you a knife, Evstigneitch? Give us the knife."

"They're sharing something, the rascals!" said the captain, coolly.

But at that very moment, with a hot, scared face, the pretty ensign ran round the corner, and waving his arms, rushed at the Cossacks.

"Don't touch it! Don't kill it!" he screamed in a childish voice.

Seeing an officer the Cossacks gave way and set free a little white kid. The young ensign was completely taken aback, he muttered something, and with a shamefaced expression stopped short before it.

Seeing the captain and me on the roof he flushed more than ever and ran lightly towards us.

"I thought they were going to kill a baby," he said with a shy smile.

X

The general with the cavalry had gone on ahead. The battalion with which I had come from Fort N—— formed the rearguard. The companies of Captain Hlopov and Lieutenant Rosenkranz were retreating together.

The captain's prediction was completely justified; as soon as we entered the copse of which he had spoken we were continually catching glimpses, on both sides of the road, of mountaineers on horse and on foot. They came so near that I could distinctly see some of them bending down, musket in hand, running from tree to tree. The captain took off his cap and reverently made the sign of the cross. Several of the elder soldiers did the same. We heard calls in the wood, and shouts of "Iay, Giaour! Iay, Urus!" The short, dry musket-shots followed one another, and bullets came whizzing from both sides. Our men answered silently with a running fire; only from time to time one heard in the ranks exclamations such as: "Where's *he** firing from?" "It's all right for *him* in the wood!" "We ought to use the cannon!"—and so forth.

The cannon were brought into line, and after a few shots from them the enemy seemed to weaken; but a minute later, at every step the troops advanced, the firing and the shouts and halloos were more incessant.

---

* The pronoun "he" is used by the Caucasian soldiers as the collective term for the enemy.

We had not gone more than six hundred yards from the village when the enemy's cannon-balls began to whistle over our heads. I saw a soldier killed by one of them . . . but why give the details of that awful scene when I would give a great deal to forget it myself?

Lieutenant Rosenkranz kept firing his own musket. He was not silent for a moment, and in a hoarse voice shouted to the soldiers, and kept galloping at full speed from one end of the line to the other. He was rather pale, which was extremely becoming to his martial countenance.

The pretty ensign was in ecstasy: his fine black eyes shone with daring; his lips wore a faint smile; he was continually riding up to the captain and asking his permission to dash into the wood.

"We shall beat them back," he said persuasively; "we shall, really!"

"No need to," the captain answered briefly; "we have to retreat."

The captain's company took up their position at the edge of the wood, and, lying down, kept off the enemy with their fire. The captain, in his shabby coat and draggled cap, slackening the rein of his white horse, sat in silence, with his legs bent from the shortness of his stirrups. (The soldiers knew, and did their business so well that there was no need to give them instructions.) Only from time to time he raised his voice and called to men who had lifted up their heads. There was nothing martial about the captain's appearance; but there was so much genuineness and simplicity that it made an extraordinary impression upon me.

"That's true courage," was the thought that rose instinctively within me.

He was exactly as I had always seen him, the same calm movements, the same quiet voice, the same guileless expression on his plain but open face; only in the unusual alertness of his glance could one detect the intentness of a man quietly absorbed in the work before him. It is easy to say "the same as always," but how many shades of difference I have observed in other people; one tries to appear more composed than usual, another tries to be sterner, a third more cheerful; but one could see by the captain's face that he did not understand why one should try to appear anything.

The Frenchman who said at Waterloo, "La garde meurt, mais ne se rend pas," and other heroes, especially French ones, who have delivered themselves of memorable utterances, were brave, and their utterances really are worth remembering. But between their bravery and the bravery of the captain there was this difference: that if, on any occasion whatsoever, some grand saying had stirred in my hero's soul, I am convinced that he would not have uttered it, in the first place, because he would have been afraid that in uttering the great saying he would be spoiling the great deed; and secondly, that when a man feels that he has the strength for a great action no word whatever is needed. This, to my thinking, is the peculiar and noble characteristic of Russian courage, and, that being so, how can a Russian help a pang at the heart when he hears among our young officers hackneyed French phrases that aim at the imitation of obsolete French chivalry?

Suddenly, on the side where the pretty ensign had been standing, was heard a shout of "hurrah!" neither loud nor unanimous. Looking in the direction of the shout I saw about thirty soldiers running laboriously over a ploughed field, with muskets in their hands and knapsacks on their backs. They kept stumbling, but still pushed on and shouted. In front of them the young ensign galloped, waving his sword.

They all vanished into the wood.

After a few minutes of shouting and musket fire a terrified horse ran out and soldiers appeared at the edge of the wood carrying the dead and the wounded; among the latter was the young ensign. Two soldiers were holding him up under the arms. He was as white as a handkerchief, and his pretty little head, on which only the faintest shadow of the martial elation of a moment before could be seen, seemed somehow fearfully sunk between his shoulders and drooping on his breast. Upon his white shirt, under his open coat, could be seen a small red spot.

"Oh, what a pity!" I said, instinctively turning away from this piteous sight.

"Of course it's a pity," said an old soldier who was standing beside me with a morose face, leaning on his musket. "He was afraid of nothing; how can anyone do so?" he added, looking intently at the wounded boy. "Still young and foolish—and so he has paid for it."

"Why, are you afraid then?" I asked.

"To be sure!"

XI

Four soldiers were carrying the ensign on a stretcher. A soldier from the fortress followed them, leading a thin, broken-down horse laden with two green boxes containing the surgical requisites. They were waiting for the doctor. The officers rode to the stretchers and tried to encourage and comfort the wounded boy.

"Well, brother Alanin, it will be some time before we dance with the castagnettes again," said Lieutenant Rosenkranz, going up to him with a smile.

He probably expected that these words would keep up the pretty ensign's courage; but as far as one could judge from the cold and mournful expression of the latter they did not produce the desired effect.

The captain, too, went up to him. He looked intently at the wounded boy and his usually unconcerned cool face expressed genuine sympathy.

"My dear Anatole Ivanovitch," he said in a voice full of affectionate tenderness, which I should never have expected of him, "it seems it was God's will."

The wounded boy looked round; his pale face was lit up by a mournful smile.

"Yes; I didn't obey you."

"Better say it was God's will," repeated the captain.

The doctor, who had arrived, took from the assistant some bandages, a probe, and other things, and turning up his sleeves with an encouraging smile went up to the ensign.

"Well, it seems they've made a little hole in a sound place," he said jokingly, in a careless tone; "show me."

The ensign obeyed; but in the expression with which he looked at the light-hearted doctor there was both wonder and reproach which the latter did not observe. He began to probe the wound and examine it from all sides; but, losing patience, the wounded boy, with a heavy groan, pushed away his hand.

"Let me be," he said, in a voice scarcely audible. "Anyway I shall die."

With those words he sank upon his back, and five minutes later when I approached the group standing round him and asked a soldier how the ensign was, he answered me, "He's passing away."

XII

It was late when the detachment, formed into a wide column, marched, singing, up to the fortress. The sun had set behind the ridge of snow-mountains, and was shedding its last rosy light on a long filmy cloud which lingered on the clear limpid horizon. The snow-mountains were beginning to be veiled by a purple mist; only their topmost outlines stood out with marvellous clearness against the red glow of the sunset. The transparent moon, which had long been up, was beginning to turn white against the dark blue of the sky. The green of the grass and the trees was turning black and was drenched with dew.

The troops moved in dark masses with steady tramp through the luxuriant meadow. Tambourines, drums and merry songs were to be heard on all sides. The singer of the sixth company was singing at the top of his voice, and the notes of his pure deep tenor, full of strength and feeling, floated far and wide in the limpid evening air.

THE SNOW-STORM*

Translated by Constance Garnett

I

IT WAS PAST six o'clock in the evening, after drinking tea, that I set out from a posting-station, the name of which I have forgotten, though I remember that it was somewhere in the Don Cossack district, near Novotcherkask. It was quite dark as I wrapped myself in my fur cloak and fur rug and settled myself beside Alyoshka in the sledge. Under the lee of the station-house it seemed warm and still. Though there was no snow falling, there was not a star to be seen overhead, and the sky seemed extraordinarily low and black in contrast with the pure, snowy plain stretched out before us.

As soon as we had driven out of the village, passing the dark figures of some windmills, one of which was clumsily waving its great sails, I noticed that the road was heavier and thicker with snow, and the wind began to blow more keenly on my left, tossed the horses' tails and manes on one side, and persistently lifted and blew away the snow as it was stirred up by the sledge-runners and the horses' hoofs. The tinkle of the bell died away, a draught of cold air made its way through some aperture in my sleeve and blew down my back, and I recalled the advice of the overseer of the station that I should do better not to start that night, or I might be out all night and get frozen on the way.

"Don't you think we might get lost?" I said to the driver. But receiving no reply, I put the question more definitely, "What do you say, shall we reach the next station? Shan't we lose the way?"

"God knows," he answered, without turning his head. "How it drives along the ground! Can't see the road a bit. Lord, 'a' mercy!"

---

* This story is printed by the kind permission of Mr. W. Heinemann.

"Well, but you tell me, do you expect to get to the next station or not?" I persisted in inquiring. "Shall we manage to get there?"

"We've got to get there," said the driver, and he said something more which I could not catch in the wind.

I did not want to turn back; but to spend the night driving in the frost and the snow-storm about the absolutely desolate steppe of that part of the Don Cossack district was a very cheerless prospect. And although in the dark I could not see my driver distinctly, I somehow did not take to him, and felt no confidence in him. He was sitting with his legs hanging down before him exactly in the middle of his seat instead of on one side. His voice sounded listless; he wore a big hat with a wavering brim, not a coachman's cap, and besides he did not drive in correct style, but held the reins in both hands, like a footman who has taken the coachman's place on the box. And what prejudiced me most of all was that he had tied a kerchief over his ears. In short, the serious, bent back before my eyes impressed me unfavourably and seemed to promise no good.

"Well, I think it would be better to turn back," said Alyoshka; "it's poor fun being lost."

"Lord, 'a' mercy! how the snow is flying; no chance of seeing the road; one's eyes choked up entirely. . . . Lord, 'a' mercy!" grumbled the driver.

We had not driven on another quarter of an hour, when the driver, pulling up the horses, handed the reins to Alyoshka, clumsily extricated his legs from the box, and walked off to look for the road, his big boots crunching in the snow.

"Where are you going? Are we off the road, eh?" I inquired, but the driver did not answer. Turning his head to avoid the wind, which was cutting straight in his face, he walked away from the sledge.

"Well, found it?" I questioned him again, when he had come back.

"No, nothing," he said with sudden impatience and annoyance, as though I were to blame for his having got off the road, and deliberately tucking his big feet back again under the box, he picked up the reins with his frozen gloves.

"What are we going to do?" I asked, as we started again.

"What are we to do? Go whither God leads us."

And we drove on at the same slow trot, unmistakably on no sort of road; at one moment in snow that was soft and deep, and the next over brittle, bare ice.

Although it was so cold, the snow on my fur collar melted very quickly; the drifting snow blew more and more thickly near the ground, and a few flakes of frozen snow began falling overhead.

It was evident that we were going astray, because after driving another quarter of an hour we had not seen a single verst post.

"Come, what do you think," I asked the driver again, "can we manage to get to the station?"

"To which station? . . . We shall get back all right if we let the horses go as they please, they'll take us there; but I doubt our getting to the other station; only lose our lives, may be."

"Well, then let us go back," said I. "And really. . . ."

"Turn back then?" repeated the driver.

"Yes, yes, turn back!"

The driver let the reins go. The horses went at a better pace, and though I did not notice that we turned round, the wind changed and soon the mills could be seen through the snow. The driver plucked up his spirits and began talking. "The other day they were driving back from the next station like this in a snow-storm," said he, "and they spent the night in some stacks and only arrived next morning. And a good job they did get into the stacks, or they'd have all been clean frozen to death—it was a frost. As it was, one had his feet frost-bitten; and he died of it three weeks after."

"But now it's not so cold and the wind seems dropping," said I; "couldn't we manage it?"

"Warmer it may be, but the snow's drifting just the same. Now it's behind us, so it seems a bit quieter, but it's blowing hard. We might have to go if we'd the mail or anything; but it's a different matter going of our own accord; it's no joke to let one's fare freeze. What if I've to answer for your honour afterwards?"

II

At that moment we heard the bells of several sledges behind us, overtaking us at a smart pace.

"It's the mail express bell," said my driver; "there's only one like that at the station."

And certainly the bells of the foremost sledge were particularly fine; their clear, rich, mellow and somewhat jangled notes reached us distinctly on the wind. As I learned afterwards, it was a set of bells such as sportsmen have on their sledges—three bells, a big one in the middle, with a "raspberry note," as it is called, and two little bells pitched at the interval of a third up and down the scale. The cadence of these thirds and the jangling fifth ringing in the air was uncommonly striking and strangely sweet in the desolate dumb steppe.

"It's the post," said my driver, when the foremost of the three sledges was level with us. "How's the road, can one get along?" he shouted to the hindmost of the drivers; but the latter only shouted to his horses without answering him.

The music of the bells quickly died away in the wind as soon as the post had passed us. I suppose my driver felt ashamed.

"Suppose we go on, sir!" he said to me; "folks have driven along the road, and now their tracks will be fresh."

I assented and we turned, facing the wind again, and pushing on through the deep snow. I watched the road at the side, that we might not go off the tracks made by the sledges. For two versts their track was distinctly visible; then only a slight unevenness could be detected below the runners, and soon I was utterly unable to say whether there was a track or simply a crease blown by the wind in the snow. My eyes were dazed by watching the snow flying monotonously by under our runners, and I began looking straight before me. The third verst post we saw, but the fourth we could not find; just as before we drove against the wind and with the wind, to the right and to the left, and at last things came to such a pass that the driver said we were too much to the right; I said too much to the left; and Alyoshka maintained that we were going straight back. Again we pulled up several times, and the driver extricated his long legs and clambered out to seek the road, but always in vain. I, too, got out once to see whether something I fancied I descried might not be the road. But scarcely had I struggled six steps against the wind and satisfied myself that there was nothing but regular, uniform white drifts of snow everywhere, and that I had seen the road only in imagination, when I lost sight of the sledge. I shouted "Driver! Alyoshka!" but my voice I felt was caught up by the wind out of my very mouth and in one second carried far away from me. I went in the direction where the sledge had been—there was no sledge there. I went to the right, it was not there. I am ashamed when I remember the loud, shrill, almost despairing, voice in which I shouted once more, "Driver!" when he was only a couple of paces from me. His black figure, with his whip and his huge hat flapping down on one side, suddenly started up before me. He led me to the sledge.

"We must be thankful, too, that it's warm," said he; "if the frost gets sharp, it's a bad look-out. . . . Lord, 'a' mercy!"

"Let the horses go, let them take us back," I said, settling myself in the sledge. "They'll take us back, driver, eh?"

"They ought to."

He put down the reins, gave the shaft horse three strokes about the pad with his whip, and we started off again. We drove for another half-hour. All at once we heard ahead of us bells, which I recognised as the sportsman's set of bells, and two others. But this time the bells were coming to meet us. The same three sledges, having delivered the post, were returning to their station with their change of horses tied on behind. The three stalwart horses of the express sledge with the sporting bells galloped swiftly in front. There was only one driver in it. He was sitting on the box-seat, shouting briskly and frequently to his horses. Behind, in the inside of the emptied sledge, there were a couple of drivers; we could hear their loud, cheerful talk. One of them was smoking a pipe, and its spark, glowing in the wind, lighted up part of his face. Looking at them I felt ashamed of having been afraid to go on, and my driver must have had the same feeling, for with one voice we said, "Let us follow them."

III

Without waiting for the hindmost sledge to get by, my driver began turning awkwardly and ran his shafts into the horses tied on at the back of it. One team of three started aside, broke their rein, and galloped away.

"Ah, the cross-eyed devil doesn't see where he's turning to—right into people! . . . The devil!" scolded a short driver in a husky, cracked voice—an old man, as I inferred from his voice and figure. He jumped nimbly out of the hindmost sledge and ran after the horses, still keeping up his coarse and cruel abuse of my driver.

But the horses would not let themselves be caught. The old man ran after them, and in one moment horses and man vanished in the white darkness of the snowstorm.

"Vassily—y! give us the bay here; there's no catching them like this," he heard his voice again.

One of the drivers, a very tall man, got out of the sledge, unyoked his three horses, pulled himself up by the head on to one of them, and crunching over the snow at a shuffling gallop vanished in the same direction.

In company with the two other sledges we pushed on without a road, following the express sledge, which ran ahead at full gallop with its ringing bells.

"What! he catch them!" said my driver, referring to the man who had run to catch the horses. "If it won't join the other horses of itself—it's a vicious beast—it'll lead him a fine dance, and he won't catch it."

From the time that he turned back, my driver seemed in better spirits and was more conversational, and as I was not sleepy I did not fail of course to take advantage of it. I began asking him where he came from, how he came here, and what he was; and soon learned that he was from my province, a Tula man, a serf from the village of Kirpitchny, that they had too little land, and that the corn had given up yielding any crop at all ever since the cholera year. There were two brothers at home, a third had gone for a soldier; they hadn't bread enough to last till Christmas, and lived on what they could earn. His younger brother, he told me, was the head of the house because he was married, while he himself was a widower. Every year gangs of men from his village came here as drivers, though he hadn't himself ever been a driver before; but now he had gone into the posting service so as to be a help to his brother. That he earned, thank God, one hundred and twenty roubles a year here, and sent a hundred of them home, and that it would be a pleasant life, too, "but the mail men were a brutal lot, very, and, indeed, all the people in these parts were a rough lot."

"Now, why did that driver abuse me? Lord, 'a' mercy on us! Did I set the horses loose on purpose? Am I a man to do anyone a mischief? And what did he gallop after them for? They'd have got home by themselves. He's only wearing out his horses, and he'll be lost himself too," repeated the God-fearing peasant.

"And what's that blackness?" I asked, noticing several black objects ahead of us.

"Why, a train of waggons. That's a pleasant way of travelling!" he went on, as we overtook the huge waggons on wheels, covered with hemp sacking, following one another. "Look, not a man to be seen—they're all asleep. The clever mare knows the way of herself, there's no making her stray off the road. . . . I've driven with a train of waggons too," he added, "so I know."

Truly it was strange to look at those huge waggons, covered with snow from their sacking top down to the wheels, moving along quite alone. But in the corner of the foremost the snow-covered sacking was lifted a little on two fingers, and a cap emerged from it for an instant when our bells were ringing close to the waggons. The big, piebald horse, stretching its neck and dragging with its back, stepped evenly along the completely buried road, and rhythmically shook its shaggy head under the whitened yoke. It pricked up one snowy ear as we came up to it.

After we had driven on another half-hour, my driver addressed me again.

"Well, what do you think, sir, are we going right?"

"I don't know," I answered.

"The wind was this way, sir, before, but now we're going with our backs to the weather. No, we're not going the right way, we're astray again," he concluded with complete serenity.

It was clear that though he was very timorous, even death, as they say, is pleasant in company; he had become perfectly composed since we were a large party, and he had not to be the guide and responsible person. With great coolness he made observations on the mistakes of the driver of the foremost sledge, as though he had not the slightest interest in the matter. I did notice, indeed, that the foremost sledge was sometimes visible in profile on my left, sometimes on the right; it positively seemed to me as though we were going round in a very small space. This might, however, have been an illusion of the senses, just as sometimes it looked to me as though the first sledge were driving up-hill, or along a slope, or downhill, though the steppe was everywhere level.

We had driven on a good while longer, when I discerned—far away, it seemed to me, on the very horizon—a long black moving streak. But a minute later it was evident to me that this was the same train of waggons we had overtaken before. Just as before, the snow lay on the creaking wheels, some of which did not turn at all, indeed. As before, all the men were asleep under the sacking covers, and as before, the piebald horse in front, with inflated nostrils, sniffed out the road and pricked up its ears.

"There, we've gone round and round, and we've come back to the same waggons again!" said my driver in a tone of dissatisfaction. "The mail horses are good ones, and so he can drive them in this mad way; but ours will come to a dead stop if we go on like this all night."

He cleared his throat.

"Let us turn back, sir, before we come to harm."

"What for? Why, we shall get somewhere."

"Get somewhere! Why, we shall spend the night on the steppe. How the snow does blow! . . . Lord, 'a' mercy on us!"

Though I was surprised that the foremost driver, who had obviously lost both the road and the direction, did not attempt to look for the road, but calling merrily to his horses drove on still at full trot, I did not feel inclined now to drop behind the other sledges.

"Follow them!" I said.

My driver went on, but he drove the horses now with less eagerness than before, and he did not address another syllable to me.

IV

The storm became more and more violent, and fine frozen snow was falling from the sky. It seemed as though it were beginning to freeze; my nose and cheeks felt the cold more keenly; more often a draught of cold air crept in under my fur cloak, and I had to wrap myself up more closely. From time to time the sledge jolted over a bare, broken crust of ice where the snow had blown away. Though I was much interested in seeing how our wanderings would end, yet, as I had been travelling six hundred versts without stopping for a night, I could not help shutting my eyes and I dropped into a doze. Once when I opened my eyes, I was struck by what seemed to me for the first minute the bright light shed over the white plain. The horizon had grown noticeably wider; the black, lowering sky had suddenly vanished; on all sides one could see the white, slanting lines of falling snow; the outlines of the horses of the front sledge were more distinctly visible, and when I looked upwards it seemed to me for the first minute that the storm-clouds had parted and that only the falling snow hid the sky. While I had been dozing, the moon had risen and cast its cold, bright light through the thin clouds and falling snow. All that I could see distinctly was my own sledge with the horse and driver and the three sledges with their horses ahead of us. In the first, the mail sledge, the one driver still sat on the box driving his horses at a smart trot. In the second there were two men, who, letting go their reins and making themselves a shelter out of a cloak, were all the time smoking a pipe, as we could see from the gleaming sparks. In the third sledge no one was to be seen; the driver was presumably asleep in the middle of it. The driver in front had, when I waked, begun stopping his horses and looking for the road. Then, as soon as we stopped the howling of the wind became more audible, and the astoundingly immense mass of snow driving in the air was more evident to me. I could see in the moonlight, veiled by the drifting snow, the short figure of the driver holding a big whip with which he was trying the snow in front of him. He moved backwards and forwards in the white darkness, came back to the sledge again, jumped sideways on the front seat, and again through the monotonous whistling of the wind we could hear his jaunty, musical calling to his horses and the ringing of the bells. Every time that the front driver got out to search for signs of the road or of stacks, a brisk self-confident voice from the second sledge shouted to him:

"I say, Ignashka, we've gone right off to the left! Keep more to the right, away from the storm." Or, "Why do you go round and round like a fool? Go the way of the snow, you'll get there all right." Or, "To the right, go on to the right, my lad! See, there's something black—a verst post may be." Or, "What are you pottering about for? Unyoke the piebald and let him go first; he'll bring you on the road in a trice. That'll be the best plan."

The man who gave this advice did not himself unyoke the trace-horse, nor get out into the snow to look for the road; he did not so much as poke his nose out beyond the shelter of the cloak, and when Ignashka, in reply to one of his counsels, shouted to him that he'd better ride on in front himself as he knew which way to go, the giver of good advice answered that, if he were driving the mail horses, he would ride on and would soon bring them on to the road. "But our horses won't lead the way in a storm!" he shouted; "they're not that sort!"

"Don't meddle then!" answered Ignashka whistling merrily to his horses.

The other driver, sitting in the same sledge as the counsellor, said nothing to Ignashka, and refrained altogether from taking part in the proceedings, though he was not yet asleep, as I concluded from his still glowing pipe, and from the fact that when we stopped I heard his regular, continuous talk. He was telling a tale. Only once, when Ignashka stopped for the sixth or seventh time, apparently vexed at the interruption in his enjoyment of the drive, he shouted to him:

"Why, what are you stopping again for? Trying to find the road, indeed! Don't you see, there's a snow-storm! The land-surveyor himself couldn't find the road now! you should drive on as long as the horses will go. We shan't freeze to death, I don't suppose. . . . Do go on!"

"I daresay! A postilion was frozen to death last year, sure enough!" my driver retorted.

The man in the third sledge did not wake up all the time. Only once, while we were halting, the counsellor shouted:

"Filip, ay . . . Filip!" And receiving no reply, he remarked, "I say, he's not frozen, is he? . . . You'd better look, Ignashka."

Ignashka, who did everything, went up to the sledge and began to poke the sleeper.

"I say, one drink has done for him. If you're frozen, just say so!" he said, shaking him.

The sleeping man muttered some words of abuse.

"Alive, lads!" said Ignashka, and he ran ahead again, and again we drove on, and so fast indeed that the little sorrel trace-horse of my sledge, who was constantly being lashed about its tail, more than once broke into a clumsy gallop.

V

It was, I think, about midnight when the old man and Vassily, who had gone in pursuit of the strayed horses, rode up to us. They had caught the horses, and found and overtook us. But how they managed to do this in the dark, blinding blizzard, across the bare steppe, has always remained a mystery to me. The old man, with his elbows and legs jogging, trotted up on the shaft-horse (the other two horses were fastened to the yoke; horses cannot be left loose in a blizzard). On overtaking us, he began railing at my driver again.

"You see, you cross-eyed devil, what a . . ."

"Hey, Uncle Mitritch," shouted the story-teller from the second sledge, "alive are you? . . . Come in to us."

But the old man, making no answer, went on scolding. When he judged he had said enough, he rode up to the second sledge.

"Caught them all?" was asked him from the sledge.

"I should think so!"

And his little figure bent forward with his breast on the horse's back while it was at full trot; then he slipped off into the snow, and without stopping an instant ran after the sledge, and tumbled into it, pulling his legs up over the side. The tall Vassily seated himself as

before, in silence, in the front sledge with Ignashka, and began looking for the road with him.

"You see what an abusive fellow . . . Lord 'a' mercy on us!" muttered my driver.

For a long while after this we drove on without a halt over the
white wilderness, in the cold, luminous, and flickering twilight of
the snow-storm.

I open my eyes. The same clumsy cap and back, covered with
snow, are standing up in front of me; the same low-arched yoke,
under which, between the tight leather reins, the head of the shaft-
horse shakes up and down always at the same distance away, with its
black mane blown rhythmically by the wind in one direction. Over
its back on the right there is a glimpse of the bay trace-horse with
its tail tied up short and the swinging bar behind it knocking now
and then against the framework of the sledge. If I look down—the
same crunching snow torn up by the sledge runners, and the wind
persistently lifting it and carrying it off, always in the same direction.
In front the foremost sledge is running on, always at the same distance;
on the right and left everything is white and wavering. In vain the
eye seeks some new object; not a post, not a stack, not a hedge—
nothing to be seen. Everywhere all is white, white and moving. At
one moment the horizon seems inconceivably remote, at the next
closed in, two paces away on all sides. Suddenly a high, white wall
shoots up on the right, and runs alongside the sledge, then all at once
it vanishes and springs up ahead, to flee further and further away,
and vanish again. One looks upwards; it seems light for the first
minute—one seems to see stars shining through a mist; but the stars
fly further and further away from the sight, and one can see nothing
but the snow, which falls past the eyes into the face and the collar of
one's cloak. Everywhere the sky is equally light, equally white,
colourless, alike and ever moving. The wind seems to shift; at one
time it blows in our faces and glues our eyes up with snow, then
teasingly it flings one's fur collar on one's head and flaps it mockingly
in one's face, then it drones behind in some chink of the sledge. One
hears the faint, never-ceasing crunch of hoofs and runners over the
snow, and the jingle of the bells, dying down as we drive over deep
snow. Only at times when we are going against the wind and over
some bare, frozen headland, Ignashka's vigorous whistling and the
melodious tinkle of the bells with the jangling fifth float clearly to
one's hearing, and these sounds make a comforting break in the

desolateness of the snowy waste, and then again the bells fall back into the same monotonous jingle, with intolerable correctness ringing ever the same phrase, which I cannot help picturing to myself in musical notes.

One of my legs began to get chilled, and when I turned over to wrap myself up closer, the snow on my collar and cap slipped down my neck and made me shiver; but on the whole, in my fur cloak, warmed through by the heat of my body, I still kept warm and was beginning to feel drowsy.

VI

Memories and fancies followed one another with increased rapidity in my imagination.

"The counsellor, that keeps on calling out advice from the second sledge, what sort of peasant is he likely to be? Sure to be a red-haired, thick-set fellow with short legs," I thought, "somewhat like Fyodor Filippitch, our old butler." And then I see the staircase of our great house and five house-serfs, who are stepping heavily, dragging along on strips of coarse linen a piano from the lodge. I see Fyodor Fillippitch, with the sleeves of his nankin coat turned up, carrying nothing but one pedal, running on ahead, pulling open bolts, tugging at a strip of linen here, shoving there, creeping between people's legs, getting in everyone's way, and in a voice of anxiety shouting assiduously:

"You now, in front, in front! That's it, the tail end upwards, upwards, upwards, through the doorway! That's it."

"You only let us be, Fyodor Filippitch, we'll do it by ourselves," timidly ventured the gardener, squeezed against the banisters, and red with exertion, as, putting out all his strength, he held up one corner of the piano.

But Fyodor Filippitch would not desist.

"And what is it?" I reflected. "Does he suppose he's necessary to the business in hand, or is he simply pleased God has given him that conceited, convincing flow of words and enjoys the exercise of it? That's what it must be."

And for some reason I recall the pond, and the tired house-serfs, knee-deep in the water, dragging the draw-net, and again Fyodor Filippitch running along the bank with the watering-pot, shouting to all of them, and only approaching the water at intervals to take hold of the golden carp, to let out the muddy water, and to pour over them fresh.

And again it is midday in July. I am wandering over the freshly-mown grass of the garden, under the burning sun straight above my head. I am still very young; there is an emptiness, a yearning for something in my heart. I walk to my favourite spot near the pond, between a thicket of wild rose and the birch-tree avenue, and lie down to go to sleep. I remember the sensation with which, as I lay there, I looked through the red, thorny stems of the rose at the black earth, dried into little clods, and at the shining, bright blue mirror of the pond. It was with a feeling of naïve self-satisfaction and melancholy. Everything around me was so beautiful; its beauty had such an intense effect on me that it seemed to me I was beautiful myself, and my only vexation was that there was no one to admire me.

It is hot. I try to console myself by going to sleep. But the flies, the intolerable flies, will not even here give me any peace; they begin to gather together about me and persistently, stolidly, as it were like pellets, they shoot from forehead to hand. A bee buzzes not far from me, right in the hottest spot; yellow butterflies flutter languidly, it seems, from stalk to stalk. I look upwards, it makes my eyes ache; the sun is too dazzling through the bright foliage of the leafy birch tree, that gently swings its branches high above me, and I feel hotter than ever. I cover my face with my handkerchief; it becomes stifling, and the flies simply stick to my moist hands. Sparrows are twittering in the thickest of the clump of roses. One of them hops on the ground a yard from me; twice he makes a feint of pecking vigorously at the earth, and with a snapping of twigs and a merry chirrup flies out of the bush. Another, too, hops on the ground, perks up his tail, looks round, and with a chirrup he too flies out like an arrow after the first. From the pond come the sounds of wet linen being beaten with washing-bats in the water, and the blows seem to echo and be carried over the surface of the pond. There is the sound of laughter, chatter, and the splashing of bathers. A gust of wind rustles in the tree-tops at a distance; it comes closer, and I hear it ruffling up the grass, and now the leaves of the wild roses tremble and beat upon the stems; and now it lifts the corner of the handkerchief and a fresh breath of air passes over me, tickling my moist face. A fly flies in under the lifted kerchief and buzzes in a frightened way about my damp mouth. A dead twig sticks into me under my spine. No, it's no good lying down; I'll go and have a bathe. But suddenly, close to my nook, I hear hurried footsteps and the frightened voices of women.

"Oh, mercy on us! What can we do! and not a man here!"

"What is it, what is it?" I ask, running out into the sunshine and addressing a serf-woman, who runs past me, groaning. She simply looks round, wrings her hands and runs on. But here comes Matrona, an old woman of seventy, holding on her kerchief as it falls back off her head, limping and dragging one leg in a worsted stocking, as she runs towards the pond. Two little girls run along, hand in hand, and a boy of ten, wearing his father's coat, hurries behind, clinging to the hempen skirt of one of them.

"What has happened?" I inquire of them.

"A peasant is drowning."

"Where?"

"In our pond."

"Who? one of ours?"

"No; a stranger."

The coachman Ivan, struggling over the newly-mown grass in his big boots, and the stout bailiff, Yakov, breathing hard, run towards the pond, and I run after them.

I recall the feeling that said to me, "Come, jump in, and pull out the man, save him, and they will all admire you," which was just what I was desiring.

"Where? where is he?" I ask of the crowd of house-serfs gathered together on the bank.

"Over yonder, near the deepest pool, towards that bank, almost at the bath-house," says a washerwoman, getting in her wet linen on a yoke. "I saw him plunge in; and he comes up so and goes down again, and comes up again and screams, 'I'm drowning, mercy!' and again he went down to the bottom, and only bubbles came up. Then I saw the man was drowning. And I yelled, 'Mercy on us, the peasant's drowning!'"

And the washerwoman hoists the yoke on to her shoulder, and bending on one side, walks along the path away from the pond.

"My word, what a shame!" says Yakov Ivanov, the bailiff, in a voice of despair: "what a to-do we shall have now with the district court—we shall never hear the last of it!"

A peasant with a scythe makes his way through the throng of women, children, and old people crowding about the bank, and hanging his scythe in the branches of a willow, begins deliberately pulling off his boots.

"Where, where did he sink?" I keep on asking, longing to throw myself in and do something extraordinary.

But they point to the smooth surface of the pond, broken into ripples here and there by the rushing wind. It is inconceivable to me that he is drowned while the water stands just as smooth and beautiful and untroubled over him, shining with glints of gold in the midday sun, and it seems to me that I can do nothing, can astonish no one, especially as I am a very poor swimmer. And the peasant is already pulling his shirt over his head, and in an instant will plunge in. Everyone watches him with hope and a sinking heart; but when he has waded in up to his shoulders, the peasant slowly turns back and puts on his shirt again—he cannot swim.

People still run up; the crowd gets bigger and bigger; the women cling to each other; but no one does anything to help. Those who have only just reached the pond give advice, and groan, and their faces express horror and despair. Of those who had arrived on the scene earlier some, tired of standing, sit down on the grass; others go back. Old Matrona asks her daughter whether she has shut the door of the oven; the boy in his father's coat flings stones with careful aim into the pond.

But now Trezorka, Fyodor Filippitch's dog, comes running downhill from the house, barking and looking round in perplexity; and the figure of Fyodor himself, running down the hill and shouting something, comes into sight behind the thicket of wild rose.

"Why are you standing still?" he shouts, taking off his coat as he runs. "A man's drowning, and they do nothing. . . . Give us a cord!"

All gaze in hope and dread at Fyodor Filippitch, while leaning on the shoulder of an obliging house-serf he kicks off his right boot with the tip of his left one.

"Over there, where the crowd is; over there, a little to the right of the willow, Fyodor Filippitch, over there," says someone.

"I know," he answers, and knitting his brows, probably in acknowledgment of symptoms of outraged delicacy in the crowd of women, he takes off his shirt and his cross, handing the latter to the gardener's boy, who stands obsequiously before him. Then, stepping vigorously over the mown grass, he goes to the pond.

Trezorka, who had stood still near the crowd, eating some blades of grass from the water's edge, and smacking his lips, looks inquiringly at his master, wondering at the rapidity of his movements. All at once, with a whine of delight, he plunges with his master into the water. For the first minute there is nothing to be seen but frothing bubbles, which float right up to us. But soon Fyodor Filippitch is seen swimming smartly towards the further bank, his arms making a graceful sweep, and his back rising and sinking regularly at every fathom's length. Trezorka, after swallowing a mouthful of water, hurriedly turns back, shakes himself in the crowd, and rolls on his back on the bank. While Fyodor Filippitch is swimming towards the further bank, the two coachmen run round to the willow with a net rolled round a pole. Fyodor Filippitch, for some reason or other, raises his hands above his head, and dives, once, twice, thrice; every time a stream of water runs out of his mouth, he tosses his hair with a fine gesture, and makes no reply to the questions which are showered upon him from all sides. At last he comes out on the bank, and, as far as I can see, simply gives orders for the casting of the net. The net is drawn up, but in it there is nothing except weed and a few carp struggling in it. While the net is being cast a second time, I walk round to that side.

Nothing is to be heard but the voice of Fyodor Filippitch giving directions, the splashing of the water through the wet cords, and sighs of horror. The wet cordage fastened to the right beam is more and more thickly covered with weed, as it comes further and further out of the water.

"Now pull together, all at once!" shouts the voice of Fyodor Filippitch. The butt-ends of the beams come into view covered with water.

"There is something; it pulls heavy, lads," says someone.

And now the beams of the net in which two or three carp struggle, splashing and crushing the weed, are dragged on to the bank. And through the shallow, shifting layer of muddy water something white comes into sight in the tightly-strained net. A sigh of horror passes over the crowd, subdued but distinctly audible in the deathlike stillness.

"Pull all together, pull it on to dry land!" cries Fyodor Filippitch's resolute voice. And with the iron hook they drag the drowned man over the cropped stalks of dock and agrimony towards the willow.

And here I see my kind old aunt in her silk gown; I see her fringed, lilac parasol, which seems somehow oddly incongruous with this scene of death, so awful in its simplicity. I see her face on the point of shedding tears. I recall her look of disappointment that in this case arnica could be of no use, and I recall the painful sense of mortification I had when she said to me with the naïve egoism of love, "Let us go, my dear. Ah, how awful it is! And you will always go bathing and swimming alone!"

I remember how glaring and hot the sun was, baking the dry earth that crumbled under our feet; how it sparkled on the mirror of the pond; how the big carp struggled on the bank; how a shoal of fish dimpled the pond's surface in the middle; how a hawk floated high up in the sky, hovering over the ducks, who swam quacking and splashing among the reeds in the centre of the water; how the white, curly storm-clouds gathered on the horizon; how the mud brought on to the bank by the net gradually slipped away; and how, as I crossed the dike, I heard the sounds of the washing-bat floating across the pond.

But the blows of the bat ring out as though there were two bats and another chiming in, a third lower in the scale; and that sound frets me, worries me, especially as I know the bat is a bell, and Fyodor Filippitch can't make it stop. And the bat, like an instrument of torture, is crushing my leg, which is chilled. I wake up.

I was waked up, it seemed to me, by our galloping very swiftly, and two voices talking quite close beside me.

"I say, Ignat, eh . . . Ignat!" said the voice of my driver; "take my fare; you've got to go anyway, and why should I go on for nothing—take him!"

The voice of Ignat close beside me answered:

"It's no treat for me to have to answer for a passenger. . . . Will you stand me a pint bottle of *vodka*?"

"Go on with your pint bottle! . . . A dram, and I'll say done."

"A dram!" shouted another voice: "a likely idea! tire your horses for a dram!"

I opened my eyes. Still the same insufferable wavering snow floating before one's eyes, the same drivers and horses, but beside me I saw a sledge. My driver had overtaken Ignat, and we had been for some time moving alongside. Although the voice from the other sledge advised him not to accept less than a pint, Ignat all at once pulled up his horses.

"Move the baggage in! Done! it's your luck. Stand me a dram when we come to-morrow. Have you much baggage, eh?"

My driver jumped out into the snow with an alacrity quite unlike him, bowed to me, and begged me to get into Ignat's sledge. I was perfectly ready to do so; but evidently the God-fearing peasant was so pleased that he wanted to lavish his gratitude and joy on someone. He bowed and thanked me, Alyoshka, and Ignashka.

"There, thank God too! Why, Lord 'a' mercy, here we've been driving half the night, and don't know ourselves where we're going! He'll take you all right, sir, but my horses are quite done up."

And he moved my things with increased energy. While they were shifting my things, with the wind at my back almost carrying me off my legs, I went towards the second sledge. The sledge was more than a quarter buried in the snow, especially on the side where a cloak had been hung over the two drivers' heads to keep off the wind; under the cloak it was sheltered and snug. The old man was lying just as before with his legs out, while the story-teller was still telling his story: "So at the very time when the general arrived in the king's name, that is, to Mariya in the prison, Mariya says to him, 'General! I don't want you, and I cannot love you, and you are not my lover; my lover is that same prince.' . . . So then"—he was going on, but, seeing me, he paused a moment, and began pulling at his pipe.

"Well, sir, are you come to listen to the tale?" said the other man, whom I have called the counsellor.

"Why, you are nice and cheerful in here!" I said.

"To be sure, it passes the time—anyway, it keeps one from thinking."

"Don't you know, really, where we are now?" This question, it struck me, was not liked by the drivers.

"Why, who's to make out where we are? Maybe we've got to the Kalmucks altogether," answered the counsellor.

"What are we going to do?" I asked.

"What are we to do? Why, we'll go on, and maybe we'll get somewhere," he said in a tone of displeasure.

"Well, but if we don't get there, and the horses can go no further in the snow, what then?"

"What then? Nothing."

"But we may freeze."

"To be sure, we may, for there are no stacks to be seen now; we must have driven right out to the Kalmucks. The chief thing is, we must look about in the snow."

"And aren't you at all afraid of being frozen, sir?" said the old man, in a trembling voice.

Although he seemed to be jeering at me, I could see that he was shivering in every bone.

"Yes, it's getting very cold," I said.

"Ah, sir! You should do as I do; every now and then take a run; that would warm you."

"It's first-rate, the way you run after the sledge," said the counsellor.

VII

"Please get in: it's all ready!" Alyoshka called to me from the front sledge.

The blizzard was so terrific that it was only by my utmost efforts, bending double and clutching the skirts of my coat in both hands, that I managed to struggle through the whirling snow, which was blown up by the wind under my feet, and to make the few steps that separated me from the sledge. My former driver was kneeling in the middle of the empty sledge, but on seeing me he took off his big cap; whereupon the wind snatched at his hair furiously. He asked me for something for drink, but most likely had not expected me to give him anything extra, for my refusal did not in the least disappoint him. He thanked me for that too, put on his cap, and said to me, "Well, good luck to you, sir!" and tugging at his reins, and clucking to his horses, he drove away from us. After that, Ignashka too, with a swing of his whole body forward, shouted to his horses. Again the sound of the crunching of the hoofs, shouting, and bells replaced the sound of the howling of the wind, which was more audible when we were standing still.

For a quarter of an hour after moving I did not go to sleep, but amused myself by watching the figures of my new driver and horses. Ignashka sat up smartly, incessantly jumping up and down, swinging his arm with the whip over the horses, shouting, knocking one leg against the other, and bending forward to set straight the shaft-horse's breech, which kept slipping to the right side. He was not tall, but seemed to be well built. Over his full coat he had on a cloak not tied in at the waist; the collar of it was open, and his neck was quite bare; his boots were not of felt, but of leather, and his cap was a small one, which he was continually taking off and shifting. His ears had no covering but his hair.

In all his actions could be detected not merely energy, but even more, it struck me, the desire to keep up his own energies. The further we went, the more and more frequently he jumped up and down on the box, shifted his position, slapped one leg against the other, and addressed remarks to me and Alyoshka. It seemed to me he was afraid of losing heart. And there was good reason; though we had good horses, the road became heavier and heavier at every step, and the horses unmistakably moved more unwillingly; he had to use the whip now, and the shaft-horse, a spirited, big, shaggy horse, stumbled twice, though at once taking fright, he darted forward and flung up his shaggy head almost to the very bells. The right trace-horse, whom I could not help watching, noticeably kept the traces slack, together with the long leather tassel of the breech, that shifted and shook up and down on the off-side. He needed the whip, but, like a good, spirited horse, he seemed vexed at his own feebleness, and angrily dropped and flung up his head, as though asking for the rein. It certainly was terrible to see the blizzard getting more and more violent, the horses growing weaker, and the road getting worse, while we hadn't a notion where we were and whether we should reach the station, or even a shelter of any sort. And ludicrous and strange it was to hear the bells ringing so gaily and unconcernedly and Ignashka calling so briskly and jauntily, as though we were driving at midday in sunny, frosty Christmas weather, along some village street on a holiday; and strangest of all it was to think that we were going on all the while and going quickly, anywhere to get away from where we were. Ignashka sang a song, in the vilest falsetto, but so loudly and with breaks in it, filled in by such whistling, that it was odd to feel frightened as one listened to him.

"Hey, hey, what are you splitting your throat for, Ignashka?" I heard the voice of the counsellor. "Do stop it for an hour."

"What?"

"Shut up!"

Ignat ceased. Again all was quiet, and the wind howled and whined, and the whirling snow began to lie thicker on our sledge. The counsellor came up to us.

"Well, what is it?"

"What, indeed; which way are we to go?"

"Who knows?"

"Why, are your feet frozen, that you keep beating them together?"

"They're quite numb."

"You should take a run. There's something over yonder; isn't it a Kalmuck encampment? It would warm your feet, anyway."

"All right. Hold the horses . . . there."

And Ignat ran in the direction indicated.

"One must keep looking and walking round, and one will find something; what's the sense of driving on like a fool?" the counsellor said to me. "See, what a steam the horses are in!"

All the time Ignat was gone—and that lasted so long that I began to be afraid he was lost—the counsellor told me in a calm, self-confident tone, how one must act during a blizzard, how the best thing of all was to unyoke a horse and let it go its own way; that as

God is holy, it would lead one right; how one could sometimes see by the stars, and how if he had been driving the leading sledge, we should have been at the station long ago.

"Well, is it?" he asked Ignat, who was coming back, stepping with difficulty almost knee-deep in the snow.

"Yes, it's an encampment," Ignat answered, panting, "but I don't know what sort of a one. We must have come right out to Prolgovsky homestead, mate. We must bear more to the left."

"What nonsense! . . . That's our encampment, behind the village!" retorted the counsellor.

"But I tell you it's not!"

"Why, I've looked, so I know. That's what it will be; or if not that, then it's Tamishevsko. We must keep more to the right, and we shall get out on the big bridge, at the eighth verst, directly."

"I tell you it's not so! Why, I've seen it!" Ignat answered with irritation.

"Hey, mate, and you call yourself a driver!"

"Yes, I do. . . . You go yourself!"

"What should I go for? I know as it is."

Ignat unmistakably lost his temper; without replying, he jumped on the box and drove on.

"I say, my legs are numb; there's no warming them," he said to Alyoshka, clapping his legs together more and more frequently, and knocking off and scraping at the snow, that had got in above his boot-tops.

I felt awfully sleepy.

VIII

"Can I really be beginning to freeze?" I wondered sleepily. "Being frozen always begins by sleepiness, they say. Better be drowned than frozen—let them drag me out in the net; but never mind, I don't care whether it's drowning or freezing, if only that stick, or whatever it is, wouldn't poke me in the back, and I could forget everything."

I lost consciousness for a second.

"How will it all end, though?" I suddenly wondered, opening my eyes for a minute and staring at the white expanse of snow; "how will it end, if we don't come across any stacks, and the horses come to a standstill, which I fancy will happen soon? We shall all be frozen." I must own that, though I was a little frightened, the desire that something extraordinary and rather tragic should happen to us was stronger than a little fear. It struck me that it would not be bad if, towards morning, the horses should reach some remote, unknown village, with us half-frozen, some of us indeed completely frozen. And dreams of something like that floated with extraordinary swiftness and clearness before my imagination. The horses stop, the snow drifts higher and higher, and now nothing can be seen of the horses but their ears and the yoke; but suddenly Ignashka appears on the top of the snow with his three horses and drives past us. We entreat him, we scream to him to take us with him; but the wind blows away our voice, there is no voice heard. Ignashka laughs, shouts to his horses, whistles, and vanishes from our sight in a deep ravine filled with snow. The old man is on horseback, his elbows jogging up and down, and he tries to gallop away, but cannot move from the spot. My old driver with his big cap rushes at him, drags him to the ground and tramples him in the snow. "You're a sorcerer," he shouts, "you're abusive, we will be lost together." But the old man pops his head out of a snowdrift; he is not so much an old man now as a hare, and he hops away from us. All the dogs are running after him. The counsellor, who is Fyodor Filippitch, says we must all sit round in a ring, that it doesn't matter if the snow does bury us; we shall be warm. And we really are warm and snug; only we are thirsty. I get out a case of wine; I treat all of them to rum with sugar in it, and I drink it myself with great enjoyment. The story-teller tells us some tale about a rainbow—and over our heads there is a ceiling made of snow and a rainbow. "Now let us make ourselves each a room in the snow and go to sleep!" I say. The snow is soft and warm like fur; I make myself a room and try to get into it, but Fyodor Filippitch, who has seen my money in the wine-case, says, "Stop, give me the money—you have to die anyway!" and he seizes me by the leg. I give him the money, and only beg him to let me go; but they will not believe it is all the money, and try to kill me. I clutch at the old man's hand, and with inexpressible delight begin kissing it; the old man's hand is soft and sweet. At first he snatches it away, but then he gives it me, and even strokes me with the other hand. But Fyodor Filippitch approaches and threatens me. I run into my room; now it is not a room, but a long, white corridor, and someone is holding me by the legs. I pull myself away. My boots and stockings, together with part of my skin, are left in the hands of the man who held me. But I only feel cold and ashamed—all the more ashamed as my aunt with her parasol and her homœopathic medicine-chest is coming to meet me, arm-in-arm with the drowned man. They are laughing, and do not understand the signs I make to them. I fling myself into a sledge, my legs drag in the snow; but the old man pursues me, his elbows jogging up and down. The old man is close upon me, but I hear two bells ringing in front of me, and I know I am safe if I can reach them. The bells ring more and more distinctly; but the old man has overtaken me and fallen with his body on my face, so that I can hardly hear the bells. I snatch his hand again, and begin kissing it, but he is not the old man but the drowned man, and he shouts, "Ignashka, stop, yonder are the Ahmetkin stacks, I do believe! Run and look!" That is too dreadful. No, I had better wake up.

I open my eyes. The wind has blown the skirt of Alyoshka's coat over my face; my knee is uncovered; we are driving over a bare surface of ice, and the chime of the bells with its jangling fifth rings out more distinctly in the air.

I look to see where there is a stack! but instead of stacks, I see now with open eyes a house with a balcony and a turreted wall like a fortress. I feel little interest in examining this house and fortress. I want most to see again the white corridor, along which I was running, to hear the church bell ringing and to kiss the old man's hand. I close my eyes again and fall asleep.

IX

I slept soundly; but the chime of the bells was audible all the while, and came into my dreams; at one time in the form of a dog barking and rushing at me, then an organ, of which I am one of the pipes, then French verses which I am composing. Then it seemed that the chime of the bell is an instrument of torture with which my right heel is being continually squeezed. This was so vivid that I woke up and opened my eyes, rubbing my foot. It was beginning to get frostbitten. The night was as light, as dim, as white as ever. The same movement jolted me and the sledge; Ignashka was sitting sideways as before, clapping his legs together. The trace-horse, as before, craning his neck and not lifting his legs high, ran trotting over the deep snow; the tassel bobbed up and down on the breech, and lashed against the horse's belly. The shaft-horse's head, with his mane flying, swayed regularly up and down, tightening and loosening the reins that were fastened to the yoke. But all this was more than ever covered, buried in snow. The snow whirled in front of us, buried the runners on one side, and the horse's legs up to the knees, and was piled up high on our collars and caps. The wind blew first on the right, then on the left, played with my collar, with the skirt of Ignashka's coat, and the trace-horse's mane, and whistled through the yoke and the shafts.

It had become fearfully cold, and I had hardly peeped out of my fur collar when the dry, frozen, whirling snow settled on my eyelashes, my nose and my mouth, and drifted down my neck. I looked round—all was white, and light and snowy; nowhere anything but dim light and snow. I felt seriously alarmed. Alyoshka was asleep at my feet, right at the bottom of the sledge; his whole back was covered by a thick layer of snow. Ignashka was not depressed, he was incessantly tugging at the reins, shouting and clapping his feet together. The bells rang as strangely as ever. The horses were panting, but they still went on, though rather more slowly, and stumbling more and more often. Ignashka jumped up and down again, brandished his gloves, and began singing a song in his shrill, strained voice. Before he had finished the song, he pulled up, flung the reins on the forepart of the sledge, and got down. The wind howled ruthlessly; the snow simply poured as it were in shovelfuls on the skirts of my fur cloak. I looked round; the third sledge was not there (it had been left behind somewhere). Beside the second sledge I could see in the snowy fog the old man hopping from one leg to the other. Ignashka walked three steps away from the sledge, sat down on the snow, undid his belt and began taking off his boots.

"What are you doing?" I asked.

"I must take my boots off; or my feet will be quite frostbitten!" he answered, going on with what he was about.

It was too cold for me to poke my neck out of my fur collar to see what he was doing. I sat up straight, looking at the trace-horse, who stood with one leg outstretched in an attitude of painful exhaustion, shaking his tied-up, snowy tail. The jolt Ignashka gave the sledge in jumping up on the box waked me up.

"Well, where are we now?" I asked. "Shall we go on till morning?"

"Don't you worry yourself, we'll take you all right," he answered. "Now my feet are grandly warm since I shifted my boots."

And he started; the bells began ringing; the sledge began swaying from side to side; and the wind whistled through the runners. And again we set off floating over the boundless sea of snow.

X

I slept soundly. When I was waked up by Alyoshka kicking me, and opened my eyes, it was morning. It seemed even colder than in the night. No snow was falling from above; but the keen, dry wind was still driving the fine snow along the ground and especially under the runners and the horse's hoofs. To the right the sky in the east was a heavy, dingy blue colour; but bright, orange-red, slanting rays were becoming more and more clearly marked in it. Overhead, behind the flying white clouds, faintly tinged with red, the pale blue sky was visible; on the left the clouds were light, bright, and moving. Everywhere around, as far as the eye could see, the country lay under deep, white snow, thrown up into sharp ridges. Here and there could be seen a greyish hillock, where the fine, dry snow had persistently blown by. Not a track of sledge, or man, or beast was visible. The outlines and colours of the driver's back and the horses could be seen clearly and distinctly against the white background. . . . The rim of Ignashka's dark blue cap, his collar, his hair, and even his boots were white. The sledge was completely buried. The grey shaft-horse's head and forelock were covered with snow on the right side; my right trace-horse's legs were buried up to the knee, and all his back, crisp with frozen sweat, was coated with snow on the off-side. The tassel was still dancing in time to any tune one liked to fancy, and the trace-horse stepped to the same rhythm. It was only from his sunken belly, that heaved and fell so often, and his drooping ears that one could see how exhausted he was. Only one new object caught my attention. That was a verst post, from which the snow was falling to the ground, and about which the wind had swept up quite a mountain on the right and kept whirling and shifting the powdery snow from one side to the other. I was utterly amazed to find that we had been driving the whole night with the same horses, twelve hours without stopping or knowing where we were going, and yet had somehow arrived. Our bells chimed more gaily than ever. Ignat kept wrapping himself round and shouting; behind us we heard the snorting of the horses and the ringing of the bells of the sledge in which were the old man and the counsellor; but the man who had been asleep had gone completely astray from us on the steppe. When we had driven on another half-verst, we came upon fresh tracks of a sledge and three horses, not yet covered by the snow, and here and there we saw a red spot of blood, most likely from a horse that had been hurt.

"That's Filip. Why, he's got in before us!" said Ignashka.

And now a little house with a signboard came into sight near the roadside, in the middle of the snow, which buried it almost to the roof and windows. Near the little inn stood a sledge with three grey horses, with their coats crisp with sweat, their legs stiffly stretched out, and their heads drooping. The snow had been cleared about the door, and a spade stood there; but the droning wind still whirled and drifted the snow from the roof.

At the sound of our bells there came out from the door a big, red-faced, red-haired driver, holding a glass of *vodka* in his hand, and shouting something to us. Ignashka turned to me and asked my permission to stop here; then, for the first time, I saw his face.

XI

His face was not swarthy, lean, and straight-nosed, as I had expected, judging from his hair and figure. It was a merry, round face, with quite a pug nose, a large mouth, and round, bright, light blue eyes. His face and neck were red, as though they had been rubbed with a polishing cloth; his eyebrows, long eyelashes, and the down that covered all the lower part of his face were stiffly coated with snow and perfectly white. It was only half a verst from the station, and we stopped.

"Only make haste," I said.

"One minute," answered Ignashka, jumping off the box and going towards Filip.

"Give it here, mate," he said, taking the glove off his right hand and flinging it with the whip on the snow, and throwing back his head, he tossed off the glass of *vodka* at one gulp.

The innkeeper, probably an old Cossack, came out of the door with a pint bottle in his hand.

"To whom shall I take some?" said he.

Tall Vassily, a thin, flaxen-headed peasant with a goat's beard, and the counsellor, a stout man with light eyebrows and a thick light beard framing his red face, came up, and drank a glass each. The old man, too, was approaching the group, but they did not offer him any, and he moved away to his horses, that were fastened at the back of the sledge, and began stroking one of them on the back.

The old man was just as I had imagined him to be—a thin little man, with a wrinkled, bluish face, a scanty beard, a sharp nose and decayed, yellow teeth. His cap was a regular driver's cap, perfectly new, but his greatcoat was shabby, smeared with tar, and torn about the shoulders and skirts. It did not cover his knees, and his coarse, hempen under-garment, which was stuffed into his huge, felt boots. He was bent and wrinkled, his face quivering, and his knees trembling. He bustled about the sledge, apparently trying to get warm.

"Why, Mitrich, have a drop; it would warm you finely," the counsellor said to him.

Mitrich gave a shrug. He straightened the breech on his horse, set the yoke right, and came up to me.

"Well, sir," said he, taking his cap off his grey hair, and bowing low, "we've been lost all night along with you, and looking for the road; you might treat me to a glass. Surely, your Excellency! Else I've nothing to warm me up," he added with a deprecating smile.

I gave him twenty-five copecks. The innkeeper brought out a glass and handed it to the old man. He took off his glove with the whip, and put his black horny little hand, blue with cold, to the glass; but his thumb was not under his control; he could not hold the glass, and let it drop, spilling the *vodka* in the snow.

All the drivers laughed.

"I say, Mitrich is so frozen he can't hold the *vodka*."

But Mitritch was greatly mortified at having spilt the drink.

They poured him out another glass, however, and put it to his lips. He became more cheerful at once, ran into the inn, lighted a pipe, began grinning, showing his decayed, yellow teeth, and at every word he uttered an oath. After drinking a last glass, the drivers got into their sledges, and we drove on.

The snow became whiter and brighter, so that it made one's eyes ache to look at it. The orange-red streaks spread higher and higher, and grew brighter and brighter in the sky overhead. The red disc of the sun appeared on the horizon through the dark blue clouds. The blue became deeper and more brilliant. Along the road near the station there was a distinct yellowish track, with here and there deep ruts in it. In the tense, frozen air there was a peculiar, refreshing lightness.

My sledge flew along very briskly. The head of the shaft-horse, with his mane floating up on the yoke above, bobbed up and down quickly under the sportsman's bell, the clapper of which did not move freely now, but somehow grated against the sides. The gallant trace-horses, pulling together at the twisted, frozen traces, trotted vigorously, and the tassel danced right under the belly and the breech.

Sometimes a trace-horse slipped off the beaten track into a snowdrift, and his eyes were all powdered with snow as he plunged smartly out of it. Ignashka shouted in a cheerful tenor; the dry frost crunched under the runners; behind us we heard the two bells ringing out with a clear, festive note, and the drunken shouts of the drivers. I looked round. The grey, crisp-haired trace-horses, breathing regularly, galloped over the snow with outstretched necks and bits askew. Filip cracked his whip and set his cap straight. The old man lay in the middle of the sledge with his legs up as before.

Two minutes later the sledge was creaking over the swept boards of the approach to the posting-station, and Ignashka turned his merry face, all covered with frost and snow, towards me.

"We've brought you safe after all, sir," said he.

THE BEAR-HUNT

[The adventure here narrated is one that happened to Tolstoy himself in 1858. More than twenty years later he gave up hunting, on humanitarian grounds.]

WE WERE OUT on a bear-hunting expedition. My comrade had shot at a bear, but only gave him a flesh-wound. There were traces of blood on the snow, but the bear had got away.

We all collected in a group in the forest, to decide whether we ought to go after the bear at once, or wait two or three days till he should settle down again. We asked the peasant bear-drivers whether it would be possible to get round the bear that day.

"No. It's impossible," said an old bear-driver. "You must let the bear quiet down. In five days' time it will be possible to surround him; but if you followed him now, you would only frighten him away, and he would not settle down."

But a young bear-driver began disputing with the old man, saying that it was quite possible to get round the bear now.

"On such snow as this," said he, "he won't go far, for he is a fat bear. He will settle down before evening; or, if not, I can overtake him on snow-shoes."

The comrade I was with was against following up the bear, and advised waiting. But I said:

"We need not argue. You do as you like, but I will follow up the track with Damian. If we get round the bear, all right. If not, we lose nothing. It is still early, and there is nothing else for us to do to-day."

So it was arranged.

The others went back to the sledges, and returned to the village. Damian and I took some bread, and remained behind in the forest.

When they had all left us, Damian and I examined our guns, and after tucking the skirts of our warm coats into our belts, we started off, following the bear's tracks.

The weather was fine, frosty and calm; but it was hard work snow-shoeing. The snow was deep and soft: it had not caked together at all in the forest, and fresh snow had fallen the day before, so that our snow-shoes sank six inches deep in the snow, and some-times more.

The bear's tracks were visible from a distance, and we could see how he had been going; sometimes sinking in up to his belly and ploughing up the snow as he went. At first, while under large trees, we kept in sight of his track; but when it turned into a thicket of small firs, Damian stopped.

"We must leave the trail now," said he. "He has probably settled somewhere here. You can see by the snow that he has been squatting down. Let us leave the track and go round; but we must go quietly. Don't shout or cough, or we shall frighten him away."

Leaving the track, therefore, we turned off to the left. But when we had gone about five hundred yards, there were the bear's traces again right before us. We followed them, and they brought us out on to the road. There we stopped, examining the road to see which way the bear had gone. Here and there in the snow were prints of the bear's paw, claws and all, and here and there the marks of a peas-ant's bark shoes. The bear had evidently gone towards the village.

As we followed the road, Damian said:

"It's no use watching the road now. We shall see where he has turned off, to right or left, by the marks in the soft snow at the side. He must have turned off somewhere; for he won't have gone on to the village."

We went along the road for nearly a mile, and then saw, ahead of us, the bear's track turning off the road. We examined it. How strange! It was a bear's track right enough, only not going from the road into the forest, but from the forest on to the road! The toes were pointing towards the road.

"This must be another bear," I said.

Damian looked at it, and considered a while.

"No," said he. "It's the same one. He's been playing tricks, and walked backwards when he left the road."

We followed the track, and found it really was so! The bear had gone some ten steps backwards, and then, behind a fir tree, had turned round and gone straight ahead. Damian stopped and said:

"Now, we are sure to get round him. There is a marsh ahead of us, and he must have settled down there. Let us go round it."

We began to make our way round, through a fir thicket. I was tired out by this time, and it had become still more difficult to get along. Now I glided on to juniper bushes and caught my snow-shoes in them, now a tiny fir tree appeared between my feet, or, from want of practise, my snow-shoes slipped off; and now I came upon a stump or a log hidden by the snow. I was getting very tired, and was drenched with perspiration; and I took off my fur cloak. And there was Damian all the time, gliding along as if in a boat, his snow-shoes moving as if of their own accord, never catching against anything, nor slipping off. He even took my fur and slung it over his shoulder, and still kept urging me on.

We went on for two more miles, and came out on the other side of the marsh. I was lagging behind. My snow-shoes kept slipping off, and my feet stumbled. Suddenly Damian, who was ahead of me, stopped and waved his arm. When I came up to him, he bent down, pointing with his hand, and whispered:

"Do you see the magpie chattering above that undergrowth? It scents the bear from afar. That is where he must be."

We turned off and went on for more than another half-mile, and presently we came on to the old track again. We had, therefore, been right round the bear, who was now within the track we had left. We stopped, and I took off my cap and loosened all my clothes. I was as hot as in a steam bath, and as wet as a drowned rat. Damian too was flushed, and wiped his face with his sleeve.

"Well, sir," he said, "we have done our job, and now we must have a rest."

The evening glow already showed red through the forest. We took off our snow-shoes and sat down on them, and got some bread and salt out of our bags. First I ate some snow, and then some bread; and the bread tasted so good, that I thought I had never in my life had any like it before. We sat there resting until it began to grow dusk, and then I asked Damian if it was far to the village.

"Yes," he said. "It must be about eight miles. We will go on there to-night, but now we must rest. Put on your fur coat, sir, or you'll be catching cold."

Damian flattened down the snow, and breaking off some fir branches made a bed of them. We lay down side by side, resting our heads on our arms. I do not remember how I fell asleep. Two hours later I woke up, hearing something crack.

I had slept so soundly that I did not know where I was. I looked around me. How wonderful! I was in some sort of a hall, all glittering and white with gleaming pillars, and when I looked up I saw, through delicate white tracery, a vault, raven black and studded with coloured lights. After a good look, I remembered that we were in the forest, and that what I took for a hall and pillars, were trees covered with snow and hoar-frost, and the coloured lights were stars twinkling between the branches.

Hoar-frost had settled in the night; all the twigs were thick with it, Damian was covered with it, it was on my fur coat, and it dropped down from the trees. I woke Damian; and we put on our snow-shoes and started. It was very quiet in the forest. No sound was heard but that of our snow-shoes pushing through the soft snow; except when now and then a tree, cracked by the frost, made the forest resound. Only once we heard the sound of a living creature. Something rustled close to us, and then rushed away. I felt sure it was the bear, but when we went to the spot whence the sound had come, we found the footmarks of hares, and saw several young aspen trees with their bark gnawed. We had startled some hares while they were feeding.

We came out on the road, and followed it, dragging our snow-shoes behind us. It was easy walking now. Our snow-shoes clattered as they slid behind us from side to side of the hard-trodden road. The snow creaked under our boots, and the cold hoar-frost settled on our faces like down. Seen through the branches, the stars seemed to be running to meet us, now twinkling, now vanishing, as if the whole sky were on the move.

I found my comrade sleeping, but woke him up, and related how we had got round the bear. After telling our peasant host to collect beaters for the morning, we had supper and lay down to sleep.

I was so tired that I could have slept on till midday, if my comrade had not roused me. I jumped up, and saw that he was already dressed, and busy doing something to his gun.

"Where is Damian?" said I.

"In the forest, long ago. He has already been over the tracks you made, and been back here, and now he has gone to look after the beaters."

I washed and dressed, and loaded my guns; and then we got into a sledge, and started.

The sharp frost still continued. It was quiet, and the sun could not be seen. There was a thick mist above us, and hoar-frost still covered everything.

After driving about two miles along the road, as we came near the forest, we saw a cloud of smoke rising from a hollow, and presently reached a group of peasants, both men and women, armed with cudgels.

We got out and went up to them. The men sat roasting potatoes, and laughing and talking with the women.

Damian was there too; and when we arrived the people got up, and Damian led them away to place them in the circle we had made the day before. They went along in single file, men and women, thirty in all. The snow was so deep that we could only see them from their waists upwards. They turned into the forest, and my friend and I followed in their track.

Though they had trodden a path, walking was difficult; but, on the other hand, it was impossible to fall: it was like walking between two walls of snow.

We went on in this way for nearly half a mile, when all at once we saw Damian coming from another direction—running towards us on his snow-shoes, and beckoning us to join him. We went towards him, and he showed us where to stand. I took my place, and looked round me.

To my left were tall fir trees, between the trunks of which I could see a good way, and, like a black patch just visible behind the trees, I could see a beater. In front of me was a thicket of young firs, about as high as a man, their branches weighed down and stuck together with snow. Through this copse ran a path thickly covered with snow, and leading straight up to where I stood. The thicket stretched away to the right of me, and ended in a small glade, where I could see Damian placing my comrade.

I examined both my guns, and considered where I had better stand. Three steps behind me was a tall fir.

"That's where I'll stand," thought I, "and then I can lean my second gun against the tree"; and I moved towards the tree, sinking up to my knees in the snow at each step. I trod the snow down, and made a clearance about a yard square, to stand on. One gun I kept in my hand; the other, ready cocked, I placed leaning up against the tree. Then I unsheathed and replaced my dagger, to make sure that I could draw it easily in case of need.

Just as I had finished these preparations, I heard Damian shouting in the forest:

"He's up! He's up!"

And as soon as Damian shouted, the peasants round the circle all replied in their different voices.

"Up, up, up! Ou! Ou! Ou!" shouted the men.

"Ay! Ay! Ay!" screamed the women in high-pitched tones.

The bear was inside the circle, and as Damian drove him on, the people all round kept shouting. Only my friend and I stood silent and motionless, waiting for the bear to come towards us. As I stood gazing and listening, my heart beat violently. I trembled, holding my gun fast.

"Now, now," I thought. "He will come suddenly. I shall aim, fire, and he will drop——"

Suddenly, to my left, but at a distance, I heard something falling on the snow. I looked between the tall fir trees, and, some fifty paces off, behind the trunks, saw something big and black. I took aim and waited, thinking:

"Won't he come any nearer?"

As I waited I saw him move his ears, turn, and go back; and then I caught a glimpse of the whole of him in profile. He was an immense brute. In my excitement, I fired, and heard my bullet go "flop" against a tree. Peering through the smoke, I saw my bear scampering back into the circle, and disappearing among the trees.

"Well," thought I. "My chance is lost. He won't come back to me. Either my comrade will shoot him, or he will escape through the line of beaters. In any case he won't give me another chance."

I reloaded my gun, however, and again stood listening. The peasants were shouting all round, but to the right, not far from where my comrade stood, I heard a woman screaming in a frenzied voice:

"Here he is! Here he is! Come here, come here! Oh! Oh! Ay! Ay!"

Evidently she could see the bear. I had given up expecting him, and was looking to the right at my comrade. All at once I saw Damian with a stick in his hand, and without his snow-shoes, running along a footpath towards my friend. He crouched down beside him, pointing his stick as if aiming at something, and then I saw my friend raise his gun and aim in the same direction. Crack! He fired.

"There," thought I. "He has killed him."

But I saw that my comrade did not run towards the bear. Evidently he had missed him, or the shot had not taken full effect.

"The bear will get away," I thought. "He will go back, but he won't come a second time towards me.—But what is that?"

Something was coming towards me like a whirlwind, snorting as it came; and I saw the snow flying up quite near me. I glanced straight before me, and there was the bear, rushing along the path through the thicket right at me, evidently beside himself with fear. He was hardly half a dozen paces off, and I could see the whole of him—his black chest and enormous head with a reddish patch. There he was, blundering straight at me, and scattering the snow about as he came. I could see by his eyes that he did not see me, but, mad with fear, was rushing blindly along; and his path led him straight at the tree under which I was standing. I raised my gun and fired. He was almost upon me now, and I saw that I had missed. My bullet had gone past him, and he did not even hear me fire, but still came headlong towards me. I lowered my gun, and fired again, almost touching his head. Crack! I had hit, but not killed him!

He raised his head, and laying his ears back, came at me, showing his teeth.

I snatched at my other gun, but almost before I had touched it, he had flown at me and, knocking me over into the snow, had passed right over me.

"Thank goodness, he has left me," thought I.

I tried to rise, but something pressed me down, and prevented my getting up. The bear's rush had carried him past me, but he had turned back, and had fallen on me with the whole weight of his body. I felt something heavy weighing me down, and something warm above my face, and I realized that he was drawing my whole face into his mouth. My nose was already in it, and I felt the heat of it, and smelt his blood. He was pressing my shoulders down with his paws so that I could not move: all I could do was to draw my head down towards my chest away from his mouth, trying to free my nose and eyes, while he tried to get his teeth into them. Then I felt that he had seized my forehead just under the hair with the teeth of his lower jaw, and the flesh below my eyes with his upper jaw, and was closing his teeth. It was as if my face were being cut with knives. I struggled to get away, while he made haste to close his jaws like a dog gnawing. I managed to twist my face away, but he began drawing it again into his mouth.

"Now," thought I, "my end has come!"

Then I felt the weight lifted, and looking up, I saw that he was no longer there. He had jumped off me and run away.

When my comrade and Damian had seen the bear knock me down and begin worrying me, they rushed to the rescue. My comrade, in his haste, blundered, and instead of following the trodden path, ran into the deep snow and fell down. While he was struggling out of the snow, the bear was gnawing at me. But Damian just as he was, without a gun, and with only a stick in his hand, rushed along the path shouting:

"He's eating the master! He's eating the master!"

And, as he ran, he called to the bear:

"Oh, you idiot! What are you doing? Leave off! Leave off!"

The bear obeyed him, and leaving me ran away. When I rose, there was as much blood on the snow as if a sheep had been killed, and the flesh hung in rags above my eyes, though in my excitement I felt no pain.

My comrade had come up by this time, and the other people collected round: they looked at my wound, and put snow on it. But I, forgetting about my wounds, only asked:

"Where's the bear? Which way has he gone?"

Suddenly I heard:

"Here he is! Here he is!"

And we saw the bear again running at us. We seized our guns, but before any one had time to fire, he had run past. He had grown ferocious, and wanted to gnaw me again, but seeing so many people he took fright. We saw by his track that his head was bleeding, and we wanted to follow him up; but, as my wounds had become very painful, we went, instead, to the town to find a doctor.

The doctor stitched up my wounds with silk, and they soon began to heal.

A month later we went to hunt that bear again, but I did not get a chance of finishing him. He would not come out of the circle, but went round and round, growling in a terrible voice.

Damian killed him. The bear's lower jaw had been broken, and one of his teeth knocked out by my bullet.

He was a huge creature, and had splendid black fur.

I had him stuffed, and he now lies in my room. The wounds on my forehead healed up so that the scars can scarcely be seen.

A PRISONER IN THE CAUCASUS

I

AN OFFICER NAMED Zhílin was serving in the army in the Caucasus.

One day he received a letter from home. It was from his mother, who wrote: "I am getting old, and should like to see my dear son once more before I die. Come and say good-bye to me and bury me, and then, if God pleases, return to service again with my blessing. But I have found a girl for you, who is sensible and good and has some property. If you can love her, you might marry her and remain at home."

Zhílin thought it over. It was quite true, the old lady was failing fast and he might not have another chance to see her alive. He had better go, and, if the girl was nice, why not marry her?

So he went to his Colonel, obtained leave of absence, said good-bye to his comrades, stood the soldiers four pailfuls of vódka as a farewell treat, and got ready to go.

It was a time of war in the Caucasus. The roads were not safe by night or day. If ever a Russian ventured to ride or walk any distance away from his fort, the Tartars killed him or carried him off to the hills. So it had been arranged that twice every week a body of soldiers should march from one fortress to the next to convoy travellers from point to point.

It was summer. At daybreak the baggage-train got ready under shelter of the fortress; the soldiers marched out; and all started along the road. Zhílin was on horseback, and a cart with his things went with the baggage-train. They had sixteen miles to go. The baggage-train moved slowly; sometimes the soldiers stopped, or perhaps a wheel would come off one of the carts, or a horse refuse to go on, and then everybody had to wait.

When by the sun it was already past noon, they had not gone half the way. It was dusty and hot, the sun was scorching, and there was no shelter anywhere: a bare plain all round—not a tree, not a bush, by the road.

Zhílin rode on in front, and stopped, waiting for the baggage to overtake him. Then he heard the signal-horn sounded behind him: the company had again stopped. So he began to think: "Hadn't I better ride on by myself? My horse is a good one: if the Tartars do attack me, I can gallop away. Perhaps, however, it would be wiser to wait."

As he sat considering, Kostílin, an officer carrying a gun, rode up to him and said:

"Come along, Zhílin, let's go on by ourselves. It's dreadful; I am famished, and the heat is terrible. My shirt is wringing wet."

Kostílin was a stout, heavy man, and the perspiration was running down his red face. Zhílin thought awhile, and then asked: "Is your gun loaded?"

"Yes, it is."

"Well, then, let's go, but on condition that we keep together."

So they rode forward along the road across the plain, talking, but keeping a look-out on both sides. They could see afar all round. But after crossing the plain the road ran through a valley between two hills, and Zhílin said: "We had better climb that hill and have a look round, or the Tartars may be on us before we know it."

But Kostílin answered: "What's the use? Let us go on."

Zhílin, however, would not agree.

"No," he said; "you can wait here if you like, but I'll go and look round." And he turned his horse to the left, up the hill. Zhílin's horse was a hunter, and carried him up the hillside as if it had wings. (He had bought it for a hundred roubles as a colt out of a herd, and had broken it in himself.) Hardly had he reached the top of the hill, when he saw some thirty Tartars not much more than a hundred yards ahead of him. As soon as he caught sight of them he turned round, but the Tartars had also seen him, and rushed after him at full gallop, getting their guns out as they went. Down galloped Zhílin as fast as the horse's legs could go, shouting to Kostílin: "Get your gun ready!"

And, in thought, he said to his horse: "Get me well out of this, my pet; don't stumble, for if you do it's all up. Once I reach the gun, they shan't take me prisoner."

But, instead of waiting, Kostílin, as soon as he caught sight of the Tartars, turned back towards the fortress at full speed, whipping his horse now on one side now on the other, and its switching tail was all that could be seen of him in the dust.

Zhílin saw it was a bad look-out; the gun was gone, and what could he do with nothing but his sword? He turned his horse towards the escort, thinking to escape, but there were six Tartars rushing to cut him off. His horse was a good one, but theirs were still better; and besides, they were across his path. He tried to rein in his horse and to turn another way, but it was going so fast it could not stop, and dashed on straight towards the Tartars. He saw a red-bearded Tartar on a grey horse, with his gun raised, come at him, yelling and showing his teeth.

"Ah," thought Zhílin, "I know you, devils that you are. If you take me alive, you'll put me in a pit and flog me. I will not be taken alive!"

Zhílin, though not a big fellow, was brave. He drew his sword and dashed at the red-bearded Tartar, thinking: "Either I'll ride him down, or disable him with my sword."

He was still a horse's length away from him, when he was fired at from behind, and his horse was hit. It fell to the ground with all its weight, pinning Zhílin to the earth.

He tried to rise, but two ill-savoured Tartars were already sitting on him and binding his hands behind his back. He made an effort and flung them off, but three others jumped from their horses and began beating his head with the butts of their guns. His eyes grew dim, and he fell back. The Tartars seized him, and, taking spare girths from their saddles, twisted his hands behind him and tied them with a Tartar knot. They knocked his cap off, pulled off his boots, searched him all over, tore his clothes, and took his money and his watch.

Zhílin looked round at his horse. There it lay on its side, poor thing, just as it had fallen; struggling, its legs in the air, unable to touch the ground. There was a hole in its head, and black blood was pouring out, turning the dust to mud for a couple of feet around.

One of the Tartars went up to the horse and began taking the saddle off; it still kicked, so he drew a dagger and cut its windpipe. A whistling sound came from its throat, the horse gave one plunge, and all was over.

The Tartars took the saddle and trappings. The red-bearded Tartar mounted his horse, and the others lifted Zhílin into the saddle behind him. To prevent his falling off, they strapped him to the Tartar's girdle; and then they all rode away to the hills.

So there sat Zhílin, swaying from side to side, his head striking against the Tartar's stinking back. He could see nothing but that muscular back and sinewy neck, with its closely shaven, bluish nape.

Zhílin's head was wounded: the blood had dried over his eyes, and he could neither shift his position on the saddle nor wipe the blood off. His arms were bound so tightly that his collar-bones ached.

They rode up and down hills for a long way. Then they reached a river which they forded, and came to a hard road leading across a valley.

Zhílin tried to see where they were going, but his eyelids were stuck together with blood, and he could not turn.

Twilight began to fall; they crossed another river, and rode up a stony hillside. There was a smell of smoke here, and dogs were barking. They had reached an Aoul (a Tartar village). The Tartars got off their horses; Tartar children came and stood round Zhílin, shrieking with pleasure and throwing stones at him.

The Tartar drove the children away, took Zhílin off the horse, and called his man. A Nogáy* with high cheek-bones, and nothing on but a shirt (and that so torn that his breast was all bare), answered the call. The Tartar gave him an order. He went and fetched shackles: two blocks of oak with iron rings attached, and a clasp and lock fixed to one of the rings.

They untied Zhílin's arms, fastened the shackles on his leg, and dragged him to a barn, where they pushed him in and locked the door.

Zhílin fell on a heap of manure. He lay still awhile, then groped about to find a soft place, and settled down.

II

That night Zhílin hardly slept at all. It was the time of year when the nights are short, and daylight soon showed itself through a chink in the wall. He rose, scratched to make the chink bigger, and peeped out.

Through the hole he saw a road leading down-hill; to the right was a Tartar hut with two trees near it, a black dog lay on the threshold, and a goat and kids were moving about wagging their tails. Then he saw a young Tartar woman in a long, loose, bright-coloured gown, with trousers and high boots showing from under it. She had a coat thrown over her head, on which she carried a large metal jug filled with water. She was leading by the hand a small, closely-shaven Tartar boy, who wore nothing but a shirt; and as she went along

---

* One of a certain Tartar tribe.

balancing herself, the muscles of her back quivered. This woman carried the water into the hut, and, soon after, the red-bearded Tartar of yesterday came out dressed in a silk tunic, with a silver-hilted dagger hanging by his side, shoes on his bare feet, and a tall black sheepskin cap set far back on his head. He came out, stretched himself, and stroked his red beard. He stood awhile, gave an order to his servant, and went away.

Then two lads rode past from watering their horses. The horses' noses were wet. Some other closely-shaven boys ran out, without any trousers, and wearing nothing but their shirts. They crowded together, came to the barn, picked up a twig, and began pushing it in at the chink. Zhílin gave a shout, and the boys shrieked and scampered off, their little bare knees gleaming as they ran.

Zhílin was very thirsty: his throat was parched, and he thought: "If only they would come and so much as look at me!"

Then he heard some one unlocking the barn. The red-bearded Tartar entered, and with him was another, a smaller man, dark, with bright black eyes, red cheeks, and a short beard. He had a merry face, and was always laughing. This man was even more richly dressed than the other. He wore a blue silk tunic trimmed with gold, a large silver dagger in his belt, red morocco slippers worked with silver, and over these a pair of thick shoes, and he had a white sheepskin cap on his head.

The red-bearded Tartar entered, muttered something as if he were annoyed, and stood leaning against the doorpost, playing with his dagger, and glaring askance at Zhílin, like a wolf. The dark one, quick and lively, and moving as if on springs, came straight up to Zhílin, squatted down in front of him, slapped him on the shoulder, and began to talk very fast in his own language. His teeth showed, and he kept winking, clicking his tongue, and repeating, "Good Russ, good Russ."

Zhílin could not understand a word, but said, "Drink! give me water to drink!"

The dark man only laughed. "Good Russ," he said, and went on talking in his own tongue.

Zhílin made signs with lips and hands that he wanted something to drink.

The dark man understood, and laughed. Then he looked out of the door, and called to some one: "Dina!"

A little girl came running in: she was about thirteen, slight, thin, and like the dark Tartar in face. Evidently she was his daughter. She, too, had clear black eyes, and her face was good-looking. She had on a long blue gown with wide sleeves, and no girdle. The hem of her gown, the front, and the sleeves, were trimmed with red. She wore trousers and slippers, and over the slippers stouter shoes with high heels. Round her neck she had a necklace made of Russian silver coins. She was bareheaded, and her black hair was plaited with a ribbon and ornamented with gilt braid and silver coins.

Her father gave an order, and she ran away and returned with a metal jug. She handed the water to Zhílin and sat down, crouching so that her knees were as high as her head; and there she sat with wide open eyes watching Zhílin drink, as though he were a wild animal.

When Zhílin handed the empty jug back to her, she gave such a sudden jump back, like a wild goat, that it made her father laugh. He sent her away for something else. She took the jug, ran out, and brought back some unleavened bread on a round board, and once more sat down, crouching, and looking on with staring eyes.

Then the Tartars went away and again locked the door.

After a while the Nogáy came and said: "*Ayda,* the master, *Ayda!*"

He, too, knew no Russian. All Zhílin could make out was that he was told to go somewhere.

Zhílin followed the Nógay, but limped, for the shackles dragged his feet so that he could hardly step at all. On getting out of the barn he saw a Tartar village of about ten houses, and a Tartar church with a small tower. Three horses stood saddled before one of the houses; little boys were holding them by the reins. The dark Tartar came out of this house, beckoning with his hand for Zhílin to follow him. Then he laughed, said something in his own language, and returned into the house.

Zhílin entered. The room was a good one: the walls smoothly plastered with clay. Near the front wall lay a pile of bright-coloured feather beds; the side walls were covered with rich carpets used as hangings, and on these were fastened guns, pistols and swords, all inlaid with silver. Close to one of the walls was a small stove on a level with the earthen floor. The floor itself was as clean as a thrashing-ground. A large space in one corner was spread over with felt, on which were rugs, and on these rugs were cushions stuffed with down. And on these cushions sat five Tartars, the dark one, the red-haired one, and three guests. They were wearing their indoor slippers, and each had a cushion behind his back. Before them were standing millet cakes on a round board, melted butter in a bowl, and a jug of *buza,* or Tartar beer. They ate both cakes and butter with their hands.

The dark man jumped up and ordered Zhílin to be placed on one side, not on the carpet but on the bare ground, then he sat down on the carpet again, and offered millet cakes and *buza* to his guests. The servant made Zhílin sit down, after which he took off his own over-shoes, put them by the door where the other shoes were standing, and sat down nearer to his masters on the felt, watching them as they ate, and licking his lips.

The Tartars ate as much as they wanted, and a woman dressed in the same way as the girl—in a long gown and trousers, with a kerchief on her head—came and took away what was left, and brought a handsome basin, and an ewer with a narrow spout. The Tartars washed their hands, folded them, went down on their knees, blew to the four quarters, and said their prayers. After they had talked for a while, one of the guests turned to Zhílin and began to speak in Russian.

"You were captured by Kazi-Mohammed," he said, and pointed at the red-bearded Tartar. "And Kazi-Mohammed has given you to Abdul Murat," pointing at the dark one. "Abdul Murat is now your master."

Zhílin was silent. Then Abdul Murat began to talk, laughing, pointing to Zhílin, and repeating, "Soldier Russ, good Russ."

The interpreter said, "He orders you to write home and tell them to send a ransom, and as soon as the money comes he will set you free."

Zhílin thought for a moment, and said, "How much ransom does he want?"

The Tartars talked awhile, and then the interpreter said, "Three thousand roubles."

"No," said Zhílin, "I can't pay so much."

Abdul jumped up and, waving his arms, talked to Zhílin, thinking, as before, that he would understand. The interpreter translated: "How much will you give?"

Zhílin considered, and said, "Five hundred roubles." At this the Tartars began speaking very quickly, all together. Abdul began to shout at the red-bearded one, and jabbered so fast that the spittle spurted out of his mouth. The red-bearded one only screwed up his eyes and clicked his tongue.

They quietened down after a while, and the interpreter said, "Five hundred roubles is not enough for the master. He paid two hundred for you himself. Kazi-Mohammed was in debt to him, and he took you in payment. Three thousand roubles! Less than that won't do. If you refuse to write, you will be put into a pit and flogged with a whip!"

"Eh!" thought Zhílin, "the more one fears them the worse it will be."

So he sprang to his feet, and said, "You tell that dog that if he tries to frighten me I will not write at all, and he will get nothing. I never was afraid of you dogs, and never will be!"

The interpreter translated, and again they all began to talk at once.

They jabbered for a long time, and then the dark man jumped up, came to Zhílin, and said: "*Dzhigit Russ, dzhigit Russ!*" (*Dzhigit* in their language means "brave.") And he laughed, and said something to the interpreter, who translated: "One thousand roubles will satisfy him."

Zhílin stuck to it: "I will not give more than five hundred. And if you kill me you'll get nothing at all."

The Tartars talked awhile, then sent the servant out to fetch something, and kept looking, now at Zhílin, now at the door. The servant returned, followed by a stout, bare-footed, tattered man, who also had his leg shackled.

Zhílin gasped with surprise: it was Kostílin. He, too, had been taken. They were put side by side, and began to tell each other what had occurred. While they talked, the Tartars looked on in silence. Zhílin related what had happened to him; and Kostílin told how his horse had stopped, his gun missed fire, and this same Abdul had overtaken and captured him.

Abdul jumped up, pointed to Kostílin, and said something. The interpreter translated that they both now belonged to one master, and the one who first paid the ransom would be set free first.

"There now," he said to Zhílin, "you get angry, but your comrade here is gentle; he has written home, and they will send five thousand roubles. So he will be well fed and well treated."

Zhílin replied: "My comrade can do as he likes; maybe he is rich, I am not. It must be as I said. Kill me, if you like—you will gain nothing by it; but I will not write for more than five hundred roubles."

They were silent. Suddenly up sprang Abdul, brought a little box, took out a pen, ink, and a bit of paper, gave them to Zhílin, slapped him on the shoulder, and made a sign that he should write. He had agreed to take five hundred roubles.

"Wait a bit!" said Zhílin to the interpreter; "tell him that he must feed us properly, give us proper clothes and boots, and let us be together. It will be more cheerful for us. And he must have these shackles taken off our feet," and Zhílin looked at his master and laughed.

The master also laughed, heard the interpreter, and said: "I will give them the best of clothes: a cloak and boots fit to be married in. I will feed them like princes; and if they like they can live together in the barn. But I can't take off the shackles, or they will run away. They shall be taken off, however, at night." And he jumped up and slapped Zhílin on the shoulder, exclaiming: "You good, I good!"

Zhílin wrote the letter, but addressed it wrongly, so that it should not reach its destination, thinking to himself: "I'll run away!"

Zhílin and Kostílin were taken back to the barn and given some maize straw, a jug of water, some bread, two old cloaks, and some worn-out military boots—evidently taken from the corpses of Russian soldiers. At night their shackles were taken off their feet, and they were locked up in the barn.

III

Zhílin and his friend lived in this way for a whole month. The master always laughed and said: "You, Iván, good! I, Abdul, good!" But he fed them badly, giving them nothing but unleavened bread of millet-flour baked into flat cakes, or sometimes only unbaked dough.

Kostílin wrote home a second time, and did nothing but mope and wait for the money to arrive. He would sit for days together in the barn sleeping, or counting the days till a letter could come.

Zhílin knew his letter would reach no one, and he did not write another. He thought: "Where could my mother get enough money to ransom me? As it is she lived chiefly on what I sent her. If she had to raise five hundred roubles, she would be quite ruined. With God's help I'll manage to escape!"

So he kept on the look-out, planning how to run away.

He would walk about the Aoul whistling; or would sit working, modelling dolls of clay, or weaving baskets out of twigs: for Zhílin was clever with his hands.

Once he modelled a doll with a nose and hands and feet and with a Tartar gown on, and put it up on the roof. When the Tartar women came out to fetch water, the master's daughter, Dina, saw the doll and called the women, who put down their jugs and stood looking and laughing. Zhílin took down the doll and held it out to them. They laughed, but dared not take it. He put down the doll and went into the barn, waiting to see what would happen.

Dina ran up to the doll, looked round, seized it, and ran away.

In the morning, at daybreak, he looked out. Dina came out of the house and sat down on the threshold with the doll, which she had dressed up in bits of red stuff, and she rocked it like a baby, singing a Tartar lullaby. An old woman came out and scolded her, and snatching the doll away she broke it to bits, and sent Dina about her business.

But Zhílin made another doll, better than the first, and gave it to Dina. Once Dina brought a little jug, put it on the ground, sat down gazing at him, and laughed, pointing to the jug.

"What pleases her so?" wondered Zhílin. He took the jug thinking it was water, but it turned out to be milk. He drank the milk and said: "That's good!"

How pleased Dina was! "Good, Iván, good!" said she, and she jumped up and clapped her hands. Then, seizing the jug, she ran away. After that, she stealthily brought him some milk every day.

The Tartars make a kind of cheese out of goat's milk, which they dry on the roofs of their houses; and sometimes, on the sly, she brought him some of this cheese. And once, when Abdul had killed a sheep, she brought Zhílin a bit of mutton in her sleeve. She would just throw the things down and run away.

One day there was a heavy storm, and the rain fell in torrents for a whole hour. All the streams became turbid. At the ford, the water rose till it was seven feet high, and the current was so strong that it rolled the stones about. Rivulets flowed everywhere, and the rumbling in the hills never ceased. When the storm was over, the water ran in streams down the village street. Zhílin got his master to lend him a knife, and with it he shaped a small cylinder, and cutting some little boards, he made a wheel to which he fixed two dolls, one on each side. The little girls brought him some bits of stuff, and he dressed the dolls, one as a peasant, the other as a peasant woman. Then he fastened them in their places, and set the wheel so that the stream should work it. The wheel began to turn and the dolls danced.

The whole village collected round. Little boys and girls, Tartar men and women, all came and clicked their tongues.

"Ah, Russ! Ah, Iván!"

Abdul had a Russian clock, which was broken. He called Zhílin and showed it to him, clicking his tongue.

"Give it me; I'll mend it for you," said Zhílin.

He took it to pieces with the knife, sorted the pieces, and put them together again, so that the clock went all right.

The master was delighted, and made him a present of one of his old tunics which was all in holes. Zhílin had to accept it. He could, at any rate, use it as a coverlet at night.

After that Zhílin's fame spread; and Tartars came from distant villages, bringing him now the lock of a gun or of a pistol, now a watch, to mend. His master gave him some tools—pincers, gimlets, and a file.

One day a Tartar fell ill, and they came to Zhílin, saying, "Come and heal him!" Zhílin knew nothing about doctoring, but he went to look, and thought to himself, "Perhaps he will get well anyway."

He returned to the barn, mixed some water with sand, and then in the presence of the Tartars whispered some words over it and gave it to the sick man to drink. Luckily for him, the Tartar recovered.

Zhílin began to pick up their language a little, and some of the Tartars grew familiar with him. When they wanted him, they would call: "Ivan! Iván!" Others, however, still looked at him askance, as at a wild beast.

The red-bearded Tartar disliked Zhílin. Whenever he saw him he frowned and turned away, or swore at him. There was also an old man there who did not live in the Aoul, but used to come up from the foot of the hill. Zhílin only saw him when he passed on his way to the Mosque. He was short, and had a white cloth wound round his hat. His beard and moustaches were clipped, and white as snow; and his face was wrinkled and brick-red. His nose was hooked like a hawk's, his grey eyes looked cruel, and he had no teeth except two tusks. He would pass, with his turban on his head, leaning on his staff, and glaring round him like a wolf. If he saw Zhílin he would snort with anger and turn away.

Once Zhílin descended the hill to see where the old man lived. He went down along the pathway and came to a little garden surrounded by a stone wall; and behind the wall he saw cherry and apricot trees, and a hut with a flat roof. He came closer, and saw hives made of plaited straw, and bees flying about and humming. The old man was kneeling, busy doing something with a hive. Zhílin stretched to look, and his shackles rattled. The old man turned round, and, giving a yell, snatched a pistol from his belt and shot at Zhílin, who just managed to shelter himself behind the stone wall.

The old man went to Zhílin's master to complain. The master called Zhílin, and said with a laugh, "Why did you go to the old man's house?"

"I did him no harm," replied Zhílin. "I only wanted to see how he lived."

The master repeated what Zhílin said.

But the old man was in a rage; he hissed and jabbered, showing his tusks, and shaking his fists at Zhílin.

Zhílin could not understand all, but he gathered that the old man was telling Abdul he ought not to keep Russians in the Aoul, but ought to kill them. At last the old man went away.

Zhílin asked the master who the old man was.

"He is a great man!" said the master. "He was the bravest of our fellows; he killed many Russians, and was at one time very rich. He had three wives and eight sons, and they all lived in one village. Then the Russians came and destroyed the village, and killed seven of his sons. Only one son was left, and he gave himself up to the Russians. The old man also went and gave himself up, and lived among the Russians for three months. At the end of that time he found his son, killed him with his own hands, and then escaped. After that he left off fighting, and went to Mecca to pray to God; that is why he wears a turban. One who has been to Mecca is called 'Hadji,' and wears a turban. He does not like you fellows. He tells me to kill you. But I can't kill you. I have paid money for you and, besides, I have grown fond of you, Iván. Far from killing you, I would not even let you go if I had not promised." And he laughed, saying in Russian, "You, Iván, good; I, Abdul, good!"

IV

Zhílin lived in this way for a month. During the day he sauntered about the Aoul or busied himself with some handicraft, but at night, when all was silent in the Aoul, he dug at the floor of the barn. It was no easy task digging, because of the stones; but he worked away at them with his file, and at last had made a hole under the wall large enough to get through.

"If only I could get to know the lay of the land," thought he, "and which way to go! But none of the Tartars will tell me."

So he chose a day when the master was away from home, and set off after dinner to climb the hill beyond the village, and to look around. But before leaving home the master always gave orders to his son to watch Zhílin, and not to lose sight of him. So the lad ran after Zhílin, shouting: "Don't go! Father does not allow it. I'll call the neighbours if you won't come back."

Zhílin tried to persuade him, and said: "I'm not going far; I only want to climb that hill. I want to find a herb—to cure sick people with. You come with me if you like. How can I run away with these shackles on? To-morrow I'll make a bow and arrows for you."

So he persuaded the lad, and they went. To look at the hill, it did not seem far to the top; but it was hard walking with shackles on his leg. Zhílin went on and on, but it was all he could do to reach the top. There he sat down and noted how the land lay. To the south, beyond the barn, was a valley in which a herd of horses was pasturing and at the bottom of the valley one could see another Aoul. Beyond that was a still steeper hill, and another hill beyond that. Between the hills, in the blue distance, were forests, and still further off were mountains, rising higher and higher. The highest of them were covered with snow, white as sugar; and one snowy peak towered above all the rest. To the east and to the west were other such hills, and here and there smoke rose from Aouls in the ravines. "Ah," thought he, "all that is Tartar country." And he turned towards the Russian side. At his feet he saw a river, and the Aoul he lived in, surrounded by little gardens. He could see women, like tiny dolls, sitting by the river rinsing clothes. Beyond the Aoul was a hill, lower than the one to the south, and beyond it two other hills well wooded; and between these, a smooth bluish plain, and far, far across the plain something that looked like a cloud of smoke. Zhílin tried to remember where the sun used to rise and set when he was living in the fort, and he saw that there was no mistake: the Russian fort must be in that plain. Between those two hills he would have to make his way when he escaped.

The sun was beginning to set. The white, snowy mountains turned red, and the dark hills turned darker; mists rose from the ravine, and the valley, where he supposed the Russian fort to be, seemed on fire with the sunset glow. Zhílin looked carefully. Something seemed to be quivering in the valley like smoke from a chimney, and he felt sure the Russian fortress was there.

It had grown late. The Mullah's cry was heard. The herds were being driven home, the cows were lowing, and the lad kept saying, "Come home!" But Zhílin did not feel inclined to go away.

At last, however, they went back. "Well," thought Zhílin, "now that I know the way, it is time to escape." He thought of running away that night. The nights were dark—the moon had waned. But as ill-luck would have it, the Tartars returned home that evening. They generally came back driving cattle before them and in good spirits. But this time they had no cattle. All they brought home was the dead body of a Tartar—the red one's brother—who had been killed. They came back looking sullen, and they all gathered together for the burial. Zhílin also came out to see it.

They wrapped the body in a piece of linen, without any coffin, and carried it out of the village, and laid it on the grass under some plane-trees. The Mullah and the old men came. They wound clothes round their caps, took off their shoes, and squatted on their heels, side by side, near the corpse.

The Mullah was in front: behind him in a row were three old men in turbans, and behind them again the other Tartars. All cast down their eyes and sat in silence. This continued a long time, until the Mullah raised his head and said: "Allah!" (which means God). He said that one word, and they all cast down their eyes again, and were again silent for a long time. They sat quite still, not moving or making any sound.

Again the Mullah lifted his head and said, "Allah!" and they all repeated: "Allah! Allah!" and were again silent.

The dead body lay immovable on the grass, and they sat as still as if they too were dead. Not one of them moved. There was no sound but that of the leaves of the plane-trees stirring in the breeze. Then the Mullah repeated a prayer, and they all rose. They lifted the body and carried it in their arms to a hole in the ground. It was not an ordinary hole, but was hollowed out under the ground like a vault. They took the body under the arms and by the legs, bent it, and let it gently down, pushing it under the earth in a sitting posture, with the hands folded in front.

The Nogáy brought some green rushes, which they stuffed into the hole, and, quickly covering it with earth, they smoothed the ground, and set an upright stone at the head of the grave. Then they trod the earth down, and again sat in a row before the grave, keeping silence for a long time.

At last they rose, said "Allah! Allah! Allah!" and sighed.

The red-bearded Tartar gave money to the old men; then he too rose, took a whip, struck himself with it three times on the forehead, and went home.

The next morning Zhílin saw the red Tartar, followed by three others, leading a mare out of the village. When they were beyond the village, the red-bearded Tartar took off his tunic and turned up his sleeves, showing his stout arms. Then he drew a dagger and sharpened it on a whetstone. The other Tartars raised the mare's head, and he cut her throat, threw her down, and began skinning her, loosening the hide with his big hands. Women and girls came and began to wash the entrails and the inwards. The mare was cut up, the pieces taken into the hut, and the whole village collected at the red Tartar's hut for a funeral feast.

For three days they went on eating the flesh of the mare, drinking *buza,* and praying for the dead man. All the Tartars were at home. On the fourth day at dinner-time Zhílin saw them preparing to go away. Horses were brought out, they got ready, and some ten of them (the red one among them) rode away; but Abdul stayed at home. It was new moon, and the nights were still dark.

"Ah!" thought Zhílin, "to-night is the time to escape." And he told Kostílin; but Kostílin's heart failed him.

"How can we escape?" he said. "We don't even know the way."

"I know the way," said Zhílin.

"Even if you do," said Kostílin, "we can't reach the fort in one night."

"If we can't," said Zhílin, "we'll sleep in the forest. See here, I have saved some cheeses. What's the good of sitting and moping here? If they send your ransom—well and good; but suppose they don't manage to collect it? The Tartars are angry now, because the Russians have killed one of their men. They are talking of killing us."

Kostílin thought it over.

"Well, let's go," said he.

V

Zhílin crept into the hole, widened it so that Kostílin might also get through, and then they both sat waiting till all should be quiet in the Aoul.

As soon as all was quiet, Zhílin crept under the wall, got out, and whispered to Kostílin, "Come!" Kostílin crept out, but in so doing he caught a stone with his foot and made a noise. The master had a very vicious watch-dog, a spotted one called Oulyashin. Zhílin had been careful to feed him for some time before. Oulyashin heard the noise and began to bark and jump, and the other dogs did the same. Zhílin gave a slight whistle, and threw him a bit of cheese. Oulyashin knew Zhílin, wagged his tail, and stopped barking.

But the master had heard the dog, and shouted to him from his hut, "Hayt, hayt, Oulyashin!"

Zhílin, however, scratched Oulyashin behind the ears, and the dog was quiet, and rubbed against his legs, wagging his tail.

They sat hidden behind a corner for awhile. All became silent again, only a sheep coughed inside a shed, and the water rippled over the stones in the hollow. It was dark, the stars were high overhead, and the new moon showed red as it set, horns upward, behind the hill. In the valleys the fog was white as milk.

Zhílin rose and said to his companion, "Well, friend, come along!"

They started; but they had only gone a few steps when they heard the Mullah crying from the roof, "Allah, Beshmillah! Ilrahman!" That meant that the people would be going to the Mosque. So they sat down again, hiding behind a wall, and waited a long time till the people had passed. At last all was quiet again.

"Now then! May God be with us!" They crossed themselves, and started once more. They passed through a yard and went down the hillside to the river, crossed the river, and went along the valley.

The mist was thick, but only near the ground; overhead the stars shone quite brightly. Zhílin directed their course by the stars. It was cool in the mist, and easy walking; only their boots were uncomfortable, being worn out and trodden down. Zhílin took his off, threw them away, and went barefoot, jumping from stone to stone, and guiding his course by the stars. Kostílin began to lag behind.

"Walk slower," he said, "these confounded boots have quite blistered my feet."

"Take them off!" said Zhílin. "It will be easier walking without them."

Kostílin went barefoot, but got on still worse. The stones cut his feet, and he kept lagging behind. Zhílin said: "If your feet get cut, they'll heal again; but if the Tartars catch us and kill us, it will be worse!"

Kostílin did not reply, but went on, groaning all the time.

Their way lay through the valley for a long time. Then, to the right, they heard dogs barking. Zhílin stopped, looked about, and began climbing the hill, feeling with his hands.

"Ah!" said he, "we have gone wrong, and have come too far to the right. Here is another Aoul, one I saw from the hill. We must turn back and go up that hill to the left. There must be a wood there."

But Kostílin said: "Wait a minute! Let me get breath. My feet are all cut and bleeding."

"Never mind, friend! They'll heal again. You should spring more lightly. Like this!"

And Zhílin ran back and turned to the left up the hill towards the wood.

Kostílin still lagged behind, and groaned. Zhílin only said "Hush!" and went on and on.

They went up the hill and found a wood as Zhílin had said. They entered the wood and forced their way through the brambles, which tore their clothes. At last they came to a path and followed it.

"Stop!" They heard the tramp of hoofs on the path, and waited, listening. It sounded like the tramping of a horse's feet, but then ceased. They moved on, and again they heard the tramping. When they paused, it also stopped. Zhílin crept nearer to it, and saw something standing on the path where it was not quite so dark. It looked like a horse, and yet not quite like one, and on it was something queer, not like a man. He heard it snorting. "What can it be?" Zhílin gave a low whistle, and off it dashed from the path into the thicket, and the woods were filled with the noise of crackling, as if a hurricane were sweeping through, breaking the branches.

Kostílin was so frightened that he sank to the ground. But Zhílin laughed and said: "It's a stag. Don't you hear him breaking the branches with his antlers? We were afraid of him, and he is afraid of us."

They went on. The Great Bear was already setting. It was near morning, and they did not know whether they were going the right way or not. Zhílin thought it was the way he had been brought by the Tartars, and that they were still some seven miles from the Russian fort; but he had nothing certain to go by, and at night one easily mistakes the way. After a time they came to a clearing. Kostílin sat down and said: "Do as you like, I can go no farther! My feet won't carry me."

Zhílin tried to persuade him.

"No, I shall never get there; I can't!"

Zhílin grew angry, and spoke roughly to him.

"Well, then, I shall go on alone. Good-bye!"

Kostílin jumped up and followed. They went another three miles. The mist in the wood had settled down still more densely; they could not see a yard before them, and the stars had grown dim.

Suddenly they heard the sound of a horse's hoofs in front of them. They heard its shoes strike the stones. Zhílin lay down flat, and listened with his ear to the ground.

"Yes, so it is! A horseman is coming towards us."

They ran off the path, crouched among the bushes, and waited. Zhílin crept to the road, looked, and saw a Tartar on horseback driving a cow and humming to himself. The Tartar rode past. Zhílin returned to Kostílin.

"God has led him past us; get up and let's go on!"

Kostílin tried to rise, but fell back again.

"I can't; on my word I can't! I have no strength left."

He was heavy and stout, and had been perspiring freely. Chilled by the mist, and with his feet all bleeding, he had grown quite limp.

Zhílin tried to lift him, when suddenly Kostílin screamed out: "Oh, how it hurts!"

Zhílin's heart sank.

"What are you shouting for? The Tartar is still near; he'll have heard you!" And he thought to himself, "He is really quite done up. What am I to do with him? It won't do to desert a comrade."

"Well, then, get up, and climb up on my back. I'll carry you if you really can't walk."

He helped Kostílin up, and put his arms under his thighs. Then he went out on to the path, carrying him.

"Only, for the love of heaven," said Zhílin, "don't throttle me with your hands! Hold on to my shoulders."

Zhílin found his load heavy; his feet, too, were bleeding, and he was tired out. Now and then he stooped to balance Kostilin better, jerking him up so that he should sit higher, and then went on again.

The Tartar must, however, really have heard Kostílin scream. Zhílin suddenly heard some one galloping behind and shouting in the Tartar tongue. He darted in among the bushes. The Tartar seized his gun and fired, but did not hit them, shouted in his own language, and galloped off along the road.

"Well, now we are lost, friend!" said Zhílin. "That dog will gather the Tartars together to hunt us down. Unless we can get a couple of miles away from here we are lost!" And he thought to himself, "Why the devil did I saddle myself with this block? I should have got away long ago had I been alone."

"Go on alone," said Kostílin. "Why should you perish because of me?"

"No, I won't go. It won't do to desert a comrade."

Again he took Kostílin on his shoulders and staggered on. They went on in that way for another half-mile or more. They were still in the forest, and could not see the end of it. But the mist was already dispersing, and clouds seemed to be gathering; the stars were no longer to be seen. Zhílin was quite done up. They came to a spring walled in with stones by the side of the path. Zhílin stopped and set Kostílin down.

"Let me have a rest and a drink," said he, "and let us eat some of the cheese. It can't be much farther now."

But hardly had he lain down to get a drink, when he heard the sound of horses' feet behind him. Again they darted to the right among the bushes, and lay down under a steep slope.

They heard Tartar voices. The Tartars stopped at the very spot where they had turned off the path. The Tartars talked a bit, and then seemed to be setting a dog on the scent. There was a sound of crackling twigs, and a strange dog appeared from behind the bushes. It stopped, and began to bark.

Then the Tartars, also strangers, came climbing down, seized Zhílin and Kostílin, bound them, put them on horses, and rode away with them.

When they had ridden about two miles, they met Abdul, their owner, with two other Tartars following him. After talking with the strangers, he put Zhílin and Kostílin on two of his own horses and took them back to the Aoul.

Abdul did not laugh now, and did not say a word to them.

They were back at the Aoul by daybreak, and were set down in the street. The children came crowding round, throwing stones, shrieking, and beating them with whips.

The Tartars gathered together in a circle, and the old man from the foot of the hill was also there. They began discussing; and Zhílin heard them considering what should be done with him and Kostílin. Some said they ought to be sent farther into the mountains; but the old man said: "They must be killed!"

Abdul disputed with him, saying: "I gave money for them, and I must get ransom for them." But the old man said: "They will pay you nothing, but will only bring misfortune. It is a sin to feed Russians. Kill them, and have done with it!"

They dispersed. When they had gone, the master came up to Zhílin and said: "If the money for your ransom is not sent within a fortnight, I will flog you; and if you try to run away again, I'll kill you like a dog! Write a letter, and write properly!"

Paper was brought to them, and they wrote the letters. Shackles were put on their feet, and they were taken behind the Mosque to a deep pit about twelve feet square, into which they were let down.

VI

Life was now very hard for them. Their shackles were never taken off, and they were not let out into the fresh air. Unbaked dough was thrown to them as if they were dogs, and water was let down in a can.

It was wet and close in the pit, and there was a horrible stench. Kostílin grew quite ill, his body became swollen and he ached all over, and moaned or slept all the time. Zhílin, too, grew downcast; he saw it was a bad look-out, and could think of no way of escape.

He tried to make a tunnel, but there was nowhere to put the earth. His master noticed it, and threatened to kill him.

He was sitting on the floor of the pit one day, thinking of freedom and feeling very downhearted, when suddenly a cake fell into his lap, then another, and then a shower of cherries. He looked up, and there was Dina. She looked at him, laughed, and ran away. And Zhílin thought: "Might not Dina help me?"

He cleared out a little place in the pit, scraped up some clay, and began modelling toys. He made men, horses, and dogs, thinking, "When Dina comes I'll throw them up to her."

But Dina did not come next day. Zhílin heard the tramp of horses; some men rode past, and the Tartars gathered in council near the Mosque. They shouted and argued; the word "Russians" was repeated several times. He could hear the voice of the old man. Though he could not distinguish what was said, he guessed that Russian troops were somewhere near, and that the Tartars, afraid they might come into the Aoul, did not know what to do with their prisoners.

After talking awhile, they went away. Suddenly he heard a rustling overhead, and saw Dina crouching at the edge of the pit, her knees higher than her head, and bending over so that the coins of her plait dangled above the pit. Her eyes gleamed like stars. She drew two cheeses out of her sleeve and threw them to him. Zhílin took them and said, "Why did you not come before? I have made some toys for you. Here, catch!" And he began throwing the toys up, one by one.

But she shook her head and would not look at them.

"I don't want any," she said. She sat silent for awhile, and then went on, "Iván, they want to kill you!" And she pointed to her own throat.

"Who wants to kill me?"

"Father; the old men say he must. But I am sorry for you!"

Zhílin answered: "Well, if you are sorry for me, bring me a long pole."

She shook her head, as much as to say, "I can't!"

He clasped his hands and prayed her: "Dina, please do! Dear Dina, I beg of you!"

"I can't!" she said, "they would see me bringing it. They're all at home." And she went away.

So when evening came Zhílin still sat looking up now and then, and wondering what would happen. The stars were there, but the moon had not yet risen. The Mullah's voice was heard; then all was silent. Zhílin was beginning to doze, thinking: "The girl will be afraid to do it!"

Suddenly he felt clay falling on his head. He looked up, and saw a long pole poking into the opposite wall of the pit. It kept poking about for a time, and then it came down, sliding into the pit. Zhílin was glad indeed. He took hold of it and lowered it. It was a strong pole, one that he had seen before on the roof of his master's hut.

He looked up. The stars were shining high in the sky, and just above the pit Dina's eyes gleamed in the dark like a cat's. She stooped with her face close to the edge of the pit, and whispered, "Iván! Iván!" waving her hand in front of her face to show that he should speak low.

"What?" said Zhílin.

"All but two have gone away."

Then Zhílin said, "Well, Kostílin, come; let us have one last try; I'll help you up."

But Kostílin would not hear of it.

"No," said he, "It's clear I can't get away from here. How can I go, when I have hardly strength to turn round?"

"Well, good-bye, then! Don't think ill of me!" and they kissed each other. Zhílin seized the pole, told Dina to hold on, and began to climb. He slipped once or twice; the shackles hindered him. Kostílin helped him, and he managed to get to the top. Dina, with her little hands, pulled with all her might at his shirt, laughing.

Zhílin drew out the pole, and said, "Put it back in its place, Dina, or they'll notice, and you will be beaten."

She dragged the pole away, and Zhílin went down the hill. When he had gone down the steep incline, he took a sharp stone and tried to wrench the lock off the shackles. But it was a strong lock and he could not manage to break it, and besides, it was difficult to get at. Then he heard some one running down the hill, springing lightly. He thought: "Surely, that's Dina again."

Dina came, took a stone, and said, "Let me try."

She knelt down and tried to wrench the lock off, but her little hands were as slender as little twigs, and she had not the strength. She threw the stone away and began to cry. Then Zhílin set to work again at the lock, and Dina squatted beside him with her hand on his shoulder.

Zhílin looked round and saw a red light to the left behind the hill. The moon was just rising. "Ah!" he thought, "before the moon has risen I must have passed the valley and be in the forest." So he rose and threw away the stone. Shackles or no, he must go on.

"Good-bye, Dina dear!" he said. "I shall never forget you!"

Dina seized hold of him and felt about with her hands for a place to put some cheeses she had brought. He took them from her.

"Thank you, my little one. Who will make dolls for you when I am gone?" And he stroked her head.

Dina burst into tears, hiding her face in her hands. Then she ran up the hill like a young goat, the coins in her plait clinking against her back.

Zhílin crossed himself, took the lock of his shackles in his hand to prevent its clattering, and went along the road, dragging his shackled leg, and looking towards the place where the moon was about to rise. He now knew the way. If he went straight he would have to walk nearly six miles. If only he could reach the wood before the moon had quite risen! He crossed the river; the light behind the hill was growing whiter. Still looking at it, he went along the valley. The moon was not yet visible. The light became brighter, and one side of the valley was growing lighter and lighter, and shadows were drawing in towards the foot of the hill, creeping nearer and nearer to him.

Zhílin went on, keeping in the shade. He was hurrying, but the moon was moving still faster; the tops of the hills on the right were already lit up. As he got near the wood the white moon appeared from behind the hills, and it became light as day. One could see all the leaves on the trees. It was light on the hill, but silent, as if nothing were alive; no sound could be heard but the gurgling of the river below.

Zhílin reached the wood without meeting any one, chose a dark spot, and sat down to rest.

He rested, and ate one of the cheeses. Then he found a stone and set to work again to knock off the shackles. He knocked his hands sore, but could not break the lock. He rose and went along the road. After walking the greater part of a mile he was quite done up, and his feet were aching. He had to stop every ten steps. "There is nothing else for it," thought he. "I must drag on as long as I have any strength left. If I sit down, I shan't be able to rise again. I can't reach the fortress; but when day breaks I'll lie down in the forest, remain there all day, and go on again at night."

He went on all night. Two Tartars on horseback passed him; but he heard them a long way off, and hid behind a tree.

The moon began to grow paler, the dew to fall. It was getting near dawn, and Zhílin had not reached the end of the forest. "Well," thought he, "I'll walk another thirty steps, and then turn in among the trees and sit down."

He walked another thirty steps, and saw that he was at the end of the forest. He went to the edge; it was now quite light, and straight before him was the plain and the fortress. To the left, quite close at the foot of the slope, a fire was dying out, and the smoke from it spread round. There were men gathered about the fire.

He looked intently, and saw guns glistening. They were soldiers—Cossacks!

Zhílin was filled with joy. He collected his remaining strength and set off down the hill, saying to himself: "God forbid that any mounted Tartar should see me now, in the open field! Near as I am, I could not get there in time."

Hardly had he said this when, a couple of hundred yards off, on a hillock to the left, he saw three Tartars.

They saw him also and made a rush. His heart sank. He waved his hands, and shouted with all his might, "Brothers, brothers! Help!"

The Cossacks heard him, and a party of them on horseback darted to cut across the Tartars' path. The Cossacks were far and the Tartars were near; but Zhílin, too, made a last effort. Lifting the shackles with his hand, he ran towards the Cossacks, hardly knowing what he was doing, crossing himself and shouting, "Brothers! Brothers! Brothers!"

There were some fifteen Cossacks. The Tartars were frightened, and stopped before reaching him. Zhílin staggered up to the Cossacks.

They surrounded him and began questioning him. "Who are you? What are you? Where from?"

But Zhílin was quite beside himself, and could only weep and repeat, "Brothers! Brothers!"

Then the soldiers came running up and crowded round Zhílin—one giving him bread, another buckwheat, a third vódka: one wrapping a cloak round him, another breaking his shackles.

The officers recognized him, and rode with him to the fortress. The soldiers were glad to see him back, and his comrades all gathered round him.

Zhílin told them all that had happened to him.

"That's the way I went home and got married!" said he. "No. It seems plain that fate was against it!"

So he went on serving in the Caucasus. A month passed before Kostílin was released, after paying five thousand roubles ransom. He was almost dead when they brought him back.

TWO OLD MEN

I

"The woman saith unto him, Sir, I perceive that thou art a prophet. Our fathers worshipped in this mountain; and ye say, that in Jerusalem is the place where men ought to worship. Jesus saith unto her, Woman, believe me, the hour cometh when neither in this mountain, nor in Jerusalem, shall ye worship the Father. . . . But the hour cometh, and now is, when the true worshippers shall worship the Father in spirit and truth: for such doth the Father seek to be his worshippers."—*John* iv. 19–21, 23.

THERE WERE ONCE two old men who decided to go on a pilgrimage to worship God at Jerusalem. One of them was a well-to-do peasant named Efím Tarásitch Shevélef. The other, Elisha Bódrof, was not so well off.

Efím was a staid man, serious and firm. He neither drank nor smoked nor took snuff, and had never used bad language in his life. He had twice served as village Elder, and when he left office his accounts were in good order. He had a large family: two sons and a married grandson, all living with him. He was hale, long-bearded and erect, and it was only when he was past sixty that a little grey began to show itself in his beard.

Elisha was neither rich nor poor. He had formerly gone out carpentering, but now that he was growing old he stayed at home and kept bees. One of his sons had gone away to find work, the other was living at home. Elisha was a kindly and cheerful old man. It is true he drank sometimes, and he took snuff, and was fond of singing; but he was a peaceable man, and lived on good terms with his family and with his neighbours. He was short and dark, with a curly beard, and, like his patron saint Elisha, he was quite bald-headed.

The two old men had taken a vow long since and had arranged to go on a pilgrimage to Jerusalem together: but Efim could never spare the time; he always had so much business on hand; as soon as one thing was finished he started another. First he had to arrange his grandson's marriage; then to wait for his youngest son's return from the army, and after that he began building a new hut.

One holiday the two old men met outside the hut and, sitting down on some timber, began to talk.

"Well," asked Elisha, "when are we to fulfil our vow?"

Efim made a wry face.

"We must wait," he said. "This year has turned out a hard one for me. I started building this hut thinking it would cost me something over a hundred roubles, but now it's getting on for three hundred and it's still not finished. We shall have to wait till the summer. In summer, God willing, we will go without fail."

"It seems to me we ought not to put it off, but should go at once," said Elisha. "Spring is the best time."

"The time's right enough, but what about my building? How can I leave that?"

"As if you had no one to leave in charge! Your son can look after it."

"But how? My eldest son is not trustworthy—he sometimes takes a glass too much."

"Ah, neighbour, when we die they'll get on without us. Let your son begin now to get some experience."

"That's true enough; but somehow when one begins a thing one likes to see it done."

"Eh, friend, we can never get through all we have to do. The other day the women-folk at home were washing and house-cleaning for Easter. Here something needed doing, there something else, and they could not get everything done. So my eldest daughter-in-law, who's a sensible woman, says: "We may be thankful the holiday comes without waiting for us, or however hard we worked we should never be ready for it.""

Efim became thoughtful.

"I've spent a lot of money on this building," he said, "and one can't start on the journey with empty pockets. We shall want a hundred roubles apiece—and it's no small sum."

Elisha laughed.

"Now, come, come, old friend!" he said, "you have ten times as much as I, and yet you talk about money. Only say when we are to start, and though I have nothing now I shall have enough by then."

Efím also smiled.

"Dear me, I did not know you were so rich!" said he. "Why, where will you get it from?"

"I can scrape some together at home, and if that's not enough, I'll sell half a score of hives to my neighbour. He's long been wanting to buy them."

"If they swarm well this year, you'll regret it."

"Regret it! Not I, neighbour! I never regretted anything in my life, except my sins. There's nothing more precious than the soul."

"That's so; still it's not right to neglect things at home."

"But what if our souls are neglected? That's worse. We took the vow, so let us go! Now, seriously, let us go!"

II

Elisha succeeded in persuading his comrade. In the morning, after thinking it well over, Efím came to Elisha.

"You are right," said he, "let us go. Life and death are in God's hands. We must go now, while we are still alive and have the strength."

A week later the old men were ready to start. Efím had money enough at hand. He took a hundred roubles himself, and left two hundred with his wife.

Elisha, too, got ready. He sold ten hives to his neighbour, with any new swarms that might come from them before the summer. He took seventy roubles for the lot. The rest of the hundred roubles he scraped together from the other members of his household, fairly clearing them all out. His wife gave him all she had been saving up for her funeral; and his daughter-in-law also gave him what she had.

Efím gave his eldest son definite orders about everything: when and how much grass to mow, where to cart the manure, and how to finish off and roof the cottage. He thought out everything, and gave his orders accordingly. Elisha, on the other hand, only explained to his wife that she was to keep separate the swarms from the hives he had sold, and to be sure to let the neighbour have them all, without any tricks. As to household affairs, he did not even mention them.

"You will see what to do and how to do it, as the needs arise," he said. "You are the masters, and will know how to do what's best for yourselves."

So the old men got ready. Their people baked them cakes, and made bags for them, and cut them linen for leg-bands*. They put on new leather shoes, and took with them spare shoes of platted bark. Their families went with them to the end of the village and there took leave of them, and the old men started on their pilgrimage.

Elisha left home in a cheerful mood, and as soon as he was out of the village forgot all his home affairs. His only care was how to please his comrade, how to avoid saying a rude word to any one, how to get to his destination and home again in peace and love. Walking along the road, Elisha would either whisper some prayer to himself or go over in his mind such of the lives of the saints as he was able to remember. When he came across any one on the road, or turned in anywhere for the night, he tried to behave as gently as possible and to say a godly word. So he journeyed on, rejoicing. One thing only he could not do, he could not give up taking snuff. Though he had left his snuff-box behind, he hankered after it. Then a man he met on the road gave him some snuff; and every now and then he would lag behind (not to lead his comrade into temptation) and would take a pinch of snuff.

Efim too walked well and firmly; doing no wrong and speaking no vain words, but his heart was not so light. Household cares weighed on his mind. He kept worrying about what was going on at home. Had he not forgotten to give his son this or that order? Would his son do things properly? If he happened to see potatoes being planted or manure carted, as he went along, he wondered if his son was doing as he had been told. And he almost wanted to turn back and show him how to do things, or even do them himself.

III

The old men had been walking for five weeks, they had worn out their home-made bark shoes, and had to begin buying new ones when they reached Little Russia†. From the time they left home they had had to pay for their food and for their night's lodging, but when

---

* Worn by Russian peasants instead of stockings.
† Little Russia is situated in the south-western part of Russia, and consists of the Governments of Kief, Poltava, Tohernigof, and part of Kharkof and Kherson.

they reached Little Russia the people vied with one another in asking them into their huts. They took them in and fed them, and would accept no payment; and, more than that, they put bread or even cakes into their bags for them to eat on the road.

The old men travelled some five hundred miles in this manner free of expense, but after they had crossed the next province, they came to a district where the harvest had failed. The peasants still gave them free lodging at night, but no longer fed them for nothing. Sometimes, even, they could get no bread: they offered to pay for it, but there was none to be had. The people said the harvest had completely failed the year before. Those who had been rich were ruined and had had to sell all they possessed; those of moderate means were left destitute, and those of the poor who had not left those parts, wandered about begging, or starved at home in utter want. In the winter they had had to eat husks and goosefoot.

One night the old men stopped in a small village; they bought fifteen pounds of bread, slept there, and started before sunrise, to get well on their way before the heat of the day. When they had gone some eight miles, on coming to a stream they sat down, and, filling a bowl with water, they steeped some bread in it, and ate it. Then they changed their leg-bands, and rested for a while. Elisha took out his snuff-box. Efim shook his head at him.

"How is it you don't give up that nasty habit?" said he.

Elisha waved his hand. "The evil habit is stronger than I," he said.

Presently they got up and went on. After walking for nearly another eight miles, they came to a large village and passed right through it. It had now grown hot. Elisha was tired out and wanted to rest and have a drink, but Efim did not stop. Efim was the better walker of the two, and Elisha found it hard to keep up with him.

"If I could only have a drink," said he.

"Well, have a drink," said Efim. "I don't want any."

Elisha stopped.

"You go on," he said, "but I'll just run in to the little hut there. I will catch you up in a moment."

"All right," said Efim, and he went on along the high road alone, while Elisha turned back to the hut.

It was a small hut plastered with clay, the bottom a dark colour, the top whitewashed; but the clay had crumbled away. Evidently it was long since it had been re-plastered, and the thatch was off the roof on one side. The entrance to the hut was through the yard. Elisha entered the yard, and saw, lying close to a bank of earth that ran round the hut, a gaunt, beardless man with his shirt tucked into his trousers, as is the custom in Little Russia*. The man must have lain down in the shade, but the sun had come round and now shone full on him. Though not asleep, he still lay there. Elisha called to him, and asked for a drink, but the man gave no answer.

"He is either ill or unfriendly," thought Elisha; and going to the door he heard a child crying in the hut. He took hold of the ring that served as a door-handle, and knocked with it.

"Hey, masters!" he called. No answer. He knocked again with his staff.

"Hey, Christians!" Nothing stirred.

"Hey, servants of God!" Still no reply.

Elisha was about to turn away, when he thought he heard a groan the other side of the door.

"Dear me, some misfortune must have happened to the people? I had better have a look."

And Elisha entered the hut.

IV

Elisha turned the ring; the door was not fastened. He opened it and went along up the narrow passage. The door into the dwelling-room was open. To the left was a brick oven; in front against the wall was an icon-stand† and a table before it; by the table was a bench on which sat an old woman, bareheaded and wearing only a single garment. There she sat with her head resting on the table, and near her was a thin, wax-coloured boy, with a protruding stomach. He was asking for something, pulling at her sleeve, and crying bitterly. Elisha entered. The air in the hut was very foul. He looked round, and saw a woman lying on the floor behind the oven: she lay flat on the ground with her eyes closed and her throat rattling, now stretching out a leg, now dragging it in, tossing from side to side; and the foul smell came from her. Evidently she could do nothing for herself and no one had been attending to her needs. The old woman lifted her head, and saw the stranger.

---

* In Great Russia the peasants let their shirt hang outside their trousers.
† An icon (properly ikón) is a representation of God, Christ, an angel, or a saint, usually painted, enamelled, or embossed.

"What do you want?" said she. "What do you want, man? We have nothing."

Elisha understood her, though she spoke in the Little-Russian dialect.

"I came in for a drink of water, servant of God," he said.

"There's no one—no one—we have nothing to fetch it in. Go your way."

Then Elisha asked:

"Is there no one among you, then, well enough to attend to that woman?"

"No, we have no one. My son is dying outside, and we are dying in here."

The little boy had ceased crying when he saw the stranger, but when the old woman began to speak, he began again, and clutching hold of her sleeve cried:

"Bread, Granny, bread."

Elisha was about to question the old woman, when the man staggered into the hut. He came along the passage, clinging to the wall, but as he was entering the dwelling-room he fell in the corner near the threshold, and without trying to get up again to reach the bench, he began to speak in broken words. He brought out a word at a time, stopping to draw breath, and gasping.

"Illness has seized us . . . ," said he, "and famine. He is dying . . . of hunger."

And he motioned towards the boy, and began to sob.

Elisha jerked up the sack behind his shoulder and, pulling the straps off his arms, put it on the floor. Then he lifted it on to the bench, and untied the strings. Having opened the sack, he took out a loaf of bread, and, cutting off a piece with his knife, handed it to the man. The man would not take it, but pointed to the little boy and to a little girl crouching behind the oven, as if to say:

"Give it to them."

Elisha held it out to the boy. When the boy smelt bread, he stretched out his arms, and seizing the slice with both his little hands, bit into it so that his nose disappeared in the chunk. The little girl came out from behind the oven and fixed her eyes on the bread. Elisha gave her also a slice. Then he cut off another piece and gave it to the old woman, and she too began munching it.

"If only some water could be brought," she said, "their mouths are parched. I tried to fetch some water yesterday—or was it to-day—I can't remember, but I fell down and could go no further, and the pail has remained there, unless some one has taken it."

Elisha asked where the well was. The old woman told him. Elisha went out, found the pail, brought some water, and gave the people a drink. The children and the old woman ate some more bread with the water, but the man would not eat.

"I cannot eat," he said.

All this time the younger woman did not show any consciousness, but continued to toss from side to side. Presently Elisha went to the village shop and bought some millet, salt, flour, and oil. He found an axe, chopped some wood, and made a fire. The little girl came and helped him. Then he boiled some soup, and gave the starving people a meal.

V

The man ate a little, the old woman had some too, and the little girl and boy licked the bowl clean, and then curled up and fell fast asleep in one another's arms.

The man and the old woman then began telling Elisha how they had sunk to their present state.

"We were poor enough before?" said they, "but when the crops failed, what we gathered hardly lasted us through the autumn. We had nothing left by the time winter came, and had to beg from the neighbours and from any one we could. At first they gave, then they began to refuse. Some would have been glad enough to help us, but had nothing to give. And we were ashamed of asking: we were in debt all round, and owed money, and flour, and bread."

"I went to look for work," the man said, "but could find none. Everywhere people were offering to work merely for their own keep. One day you'd get a short job, and then you might spend two days looking for work. Then the old woman and the girl went begging, further away. But they got very little; bread was so scarce. Still we scraped food together somehow, and hoped to struggle through till next harvest, but towards spring people ceased to give anything. And then this illness seized us. Things became worse and worse. One day we might have something to eat, and then nothing for two days. We began eating grass. Whether it was the grass, or what, made my wife ill, I don't know. She could not keep on her legs, and I had no strength left, and there was nothing to help us to recovery."

"I struggled on alone for a while," said the old woman, "but at last I broke down too for want of food, and grew quite weak. The girl also grew weak and timid. I told her to go to the neighbours—she would not leave the hut, but crept into a corner and sat there. The day before yesterday a neighbour looked in, but seeing that we were ill and hungry she turned away and left us. Her husband has had to go away, and she has nothing for her own little ones to eat. And so we lay, waiting for death."

Having heard their story, Elisha gave up the thought of overtaking his comrade that day, and remained with them all night. In the morning he got up and began doing the housework, just as if it were his own home. He kneaded the bread with the old woman's help, and lit the fire. Then he went with the little girl to the neighbours to get the most necessary things; for there was nothing in the hut: everything had been sold for bread—cooking utensils, clothing, and all. So Elisha began replacing what was necessary, making some things himself, and buying some. He remained there one day, then another, and then a third. The little boy picked up strength and, whenever Elisha sat down, crept along the bench and nestled up to him. The little girl brightened up and helped in all the work, running after Elisha and calling,

"Daddy, daddy."

The old woman grew stronger, and managed to go out to see a neighbour. The man too improved, and was able to get about, holding on to the wall. Only the wife could not get up, but even she regained consciousness on the third day, and asked for food.

"Well," thought Elisha, "I never expected to waste so much time on the way. Now I must be getting on."

VI

The fourth day was the feast day after the summer fast, and Elisha thought:

"I will stay and break the fast with these people. I'll go and buy them something, and keep the feast with them, and to-morrow evening I will start."

So Elisha went into the village, bought milk, wheat-flour and dripping, and helped the old woman to boil and bake for the morrow. On the feast day Elisha went to church, and then broke the fast with his friends at the hut. That day the wife got up, and managed to move about a bit. The husband had shaved and put on a clean shirt, which the old woman had washed for him; and he went to beg for mercy of a rich peasant in the village to whom his plough-land and meadow were mortgaged. He went to beg the rich peasant to grant him the use of the meadow and field till after the harvest; but in the evening he came back very sad, and began to weep. The rich peasant had shown no mercy, but had said: "Bring me the money."

Elisha again grew thoughtful. "How are they to live now?" thought he to himself. "Other people will go haymaking, but there will be nothing for these to mow, their grass land is mortgaged. The rye will ripen. Others will reap (and what a fine crop mother-earth is giving this year), but they have nothing to look forward to. Their three acres are pledged to the rich peasant. When I am gone, they'll drift back into the state I found them in."

Elisha was in two minds, but finally decided not to leave that evening, but to wait until the morrow. He went out into the yard to sleep. He said his prayers, and lay down; but he could not sleep. On the one hand he felt he ought to be going, for he had spent too much time and money as it was; on the other hand he felt sorry for the people.

"There seems to be no end to it," he said. "First I only meant to bring them a little water and give them each a slice of bread: and just see where it has landed me. It's a case of redeeming the meadow and the cornfield. And when I have done that, I shall have to buy a cow for them, and a horse for the man to cart his sheaves. A nice coil you've got yourself into, brother Elisha! You've slipped your cables and lost your reckoning!"

Elisha got up, lifted his coat which he had been using for a pillow, unfolded it, got out his snuff-box and took a pinch, thinking that it might perhaps clear his thoughts.

But no! He thought and thought, and came to no conclusion. He ought to be going; and yet pity held him back. He did not know what to do. He refolded his coat and put it under his head again. He lay thus for a long time, till the cocks had already crowed once: then he was quite drowsy. And suddenly it seemed as if some one had roused him. He saw that he was dressed for the journey, with the sack on his back and the staff in his hand, and the gate stood ajar so that he could just squeeze through. He was about to pass out, when his sack caught against the fence on one side: he tried to free it, but then his leg-band caught on the other side and came undone. He pulled at the sack, and saw that it had not caught on the fence, but that the little girl was holding it and crying,

"Bread, daddy, bread!"

He looked at his foot, and there was the tiny boy holding him by the leg-band, while the master of the hut and the old woman were looking at him through the window.

Elisha awoke, and said to himself in an audible voice:

"To-morrow I will redeem their cornfield, and will buy them a horse, and flour to last till the harvest, and a cow for the little ones; or else while I go to seek the Lord beyond the sea, I may lose Him in myself."

Then Elisha fell asleep, and slept till morning. He awoke early, and going to the rich peasant, redeemed both the cornfield and the meadow land. He bought a scythe (for that also had been sold) and brought it back with him. Then he sent the man to mow, and himself went into the village. He heard that there was a horse and cart for sale at the public-house, and he struck a bargain with the owner, and bought them. Then he bought a sack of flour, put it in the cart, and went to see about a cow. As he was going along he overtook two women talking as they went. Though they spake the Little-Russian dialect, he understood what they were saying.

"At first, it seems, they did not know him; they thought he was just an ordinary man. He came in to ask for a drink of water, and then he remained. Just think of the things he has bought for them! Why they say he bought a horse and cart for them at the publican's, only this morning! There are not many such men in the world. It's worth while going to have a look at him."

Elisha heard and understood that he was being praised, and he did not go to buy the cow, but returned to the inn, paid for the horse, harnessed it, drove up to the hut, and got out. The people in the hut were astonished when they saw the horse. They thought it might be for them, but dared not ask. The man came out to open the gate.

"Where did you get a horse from, grandfather," he asked.

"Why, I bought it," said Elisha. "It was going cheap. Go and cut some grass and put it in the manger for it to eat during the night. And take in the sack."

The man unharnessed the horse, and carried the sack into the barn. Then he mowed some grass and put it in the manger. Everybody lay down to sleep. Elisha went outside and lay by the roadside. That evening he took his bag out with him. When every one was asleep, he got up, packed and fastened his bag, wrapped the linen bands round his legs, put on his shoes and coat, and set off to follow Efim.

VII

When Elisha had walked rather more than three miles it began to grow light, He sat down under a tree, opened his bag, counted his money, and found he had only seventeen roubles and twenty kopeks left.

"Well," thought he, "it is no use trying to cross the sea with this. If I beg my way it may be worse than not going at all. Friend Efim will get to Jerusalem without me, and will place a candle at the shrines in my name. As for me, I'm afraid I shall never fulfil my vow in this life. I must be thankful it was made to a merciful Master, and to one who pardons sinners."

Elisha rose, jerked his bag well up on his shoulders, and turned back. Not wishing to be recognized by any one, he made a circuit to avoid the village, and walked briskly homeward. Coming from home the way had seemed difficult to him, and he had found it hard to keep up with Efim, but now on his return journey, God helped him to get over the ground so that he hardly felt fatigue. Walking seemed like child's play. He went along swinging his staff, and did his forty to fifty miles a day.

When Elisha reached home the harvest was over. His family were delighted to see him again, and all wanted to know what had happened: Why and how he had been left behind? And why he had returned without reaching Jerusalem? But Elisha did not tell them.

"It was not God's will that I should get there," said he. "I lost my money on the way, and lagged behind my companion. Forgive me, for the Lord's sake!"

Elisha gave his old wife what money he had left. Then he questioned them about home affairs. Everything was going on well; all the work had been done, nothing neglected, and all were living in peace and concord.

Efim's family heard of his return the same day, and came for news of their old man; and to them Elisha gave the same answers.

"Efim is a fast walker. We parted three days before St. Peter's day, and I meant to catch him up again, but all sorts of things happened. I lost my money, and had no means to get any further, so I turned back."

The folks were astonished that so sensible a man should have acted so foolishly: should have started and not got to his destination, and should have squandered all his money. They wondered at it for a while, and then forgot all about it; and Elisha forgot it too. He set to work again on his homestead. With his son's help he cut wood for fuel for the winter. He and the women threshed the corn. Then he mended the thatch on the outhouses, put the bees under cover, and handed over to his neighbour the ten hives he had sold him in spring, and all the swarms that had come from them. His wife tried not to tell how many swarms there had been from these hives, but Elisha knew well enough from which there had been swarms and from which not. And instead of ten, he handed over seventeen swarms to his neighbour. Having got everything ready for the winter, Elisha sent his son away to find work, while he himself took to platting shoes of bark, and hollowing out logs for hives.

VIII

All that day while Elisha stopped behind in the hut with the sick people, Efim waited for him. He only went on a little way before he sat down. He waited and waited, had a nap, woke up again, and again sat waiting; but his comrade did not come. He gazed till his eyes ached. The sun was already sinking behind a tree, and still no Elisha was to be seen.

"Perhaps he has passed me," thought Efim, "or perhaps some one gave him a lift and he drove by while I slept, and did not see me. But how could he help seeing me? One can see so far here in the steppe. Shall I go back? Suppose he is on in front, we shall then miss each other completely and it will be still worse. I had better go on, and we shall be sure to meet where we put up for the night."

He came to a village, and told the watchman, if an old man of a certain description came along, to bring him to the hut where Efim stopped. But Elisha did not turn up that night. Efim went on, asking all he met whether they had not seen a little, bald-headed, old man? No one had seen such a traveller. Efim wondered, but went on alone, saying:

"We shall be sure to meet in Odessa, or on board the ship," and he did not trouble more about it.

On the way, he came across a pilgrim wearing a priest's coat, with long hair and a skull-cap such as priests wear. This pilgrim had been to Mount Athos, and was now going to Jerusalem for the second time. They both stopped at the same place one night, and, having met, they travelled on together.

They got safely to Odessa, and there had to wait three days for a ship. Many pilgrims from many different parts were in the same case. Again Efim asked about Elisha, but no one had seen him.

Efím got himself a foreign passport, which cost him five roubles. He paid forty roubles for a return ticket to Jerusalem, and bought a supply of bread and herrings for the voyage.

The pilgrim began explaining to Efím how he might get on to the ship without paying his fare; but Efím would not listen. "No, I came prepared to pay, and I shall pay," said he.

The ship was freighted, and the pilgrims went on board, Efím and his new comrade among them. The anchors were weighed, and the ship put out to sea.

All day they sailed smoothly, but towards night a wind arose, rain came on, and the vessel tossed about and shipped water. The people were frightened: the women wailed and screamed, and some of the weaker men ran about the ship looking for shelter. Efím too was frightened, but he would not show it, and remained at the place on deck where he had settled down when first he came on board, beside some old men from Tambóf. There they sat silent, all night and all next day, holding on to their sacks. On the third day it grew calm, and on the fifth day they anchored at Constantinople. Some of the pilgrims went on shore to visit the Church of St. Sophia, now held by the Turks. Efím remained on the ship, and only bought some white bread. They lay there for twenty-four hours, and then put to sea again. At Smyrna they stopped again; and at Alexandria; but at last they arrived safely at Jaffa, where all the pilgrims had to disembark. From there still it was more than forty miles by road to Jerusalem. When disembarking the people were again much frightened. The ship was high, and the people were dropped into boats, which rocked so much that it was easy to miss them and fall into the water. A couple of men did get a wetting, but at last all were safely landed.

They went on on foot, and at noon on the third day reached Jerusalem. They stopped outside the town, at the Russian inn, where their passports were indorsed. Then, after dinner, Efím visited the Holy Places with his companion, the pilgrim. It was not the time when they could be admitted to the Holy Sepulchre, but they went to the Patriarchate. All the pilgrims assembled there. The women were separated from the men, who were all told to sit in a circle, barefoot. Then a monk came in with a towel to wash their feet. He washed, wiped, and then kissed their feet, and did this to every one in the circle. Efím's feet were washed and kissed, with the rest. He stood through vespers and matins, prayed, placed candles at the shrines, handed in booklets inscribed with his parents' names, that they might be mentioned in the church prayers. Here at the Patriarchate food

and wine were given them. Next morning they went to the cell of
Mary of Egypt, where she had lived doing penance. Here too they
placed candles and had prayers read. From there they went to Abraham's Monastery, and saw the place where Abraham intended to slay
his son as an offering to God. Then they visited the spot where Christ
appeared to Mary Magdalene, and the Church of James, the Lord's
brother. The pilgrim showed Efím all these places, and told him how
much money to give at each place. At mid-day they returned to the
inn and had dinner. As they were preparing to lie down and rest,
the pilgrim cried out, and began to search his clothes, feeling them
all over.

"My purse has been stolen, there were twenty-three roubles in
it," said he, "two ten-rouble notes and the rest in change."

He sighed and lamented a great deal, but as there was no help for
it, they lay down to sleep.

IX

As Efím lay there, he was assailed by temptation.

"No one has stolen any money from this pilgrim," thought he, "I
do not believe he had any. He gave none away anywhere, though
he made me give, and even borrowed a rouble of me."

This thought had no sooner crossed his mind, than Efím rebuked
himself, saying: "What right have I to judge a man? It is a sin. I will
think no more about it." But as soon as his thoughts began to wan-
der, they turned again to the pilgrim: how interested he seemed to
be in money, and how unlikely it sounded when he declared that
his purse had been stolen.

"He never had any money," thought Efím. "It's all an invention."

Towards evening they got up, and went to midnight Mass at the
great Church of the Resurrection, where the Lord's Sepulchre is.
The pilgrim kept close to Efím and went with him everywhere.
They came to the Church; a great many pilgrims were there; some
Russians and some of other nationalities: Greeks, Armenians, Turks,
and Syrians. Efím entered the Holy Gates with the crowd. A monk
led them past the Turkish sentinels, to the place where the Saviour
was taken down from the cross and anointed, and where candles
were burning in nine great candlesticks. The monk showed and
explained everything. Efím offered a candle there. Then the monk
led Efím to the right, up the steps to Golgotha, to the place where

the cross had stood. Efím prayed there. Then they showed him the cleft where the ground had been rent asunder to its nethermost depths; then the place where Christ's hands and feet were nailed to the cross; then Adam's tomb, where the blood of Christ had dripped on to Adam's bones. Then they showed him the stone on which Christ sat when the crown of thorns was placed on His head; then the post to which Christ was bound when He was scourged. Then Efím saw the stone with two holes for Christ's feet. They were going to show him something else, but there was a stir in the crowd, and the people all hurried to the church of the Lord's Sepulchre itself. The Latin Mass had just finished there, and the Russian Mass was beginning. And Efím went with the crowd to the tomb cut in the rock.

He tried to get rid of the pilgrim, against whom he was still sinning in his mind, but the pilgrim would not leave him, but went with him to the Mass at the Holy Sepulchre. They tried to get to the front, but were too late. There was such a crowd that it was impossible to move either backwards or forwards. Efím stood looking in front of him, praying, and every now and then feeling for his purse. He was in two minds: sometimes he thought that the pilgrim was deceiving him, and then again he thought that if the pilgrim spoke the truth and his purse had really been stolen, the same thing might happen to himself.

X

Efím stood there gazing into the little chapel in which was the Holy Sepulchre itself with thirty-six lamps burning above it. As he stood looking over the people's heads, he saw something that surprised him. Just beneath the lamps in which the sacred fire burns, and in front of every one, Efím saw an old man in a grey coat, whose bald, shining head was just like Elisha Bódrof.

"It is like him," thought Efím, "but it cannot be Elisha. He could not have got ahead of me. The ship before ours started a week sooner. He could not have caught that; and he was not on ours, for I saw every pilgrim on board."

Hardly had Efím thought this, when the little old man began to pray, and bowed three times: once forwards to God, then once on each side—to the brethren. And as he turned his head to the right, Efím recognized him. It was Elisha Bódrof himself, with his dark, curly beard turning grey at the cheeks, with his brows, his eyes and nose, and his expression of face. Yes, it was he!

Efím was very pleased to have found his comrade again, and wondered how Elisha had got ahead of him.

"Well done, Elisha!" thought he. "See how he has pushed ahead. He must have come across some one who showed him the way. When we get out, I will find him, get rid of this fellow in the skull-cap, and keep to Elisha. Perhaps he will show me how to get to the front also."

Efím kept looking out, so as not to lose sight of Elisha. But when the Mass was over, the crowd began to sway, pushing forward to kiss the tomb, and pushed Efím aside. He was again seized with fear lest his purse should be stolen. Pressing it with his hand, he began elbowing through the crowd, anxious only to get out. When he reached the open, he went about for a long time searching for Elisha both outside and in the Church itself. In the cells of the Church he saw many people of all kinds, eating, and drinking wine, and reading and sleeping there. But Elisha was nowhere to be seen. So Efím returned to the inn without having found his comrade. That evening the pilgrim in the skull-cap did not turn up. He had gone off without repaying the rouble, and Efím was left alone.

The next day Efím went to the Holy Sepulchre again, with an old man from Tambóf, whom he had met on the ship. He tried to get to the front, but was again pressed back; so he stood by a pillar and prayed. He looked before him, and there in the foremost place under the lamps, close to the very Sepulchre of the Lord, stood Elisha, with his arms spread out like a priest at the altar, and with his bald head all shining.

"Well, now," thought Efím, "I won't lose him!"

He pushed forward to the front, but when he got there, there was no Elisha: he had evidently gone away.

Again on the third day Efím looked, and saw at the Sepulchre, in the holiest place, Elisha standing in the sight of all men, his arms outspread, and his eyes gazing upwards as if he saw something above. And his bald head was all shining.

"Well, this time," thought Efím, "he shall not escape me! I will go and stand at the door, then we can't miss one another!"

Efím went out and stood by the door till past noon. Every one had passed out, but still Elisha did not appear.

Efím remained six weeks in Jerusalem, and went everywhere: to Bethlehem, and to Bethany, and to the Jordan. He had a new shirt sealed at the Holy Sepulchre for his burial, and he took a bottle of water from the Jordan, and some holy earth, and bought candles that had been lit at the sacred flame. In eight places he inscribed names to be prayed for, and he spent all his money, except just enough to get home with. Then he started homeward. He walked to Jaffa, sailed thence to Odessa, and walked home from there on foot.

XI

Efim travelled the same road he had come by; and as he drew nearer home his former anxiety returned, as to how affairs were getting on in his absence. "Much water flows away in a year," the proverb says. It takes a lifetime to build up a homestead, but not long to ruin it, thought he. And he wondered how his son had managed without him, what sort of spring they were having, how the cattle had wintered, and whether the cottage was well finished. When Efim came to the district where he had parted from Elisha the summer before, he could hardly believe that the people living there were the same. The year before they had been starving, but now they were living in comfort. The harvest had been good, and the people had recovered, and had forgotten their former misery.

One evening Efim reached the very place where Elisha had remained behind; and as he entered the village, a little girl in a white smock ran out of a hut.

"Daddy, daddy, come to our house!"

Efim meant to pass on, but the little girl would not let him. She took hold of his coat, laughing, and pulled him towards the hut, where a woman with a small boy came out into the porch and beckoned to him.

"Come in, grandfather," she said. "Have supper and spend the night with us."

So Efim went in.

"I may as well ask about Elisha," he thought. "I fancy this is the very hut he went to for a drink of water."

The woman helped him off with the bag he carried, and gave him water to wash his face. Then she made him sit down to table, and set milk, curd-cakes and porridge before him. Efim thanked her, and praised her for her kindness to a pilgrim. The woman shook her head.

"We have good reason to welcome pilgrims," she said. "It was a pilgrim who showed us what life is. We were living forgetful of God, and God punished us almost to death. We reached such a pass last summer, that we all lay ill and helpless with nothing to eat. And we should have died, but that God sent an old man to help us—just such a one as you. He came in one day to ask for a drink of water, saw the state we were in, took pity on us, and remained with us. He gave us food and drink, and set us on our feet again; and he redeemed our land, and bought a cart and horse and gave them to us."

Here the old woman entering the hut, interrupted the younger one and said:

"We don't know whether it was a man, or an angel from God. He loved us all, pitied us all, and went away without telling us his name, so that we don't even know whom to pray for. I can see it all before me now! There I lay waiting for death, when in comes a bald-headed old man. He was not anything much to look at, and he asked for a drink of water. I, sinner that I am, thought to myself: 'What does he come prowling about here for?' And just think what he did! As soon as he saw us, he let down his bag, on this very spot, and untied it."

Here the little girl joined in.

"No, Granny," said she, "first he put it down here in the middle of the hut, and then he lifted it on to the bench."

And they began discussing and recalling all he had said and done, where he sat and slept, and what he had said to each of them.

At night the peasant himself came home on his horse, and he too began to tell about Elisha and how he had lived with them.

"Had he not come we should all have died in our sins. We were dying in despair, murmuring against God and man. But he set us on our feet again; and through him we learned to know God, and to believe that there is good in man. May the Lord bless him! We used to live like animals; he made human beings of us."

After giving Efim food and drink, they showed him where he was to sleep; and lay down to sleep themselves.

But though Efim lay down, he could not sleep. He could not get Elisha out of his mind, but remembered how he had seen him three times at Jerusalem, standing in the foremost place.

"So that is how he got ahead of me," thought Efim. "God may or may not have accepted my pilgrimage, but He has certainly accepted his!"

Next morning Efim bade farewell to the people, who put some patties in his sack before they went to their work, and he continued his journey.

XII

Efim had been away just a year, and it was spring again when he reached home one evening. His son was not at home, but had gone to the public-house, and when he came back, he had had a drop too much. Efim began questioning him. Everything showed that the young fellow had been unsteady during his father's absence. The money had all been wrongly spent, and the work had been neglected. The father began to upbraid the son; and the son answered rudely.

"Why didn't you stay and look after it yourself?" he said. "You go off, taking the money with you, and now you demand it of me!"

The old man grew angry, and struck his son.

In the morning Efim went to the village Elder to complain of his son's conduct. As he was passing Elisha's house, his friend's wife greeted him from the porch.

"How do you do, neighbour," she said. "How do you do, dear friend? Did you get to Jerusalem safely?"

Efim stopped.

"Yes, thank God," he said. "I have been there. I lost sight of your old man, but I hear he got home safely."

The old woman was fond of talking:

"Yes, neighbour, he has come back," said she. "He's been back a long time. Soon after Assumption, I think it was, he returned. And we were glad the Lord had sent him back to us! We were dull without him. We can't expect much work from him any more, his years for work are past; but still he is the head of the household and it's more cheerful when he's at home. And how glad our lad was! He said, 'It's like being without sunlight, when father's away!' It was dull without him, dear friend. We're fond of him, and take good care of him."

"Is he at home now?"

"He is, dear friend. He is with his bees. He is hiving the swarms. He says they are swarming well this year. The Lord has given such strength to the bees that my husband doesn't remember the like. 'The Lord is not rewarding us according to our sins,' he says. Come in, dear neighbour, he will be so glad to see you again."

Efim passed through the passage into the yard and to the apiary, to see Elisha. There was Elisha in his grey coat, without any face-net or gloves, standing under the birch trees, looking upwards, his arms stretched out and his bald head shining, as Efim had seen him at the Holy Sepulchre in Jerusalem: and above him the sunlight shone through the birches as the flames of fire had done in the holy place, and the golden bees flew round his head like a halo, and did not sting him.

Efim stopped. The old woman called to her husband.

"Here's your friend come," she cried.

Elisha looked round with a pleased face, and came towards Efim, gently picking bees out of his own beard.

"Good-day, neighbour, good-day, dear friend. Did you get there safely?"

"My feet walked there, and I have brought you some water from the river Jordan. You must come to my house for it. But whether the Lord accepted my efforts. . . ."

"Well the Lord be thanked! May Christ bless you!" said Elisha.

Efim was silent for a while, and then added:

"My feet have been there, but whether my soul, or another's, has been there more truly . . ."

"That's God's business, neighbour, God's business," interrupted Elisha.

"On my return journey I stopped at the hut where you remained behind. . . ."

Elisha was alarmed, and said hurriedly:

"God's business, neighbour, God's business! Come into the cottage, I'll give you some of our honey." And Elisha changed the conversation, and talked of home affairs.

Efim sighed, and did not speak to Elisha of the people in the hut, nor of how he had seen him in Jerusalem. But he now understood that the best way to keep one's vows to God and to do His will, is for each man while he lives to show love and do good to others.

THE GODSON

"Ye have heard that it hath been said, an eye for an eye, and a tooth for a tooth : but I say unto you, that ye resist not evil."

(Matt. v. 38, 39.)

"Vengeance is mine, I will repay."

(Rom. xii. 19.)

I

A POOR PEASANT had a son born to him. Greatly delighted, he went off to a neighbour's to ask him to stand godfather; but the neighbour refused, since he was unwilling to stand godfather to a poor man's son. Then the father went to another neighbour with the same request, but this man too refused.

In fact, the peasant made the round of the village, but no one would stand godfather, and he was driven to pursue his quest elsewhere. On the way to another village he fell in with a chance wayfarer, who stopped when he met him.

"Good-day to you, friend peasant," he said. "Whither is God taking you?"

"He has just given me a child," replied the peasant, "that it may be a joy to me in my prime, a comfort to me in my old age, and a memorial to my soul when I am dead. Yet, because of my poverty, no one in our village will stand godfather, and I am just off to seek godparents elsewhere."

"Take myself as godfather," said the stranger.

The peasant was delighted, and, thanking him for the offer, inquired: "Whom, then, shall I ask to be godmother?"

"A merchant's daughter whom I know," replied the other. "Go to the town, to the stone building with the shops in it which fronts the square. Enter and ask the proprietor to give his daughter leave to stand godmother."

The peasant demurred to this.

"But, my good friend," he said, "who am I that I should go and call upon a rich merchant? He will only turn away from me in disgust, and refuse his daughter leave."

"That will not be *your* fault. Go and ask him. Arrange the christening for to-morrow morning, and I will be there."

So the poor peasant returned home, first of all, and then set out to the merchant's in the town. He was fastening up his horse in the courtyard when the merchant himself came out.

"What do you want?" he said.

"This, sir," replied the peasant. "God has just given to me a child, that it may be a joy to me in my prime, a comfort to me in my old age, and a memorial to my soul when I am dead. Pray give your daughter leave to stand godmother."

"When is the christening to be?"

"To-morrow morning."

"So be it. God go with you. To-morrow my daughter will be at the christening Mass."

And, sure enough, on the following morning both the godfather and the godmother arrived, and the child was christened; but as soon as ever the christening was over, the godfather departed without revealing his identity, and they never saw him again.

II

The child grew up to be a delight to his parents, for he was strong, industrious, intelligent and peaceable. When he was ten years old his parents sent him to learn his letters, and he learnt in a year what others took five years to master. His education was soon completed.

One Holy Week the boy went as usual to visit his godmother and give her the Easter embrace. But when he had returned home he said:

"Dear father and mother, where does my godfather live? I should like to go and give him the Easter greeting."

But his father said: "We do not know, little son, where your godfather lives. We ourselves have often been troubled about that. Never since the day of your christening have we set eyes upon him, nor heard of him; so that we neither know where he lives nor whether he be alive at all."

Then the boy knelt down before his father and mother.

"Let me go and look for him, dear parents," he said. "I might find him and give him the Easter greeting."

So the father and mother gave their boy leave to go, and he set off in quest of his godfather.

III

Leaving the hut, he started along the highroad, and had been walking about half the day when he met a stranger.

The stranger stopped.

"Good-day to you, my boy," he said. "And whither is God taking you?"

"This morning," answered the boy, "I went to visit my godmother and give her the Easter greeting, after which I returned home and asked my parents: 'Where does my godfather live? I should like to go and give him also the Easter greeting.' But my parents said to me: 'Little son, we do not know where your godfather lives. As soon as ever you had been christened he left our house, so that we know nothing about him nor whether he be alive at all.' Yet I felt a great longing to see my godfather, and now have come out to seek him."

Then the stranger said, "I am your godfather."

The boy was overjoyed, and straightway gave his godfather the Easter embrace.

"But where are you going now, dear godfather?" he asked. "If in our direction, come with me to our hut; and if to your own home, let me come with you."

"Nay, I have no time now to go to your home," replied his godfather, "for I have business to do in the villages; but I shall be back at my own home to-morrow, and you may come to me then."

"And how shall I find the way to you, dear godfather?"

"Walk straight towards the rising sun, and you will come to a forest, and in the middle of the forest to a clearing. Sit down there and rest yourself, and observe what happens in that spot. Then come out of the forest, and you will see in front of you a garden, and in that garden a pavilion with a golden roof to it. That is my home. Walk straight up to the garden gates, and I will meet you there."

Thus spake the godfather, and then vanished from his godson's eyes.

IV

So the boy went by the way that his godfather had told him. On and on he went, until he reached the forest, and then a little clearing in the middle of it. In the centre of this clearing stood a pine tree, to one branch of which a rope was fastened, and to the other end of the rope an oaken log some three poods* in weight. Exactly beneath the log there was placed a pail of honey. Just as the boy was wondering why the honey had been put there, there came a crackling sound from the forest, and he saw some bears approaching. In front walked the mother bear, behind her a young yearling bear, and behind him again three little bear cubs. The mother bear raised her muzzle and sniffed, and then made straight for the pail, with the young ones behind her. First she plunged her own nose into the pail, and then called the young ones. Up they ran, and fell to work on the honey; but their doing so caused the log to swing a little, and to thrust the cubs away as it swung back. Seeing this, the old she-bear thrust it away again with her paw. It swung further this time, and, returning, struck two of the cubs—one of them on the head, and the other one on the back—so that they squealed and jumped aside. This angered the mother bear, and, raising both paws to the log, she lifted it above her head and flung it far away from her. High up it swung, and immediately the yearling bear leapt to the pail, buried his nose in the honey, and munched away greedily, while the cubs also began to return. Before, however, they had reached the pail the log came flying back, struck the yearling bear on the head, and killed him outright. The mother bear growled more fiercely than ever as she seized the log and flung it away from her with all her strength. Up, up it flew—higher than the branch itself, and well-nigh breaking the rope. Then the she-bear approached the pail, and the cubs after her. The log had gone flying upwards and upwards, but now it stopped, and began to descend. The lower it came, the faster it travelled. Faster and faster it flew, until it struck the mother bear and crashed against her head. She turned over, stretched out her paws, and died, while the cubs ran away.

---

* The *pood* = 40 Russian pounds.

V

The boy marvelled at what he saw, and then went on until he came
to a large garden, in the middle of which stood a lofty pavilion with
a golden roof to it. At the entrance gates of the garden stood his
godfather smiling, who greeted his godson, drew him within, and
led him through the grounds. Never, even in a dream, had the boy
seen such beauty and delight as were contained in that garden.

Next, his godfather conducted him into the pavilion, the interior
of which was even more beautiful than the garden had been. Through
every room did his godfather lead him—each one more magnificent,
more enchanting than the last—until he had brought him to a sealed
door.

"Do you see this door?" he said. "There is no lock upon it—only
seals. Yet, although it can be opened, I bid you not do so. You may
live here and play here, where you like and how you like, and enjoy
all these delights; but this one charge do I lay upon you—that you
do not enter that door. If ever you should do so, you will remember
what you have so lately seen in the forest."

Thus his godfather spake, and disappeared. Left alone, his godson
lived so happily and contentedly that he seemed only to have been
there three hours when in reality he had been there thirty years. At
the end of those thirty years the godson drew near to the sealed door
and thought within himself, "Why did my godfather forbid me to
enter that room? Suppose I go in now and see what it contains?"

So he pushed at the door, the seals parted, and the door flew open.
As he entered he could see rooms larger and more splendid even than
the others, and that in the midst of them there was set a golden throne.
On and on he walked through those rooms, until he had come to the
throne. Ascending the steps, he sat down upon it. Hardly had he done
so when he perceived a sceptre resting against the throne. He took
this sceptre into his hand—and lo! in a moment all the four walls of
all the surrounding rooms had rolled away, and he could look right
round him, and see the whole world at a glance and all that men were
doing in it. In front of him he could see the sea and the ships sailing
over it. To his right he could view the life of all foreign, non-
Christian nations. To his left he could watch the doings of all Christian
nations other than the Russian. And lastly, on the fourth side, he
could behold how our own—the Russian—nation was living.

"Suppose," he said to himself, "I look to see what is happening
in my own home, and whether the crop has come up well?"

So he looked towards his own native field, and saw sheaves stand-ing there; whereupon he began to count them, to see how many there were. While he was doing this he caught sight of a cart going across the field, with a peasant sitting in it. At first he thought it must be his father going to carry sheaves home by night, but when he looked again he saw that it was Vassili Kudnishoff, the thief, who was driving the cart. Up to the sheaves he drove, and began to load them on to the cart. The godson was enraged at this, and cried out: "Father dear! they are stealing sheaves from your field!"

His father awoke in the middle of the night. "Somehow I dreamt that my sheaves were being stolen," he said. "Suppose I go and look?" So he mounted his horse and set off. As soon as he came to the field he perceived Vassili there, and raised the hue and cry. Other peasants came, and Vassili was beaten, bound, and carried off to prison.

Next, the godson looked towards the town where his godmother was living, and saw that she was now married to a merchant. There she lay asleep, while her husband had got out of bed and was sneak-ing off to his paramour's room. So the godson cried out to the merchant's wife: "Arise! your husband is about an evil business."

His godmother leapt out of bed, dressed herself and went to look for her husband. She shamed him utterly, beat his paramour, and turned him out of doors.

Then the godson looked to see how his mother was faring, and saw her lying asleep in the hut. Presently a robber entered, and began to break open her strongbox. At this moment she awoke and cried out, whereupon the robber seized a hatchet, flourished it over her, and seemed on the point of killing her.

The godson could not restrain himself, but flung the sceptre towards the robber. Striking him right on the temple, it killed him on the spot.

VI

Instantly that the godson had killed the robber the walls of the pavil-ion closed in again, and the place became as before.

Then the door opened, and the godfather entered. He went up to his godson, and, taking him by the hand, led him down from the throne.

"You have not obeyed my commands," he said. "One thing you have done which you ought not: you have opened the forbidden door. A second thing you have done which you ought not: you have ascended the throne and taken my sceptre into your hands. And a third thing you have done which you ought not: you have caused much evil in the world. Had you sat there but another hour you would have ruined the half of mankind."

Then the godfather led his godson back to the throne, and took the sceptre into his hands. Once again the walls rolled back, and all the world became visible.

"Look first at what you have done to your father," said the godfather. "Vassili lay for a year in prison, and there learnt every kind of villainy and became embittered against his fellow-man. Now, look you, he has just stolen two of your father's horses, and is at this very moment in the act of firing his farm also. That is what you have done to your father."

Yet, hardly had the godson perceived that his father's farm was blazing up before his godfather hid the spectacle from him and bade him look in another direction.

"Look there," he said. "It is just a year since your godmother was deserted by her husband for an unlawful love, and she has been driven by her grief to drink, and her husband's paramour to utter ruin. That is what you have done to your godmother."

Then this picture also was hid from the godson by his godfather as he pointed towards the godson's own home. In it sat his mother, weeping tears of remorse for her sins and saying: "Far better had it been had the robber killed me, for then I should have sinned the less."

"That is what you have done to your mother," added the godfather. Then he hid this spectacle also from his godson, and pointed below it. There the godson saw the robber standing before a dungeon, with a warder holding him on either side.

And the godfather said to his godson: "This man has taken nine lives during his career. For those sins he would have had to atone had you not killed him. But now you have transferred those sins to yourself, and for them all you must answer. That is what you have done to *yourself*."

Then the godfather went on:

"The first time that the old she-bear pushed away the log, she only frightened her cubs a little. The second time that she pushed it away, she killed the yearling bear by doing so. But the third time that she pushed the log away, she killed herself. So also have you done. Yet I will set you now a term of thirty years in which to go forth into the world and atone for the sins of that robber. Should you not atone for them within that time, then it will be your fate to go where he has gone."

And the godson said: "In what manner shall I atone for his sins?"

To this the godfather replied: "When you have relieved the world of as much evil as you have brought into it, then will you have atoned for the sins of that robber."

"But in what manner," asked his godson again, "am I to relieve the world of evil?"

"Go you towards the rising sun," replied his godfather, "until you come to a field with men in it. Note carefully what those men do, and teach them what you yourself have learnt. Then go forward again, still noting what you see, and on the fourth day you will come to a forest. Within that forest there stands a hermit's cell, and in that cell there lives an old man. Tell him all that has befallen you, and he will instruct you. When you have done all that he bids you do, then will you have atoned both for the sins of that robber and for your own."

Thus spoke his godfather, and dismissed him from the entrance gates.

VII

The godson went on and on, and as he walked he kept thinking to himself: "How am I to relieve the world of evil? The world relieves itself of evil by sending evil men into exile, by casting them into prison, by executing them upon the scaffold. How, then, will it be possible for me to rid the world of evil without taking upon myself the sins of others?"

Thus did he ponder and ponder, yet could not resolve the problem.

On and on he went, until he came to a field in which the corn had grown up rich and thick, and was now ready for the harvest. Suddenly he perceived that a calf had wandered into the corn, and that some peasants, having also seen it, had mounted their horses and were now chasing the calf from one side of the field to the other through the corn. Whenever the calf was on the point of breaking out of the corn a man would come riding up and the calf would double back in terror. Then once more the riders would go galloping about through the crop in pursuit of it. Yet all this time an old woman was standing weeping on the highway and crying out: "My calf is being driven to death!"

So the godson called out to the peasants:

"Why ride about like that? Come out of the corn, all of you, and then the old woman will call her calf back to her."

The peasants listened to his urging, and, advancing to the edge of the corn, the old woman cried aloud, "Here, here, little madcap! Come here, then!" The calf pricked up its ears and listened. For a little while it listened, and then ran to the old woman and thrust its head against her skirt, almost pushing her from her feet. And it all ended in the peasants being pleased, and the old woman likewise, and the calf as well.

As the godson went on he thought to himself:

"I see now that evil cannot be removed by evil. The more that men requite evil, the more does evil spread. Thus it is manifest that evil is powerless against evil. Yet how to remove it I know not. It was pleasant to see the calf listen to the old woman's voice. Yet, had it not listened, how could she ever have recovered it from the corn?"

Thus the godson pondered and pondered as he went.

VIII

On and on he walked, until he came to a village, where he asked at the first hut for a night's lodging, and was admitted by the goodwife. She was all alone in the hut, and engaged in washing it and the furniture.

Having entered, the godson went quietly to the stove, and stood watching what the woman was doing. She had finished the floor and was now starting to wash the table. First of all she swilled it over, and then began wiping it with a dirty clout. She rubbed it vigorously one way, but still it was not clean, since the dirty clout left streaks upon its surface. Then she rubbed it the other way about, and cleared off some of the streaks, while making fresh ones. Lastly, she rubbed it lengthways, and back again, yet only with the result of streaking its surface afresh with the dirty clout. One piece of dirt might be wiped away here and there, yet others would be rubbed in all the firmer.

The godson watched her for a time, and at last said:

"My good woman, what are you doing?"

"Do you not see?" she said. "I am cleaning against the festival day, but, although I am tired out, I cannot get this table clean."

"But you should first of all rinse the clout, and *then* rub the table with it."

The woman did so, and very soon had the table clean.

"I thank you," she said, "for what you have taught me."

In the morning the godson took leave of his hostess, and went on. He walked and walked, until he came to a forest. There he saw some peasants bending felloes. The godson drew near them and saw that, however much they kept walking round the felloe-block, a felloe would not bend. So he watched them, and perceived that this was because the felloe-block kept turning with them, since it lacked a stay-pin. As soon as he saw this he said:

"My brothers, what are you doing?"

"We are bending felloes," they replied. "Twice have we soaked these felloes, and worn ourselves out, yet they will not bend."

"But you should first of all make fast the felloe-block," said the godson, "and then the felloe will bend as you circle round."

Hearing this, the peasants made fast the felloe-block, and thereafter their work prospered.

The godson spent the night with them, and then went on again. A whole day and a night did he walk, until just before dawn he came up with some cattle-drovers, and lay down beside them. He saw that they had picketed their cattle and were now trying to light a fire. They kept taking dry twigs and setting fire to them, yet the flames had no sooner sprung up than they put wet brushwood upon them. The brushwood only gave a hiss, and the flames went out. Again and again the drovers took dry twigs and lit them, yet always piled wet brushwood on the top, and so extinguished the flames. For a long time they laboured at this, yet could not make the fire burn up.

At length the godson said, "Do not be so hasty in piling on the brushwood. First draw up the fire into a good flame. When it is burning fiercely, *then* put on the brushwood."

The drovers did so. First of all they drew up the flames to a good heat, and then applied the brushwood, so that the latter caught successfully, and the whole pile burst into a blaze.

The godson stayed with them for a while, and then went on again. He kept wondering and wondering why he should have seen these three incidents, yet could not discern the reason.

IX

For the whole of that day he pressed on, until he came to the forest in which stood the hermit's cell. He approached the cell and knocked at the door, whereupon a voice from within called out to him: "Who is there?"

"A great sinner," replied the godson, "who has come hither to atone for the sins of another."

Then an old man came out and asked him further:

"What sins of another are those which have been laid upon you?"

So the godson told him all—about his godfather, and the bear and her young, and the throne in the sealed room, and the command which his godfather had given him, and the peasants whom he had seen in the field, and their trampling of the corn, and the calf running to the old woman of its own accord.

"It was then," said the godson, "that I understood that evil cannot be removed by evil. Yet still I know not how to remove it. I pray you, teach me."

And the old man said: "Yet tell me first what else you have seen by the wayside as you came."

So the godson told him about the woman and the washing of the table, as also about the peasants who were bending felloes and the drovers who were lighting a fire. The old man heard him out, and then, turning back into the cell, brought out thence a little notched axe.

"Come with me," he said.

He went across the clearing from the cell, and pointed to a tree.

"Cut that down," he said.

So the godson applied the axe until the tree fell.

"Now split it into three."

The godson did so. Then the old man went back to the cell, and returned thence with a lighted torch.

"Set fire," he said, "to those three logs."

So the godson took the torch, and set fire to the three logs, until there remained of them only three charred stumps.

"Now, bury them half their length in the ground. So."

The godson buried them as directed.

"Under that hill," went on the old man, "there runs a river. Go and bring thence some water in your mouth, and sprinkle these stumps with it. Sprinkle the first stump even as you taught the woman in the hut. Sprinkle the second one even as you taught the felloes-makers.

And sprinkle the third one even as you taught the drovers. When all these three stumps shall sprout, and change from stumps to apple trees, then shall you know how evil may be removed from among men, and then also will you have atoned for your sins."

Thus spoke the old man, and retreated to his cell again, while the godson pondered and pondered, and yet could not understand what the old man had said to him. Nevertheless, he set about doing as he had been bidden.

X

Going to the river, and taking a full mouthful of water, he returned and sprinkled the first stump. Again, and yet again, he went, and sprinkled the other two. Now he began to feel tired and hungry, so he went to the cell to beg bite and sup of the old man; yet, hardly had he opened the door, when he saw the old man lying dead across his praying-stool. The godson looked about until he found some dry biscuits, which he ate. Then he found also a spade, and began to dig a grave for the old man. By night he brought water and sprinkled the stumps, and by day he went on digging the grave. Just when he had finished it and was about to bury the old man, some peasants from a neighbouring village arrived with presents of food for the aged hermit.

Learning that the old man was dead, and believing that he had blessed the godson as his successor, they helped to inter the body, left the food for the godson's use, and departed after promising to bring him some more.

So the godson lived in the old man's cell, subsisting upon food brought him by the people, and doing as he had been bidden—that is to say, bringing water in his mouth from the river and sprinkling with it the stumps.

He lived thus for a year, and many people began to come to him, since it had got abroad that a holy man was living the devout life in the forest who brought water in his mouth from under the hill to sprinkle with it three charred stumps. Very many folk visited him, and even rich merchants brought presents, but the godson would accept nothing for himself beyond necessaries. All other things which were given him he handed to the poor.

Thus his order of life became as follows. Half the day he would spend in fetching water in his mouth for the sprinkling of the stumps, and the other half he would spend in resting or receiving visitors. In time he began to believe that this must really be the way in which it was appointed him to live, and that by this very mode of life he would succeed both in removing evil from the world and in atoning for his own sins.

A second year passed without his once omitting, on any single day, to sprinkle the stumps: yet none of the three had yet begun to sprout.

Once he was sitting in his cell, when he heard a man ride by on horseback, singing to himself as he went. Going out to see what manner of man this was, the godson beheld a fine, strong young man, well-dressed, and mounted on a valuable horse and saddle. So the godson hailed him, and asked him what his business was, and whither he was going. The man drew rein.

"I am a highwayman," he said, "and ride the roads and kill people. The more I kill, the merrier is my singing."

The godson was horrified, and thought to himself: "How am I to remove the evil that must lie in such a man? It is easy for me to counsel those who visit me, because they are themselves repentant, but this man glories in his wickedness."

However, he said nothing, but went on reflecting as he walked beside the man:

"What is to be done now? If this highwayman takes to riding this way, he will frighten the people, and they will cease to visit me. What use will it be for me then to go on living here?"

So he stopped, and said to the highwayman:

"People come here to visit me—not to glory in their wickedness, but to repent and to pray for their sins' forgiveness. Do you also repent if you have any fear of God. But, if you will not, then ride the roads elsewhere, and never come this way again, so that you may not trouble my peace and terrify the people. Should you not hearken to me, assuredly God will chastise you."

The highwayman laughed.

"I neither fear God nor will listen to *you*," he said. "You are not my master. *You* live by your prayers and piety, and *I* by murder. Everyone must live somehow. Do you go on with your teaching of the old women who come to you, but do not attempt to teach *me*. Yet because you have reminded me of God this day, I will kill two people the more to-morrow. I would have killed you yourself this instant, but that I do not wish to soil my hands. For the rest, keep out of my way."

Having uttered these threats, the highwayman rode away. Yet he came no more in that direction, and the godson went on living quietly as of old for another eight years.

XI

One night the godson had been sprinkling the stumps, and then returned to his cell to sit and rest a while. As he sat there he kept looking along the little forest path to see if any of the peasants were coming to visit him. Yet none came that day, and the godson sat alone until evening. Growing weary, he began to think over his past life. He remembered how the highwayman had reproached him for living by his piety, and began to recall his whole career.

"I am not living as God meant me to," he thought. "The old man laid upon me a penance, but that penance I have turned into a source both of bread and of public repute. I have been so led into temptation by it that I find time hang heavy on my hands if no visitors come. Yet, when they come, I am pleased only if they extol my piety! It is not thus that I must live. I have been led astray by the praise of men. So far from atoning for my past sins, I have been incurring new ones. I will go away into the forest—away to some new spot where the people cannot find me, and there I will live entirely alone, so that I may both atone for my past sins and incur no fresh ones."

Thus the godson pondered in his heart. Then he took a little bag of biscuits and the spade, and set out from the cell towards a ravine, in some remote corner of which he hoped to dig for himself an earthen hut, and so hide himself from the people.

As he was walking along with the bag of biscuits and the spade, there came riding towards him the highwayman. The godson was afraid, and tried to flee, but the highwayman overtook him.

"Whither are you going?" asked the brigand.

The godson replied that he wished to hide himself in some spot where no one could visit him. The highwayman was surprised at this.

"But how will you subsist," he asked, "when no one can come to visit you?"

The godson had not thought of this before, but as soon as the highwayman put the question he remembered the matter of food.

"Surely God will give me the wherewithal," he replied.

The highwayman said nothing more, but started to ride on his way.

"What can I be thinking of?" said the godson suddenly to himself. "I have said not a word to him about his mode of life. Maybe he is repentant now. He seemed softened to-day, and never once threatened to kill me."

So he called after the highwayman:

"Yet I beseech you to repent, for never can you escape God."

Upon this the highwayman turned his horse, seized a dagger from his belt, and brandished it at the godson, who straightway fled in terror into the forest. The highwayman did not pursue him, but said:

"Twice now have I let you go, old man; but the third time, look to yourself, for I will kill you."

This said, he rode away.

That evening the godson went to sprinkle the stumps as usual—and, behold! one of them had put forth shoots, and a little apple tree was growing from it!

XII

So the godson hid himself from men, and entered upon a life wholly solitary. When his small stock of biscuits came to an end he bethought him: "I must go out and search for roots." Yet, hardly had he set forth upon this quest, when he saw hanging from a bough in front of him a little bag of biscuits. He took them down and ate them. No sooner had he done so than he saw another little bag hanging on the same bough.

Thus the godson lived on, with no anxieties to trouble him, save one—fear of the highwayman. Whenever he heard him coming he would hide himself, thinking: "If he were to kill me I should die with my sins unpurged."

He lived in this manner for ten years. The apple tree on the one stump grew apace, but the other two stumps remained as they had always been.

One day he rose early, and went out to perform his task of sprinkling the stumps. He had done this, when he felt weariness overcome him, and sat down to rest. As he sat resting there, the thought occurred to him: "Surely I have sinned the more, since now I have begun to fear death. Yet it may be that it is by death itself that God means me to atone for my sins."

Hardly had he thought this, when of a sudden he heard the high-wayman riding towards him, and cursing as he came. As soon as he heard him the godson thought: "None but God Himself can work me weal or woe," and so went straight to meet the robber.

Then he saw that the highwayman was not riding alone, but was carrying a man behind him, and that the man's hands were bound and his mouth gagged. The man could utter no word, but the high-wayman was cursing him without ceasing. The godson advanced towards them, and stood in the horse's path.

"Whither are you carrying this man?" he said.

"Into the forest," replied the highwayman. "He is a merchant's son, and refuses to say where his father's money is concealed, so I am going to flog him until he tells me."

And the highwayman tried to ride on, but the godson seized his bridle, and would not let him pass. "Let the man go," he said.

The highwayman was enraged at this, and shook his fist at the godson.

"Do you want the same as he?" he asked him. "I promised you long ago that I would kill you. Let me pass."

But the godson felt no fear now.

"I will *not* let you pass," he said. "I fear not you, but only God, and God has bidden me detain you. Let this man go."

The highwayman knit his brows, then seized his dagger, cut the bonds, and released the merchant's son.

"Away with you both," he said, "and never cross my path again."

The merchant's son leapt to the ground and fled, but when the highwayman tried to ride on again the godson still detained him, and told him that he must abandon his wicked life. The highwayman sat quietly listening, but said nothing in reply, and then departed.

In the morning the godson went to sprinkle the stumps as usual—and behold! another one of them had sprouted, and from it a second little apple tree was growing.

XIII

Another ten years passed, and one day, as he was sitting free from anxiety or fear of any kind, and with his heart light within him, the godson thought to himself: "What blessings are given to men by God! Yet they vex themselves in vain when all the time they should be living in peace."

He thought of the vast sum of human wickedness, and how men distressed themselves to no purpose. And he felt a great pity for men.

"I ought not to be living thus," he thought. "Rather ought I to go forth and tell men what I know."

Just as this had passed through his mind he heard once more the highwayman approaching. At first he was for avoiding the brigand, thinking: "It is bootless to say anything to this man."

Thus he thought at first, but presently he changed his mind, and stepped forth into the road. The highwayman was riding along with downcast mien and with his eyes fixed upon the ground. As the godson looked upon him he felt a great pity for him, and, running to his side, clasped him by the knee.

"Dear brother," he cried, "have mercy upon your own soul, for in you too there dwells a God-given spirit. If you continue thus to torment yourself and to torment others, assuredly worse torments than all await you. Yet think how God yearns towards you, and what blessings He has laid up for you! Do not destroy yourself, my brother, but change your way of life."

But the highwayman only frowned and turned away. "Leave me," he said.

Yet the godson clasped him still closer by the knee, and burst into tears.

At that the highwayman raised his eyes and looked at the godson. He looked and looked, and then suddenly slid from his horse and threw himself upon his knees on the ground.

"Old man," he said, "you have overcome me at last. Twenty years have I striven with you, but you have gradually taken away my strength, until now I am not master of myself. Do what you will with me. The first time that you pleaded with me I was but the more enraged. It was not until you withdrew from the eyes of men, and recognised that you needed not their help, that I began to think over your words. But from that moment I began to hang the bags of biscuits for you on the bough."

Then the godson remembered how it was only when the clout was rinsed the table was cleaned. Even so, he saw it was only when he had ceased to take thought for himself that his heart had been purified, and he had been able to purify the hearts of others.

And the highwayman went on:

"But the first real change of heart took place in me when you ceased to fear death at my hands."

Instantly the godson remembered that it was only when the felloes-makers had fastened firmly the felloes-block that they had been able to bend the felloes. Even so, he saw it was only when he had established firmly his life in God and humbled his presumptuous heart that he had ceased to have any fear of death.

"And," said the highwayman, in conclusion, "it was when your heart went out to me in pity, and you wept before me, that my own heart was changed entirely."

Rejoicing greatly, the godson led the highwayman to the spot where the three stumps were—and behold! from the third stump also an apple tree had sprouted!

Then the godson remembered that it was only when the drovers' fire had kindled to a blaze that the wet brushwood had kindled with it. So also, he saw, had his heart within him kindled to a blaze, and with its flame had set fire to the heart of another.

With joy he recognised that his sins were at last redeemed.

All this he related to the highwayman and died. The highwayman laid him in his grave, and lived thereafter as the godson had bidden him, and taught men to do likewise.

THE FORGED COUPON

PART FIRST

I

FEDOR MIHAILOVICH SMOKOVNIKOV, the president of the local Income Tax Department, a man of unswerving honesty—and proud of it, too—a gloomy Liberal, a free-thinker, and an enemy to every manifestation of religious feeling, which he thought a relic of superstition, came home from his office feeling very much annoyed. The Governor of the province had sent him an extraordinarily stupid minute, almost assuming that his dealings had been dishonest.

Fedor Mihailovich felt embittered, and wrote at once a sharp answer. On his return home everything seemed to go contrary to his wishes.

It was five minutes to five, and he expected the dinner to be served at once, but he was told it was not ready. He banged the door and went to his study. Somebody knocked at the door. "Who the devil is that?" he thought; and shouted,—

"Who is there?"

The door opened and a boy of fifteen came in, the son of Fedor Mihailovich, a pupil of the fifth class of the local school.

"What do you want?"

"It is the first of the month to-day, father."

"Well! You want your money?"

It had been arranged that the father should pay his son a monthly allowance of three roubles as pocket money. Fedor Mihailovich frowned, took out of his pocket-book a coupon of two roubles fifty kopeks which he found among the banknotes, and added to it fifty kopeks in silver out of the loose change in his purse. The boy kept silent, and did not take the money his father proffered him.

"Father, please give me some more in advance."

"What?"

"I would not ask for it, but I have borrowed a small sum from a friend, and promised upon my word of honour to pay it off. My honour is dear to me, and that is why I want another three roubles. I don't like asking you; but, please, father, give me another three roubles."

"I have told you—"

"I know, father, but just for once."

"You have an allowance of three roubles and you ought to be content. I had not fifty kopeks when I was your age."

"Now, all my comrades have much more. Petrov and Ivanitsky have fifty roubles a month."

"And I tell you that if you behave like them you will be a scoundrel. Mind that."

"What is there to mind? You never understand my position. I shall be disgraced if I don't pay my debt. It is all very well for you to speak as you do."

"Be off, you silly boy! Be off!"

Fedor Mihailovich jumped from his seat and pounced upon his son. "Be off, I say!" he shouted. "You deserve a good thrashing, all you boys!"

His son was at once frightened and embittered. The bitterness was even greater than the fright. With his head bent down he hastily turned to the door. Fedor Mihailovich did not intend to strike him, but he was glad to vent his wrath, and went on shouting and abusing the boy till he had closed the door.

When the maid came in to announce that dinner was ready, Fedor Mihailovich rose.

"At last!" he said. "I don't feel hungry any longer."

He went to the dining-room with a sullen face. At table his wife made some remark, but he gave her such a short and angry answer that she abstained from further speech. The son also did not lift his eyes from his plate, and was silent all the time. The trio finished their dinner in silence, rose from the table and separated, without a word.

After dinner the boy went to his room, took the coupon and the change out of his pocket, and threw the money on the table. After that he took off his uniform and put on a jacket.

He sat down to work, and began to study Latin grammar out of a dog's-eared book. After a while he rose, closed and bolted the door, shifted the money into a drawer, took out some cigarette papers, rolled one up, stuffed it with cotton wool, and began to smoke.

He spent nearly two hours over his grammar and writing books without understanding a word of what he saw before him; then he rose and began to stamp up and down the room, trying to recollect all that his father had said to him. All the abuse showered upon him, and worst of all his father's angry face, were as fresh in his memory as if he saw and heard them all over again. "Silly boy! You ought to get a good thrashing!" And the more he thought of it the angrier he grew. He remembered also how his father said: "I see what a scoundrel you will turn out. I know you will. You are sure to become a cheat, if you go on like that. . . ." He had certainly forgotten how he felt when he was young! "What crime have I committed, I wonder? I wanted to go to the theatre, and having no money borrowed some from Petia Grouchetsky. Was that so very wicked of me? Another father would have been sorry for me; would have asked how it all happened; whereas he just called me names. He never thinks of anything but himself. When it is he who has not got something he wants—that is a different matter! Then all the house is upset by his shouts. And I—I am a scoundrel, a cheat, he says. No, I don't love him, although he is my father. It may be wrong, but I hate him."

There was a knock at the door. The servant brought a letter—a message from his friend. "They want an answer," said the servant.

The letter ran as follows: "I ask you now for the third time to pay me back the six roubles you have borrowed; you are trying to avoid me. That is not the way an honest man ought to behave. Will you please send the amount by my messenger? I am myself in a frightful fix. Can you not get the money somewhere?—Yours, according to whether you send the money or not, with scorn, or love, Grouchetsky."

"There we have it! Such a pig! Could he not wait a while? I will have another try."

Mitia went to his mother. This was his last hope. His mother was very kind, and hardly ever refused him anything. She would probably have helped him this time also out of his trouble, but she was in great anxiety: her younger child, Petia, a boy of two, had fallen ill. She got angry with Mitia for rushing so noisily into the nursery, and refused him almost without listening to what he had to say. Mitia muttered something to himself and turned to go. The mother felt sorry for him. "Wait, Mitia," she said; "I have not got the money you want now, but I will get it for you to-morrow."

But Mitia was still raging against his father.

"What is the use of having it to-morrow, when I want it to-day? I am going to see a friend. That is all I have got to say."

He went out, banging the door. . . . "Nothing else is left to me. He will tell me how to pawn my watch," he thought, touching his watch in his pocket.

Mitia went to his room, took the coupon and the watch from the drawer, put on his coat, and went to Mahin.

II

Mahin was his schoolfellow, his senior, a grown-up young man with a moustache. He gambled, had a large feminine acquaintance, and always had ready cash. He lived with his aunt. Mitia quite realised that Mahin was not a respectable fellow, but when he was in his company he could not help doing what he wished. Mahin was in when Mitia called, and was just preparing to go to the theatre. His untidy room smelt of scented soap and eau-de-Cologne.

"That's awful, old chap," said Mahin, when Mitia telling him about his troubles, showed the coupon and the fifty kopeks, and added that he wanted nine roubles more. "We might, of course, go and pawn your watch. But we might do something far better." And Mahin winked an eye.

"What's that?"

"Something quite simple." Mahin took the coupon in his hand. "Put *one* before the 2.50 and it will be 12.50."

"But do such coupons exist?"

"Why, certainly; the thousand roubles notes have coupons of 12.50. I have cashed one in the same way."

"You don't say so?"

"Well, yes or no?" asked Mahin, taking the pen and smoothing the coupon with the fingers of his left hand.

"But it is wrong."

"Nonsense!"

"Nonsense, indeed," thought Mitia, and again his father's hard words came back to his memory. "Scoundrel! As you called me that, I might as well be it." He looked into Mahin's face. Mahin looked at him, smiling with perfect ease.

"Well?" he said.

"All right. I don't mind."

Mahin carefully wrote the unit in front of 2.50.

"Now let us go to the shop across the road; they sell photographers' materials there. I just happen to want a frame—for this young person here." He took out of his pocket a photograph of a young lady with large eyes, luxuriant hair, and an uncommonly well-developed bust.

"Is she not sweet? Eh?"

"Yes, yes . . . of course . . ."

"Well, you see.—But let us go."

Mahin took his coat, and they left the house.

III

The two boys, having rung the door-bell, entered the empty shop, which had shelves along the walls and photographic appliances on them, together with show-cases on the counters. A plain woman, with a kind face, came through the inner door and asked from behind the counter what they required.

"A nice frame, if you please, madam."

"At what price?" asked the woman; she wore mittens on her swollen fingers with which she rapidly handled picture-frames of different shapes.

"These are fifty kopeks each; and these are a little more expensive. There is rather a pretty one, of quite a new style; one rouble and twenty kopeks."

"All right, I will have this. But could not you make it cheaper? Let us say one rouble."

"We don't bargain in our shop," said the shopkeeper with a dignified air.

"Well, I will take it," said Mahin, and put the coupon on the counter. "Wrap up the frame and give me change. But please be quick. We must be off to the theatre, and it is getting late."

"You have plenty of time," said the shopkeeper, examining the coupon very closely because of her shortsightedness.

"It will look lovely in that frame, don't you think so?" said Mahin, turning to Mitia.

"Have you no small change?" asked the shop-woman.

"I am sorry, I have not. My father gave me that, so I have to cash it."

"But surely you have one rouble twenty?"

"I have only fifty kopeks in cash. But what are you afraid of? You don't think, I suppose, that we want to cheat you and give you bad money?"

"Oh, no; I don't mean anything of the sort."

"You had better give it to me back. We will cash it somewhere else."

"How much have I to pay you back? Eleven and something."

She made a calculation on the counter, opened the desk, took out a ten-roubles note, looked for change and added to the sum six twenty-kopeks coins and two five-kopek pieces.

"Please make a parcel of the frame," said Mahin, taking the money in a leisurely fashion.

"Yes, sir." She made a parcel and tied it with a string.

Mitia only breathed freely when the door bell rang behind them, and they were again in the street.

"There are ten ten roubles for you, and let me have the rest I will give it back to you."

Mahin went off to the theatre, and Mitia called on Grouchetsky to repay the money he had borrowed from him.

IV

An hour after the boys were gone Eugene Mihailovich, the owner of the shop, came home, and began to count his receipts.

"Oh, you clumsy fool! Idiot that you are!" he shouted, addressing his wife, after having seen the coupon and noticed the forgery.

"But I have often seen you, Eugene, accepting coupons in payment, and precisely twelve rouble ones," retorted his wife, very humiliated, grieved, and all but bursting into tears. "I really don't know how they contrived to cheat me," she went on. "They were pupils of the school, in uniform. One of them was quite a handsome boy, and looked so *comme il faut*."

"A *comme il faut* fool, that is what you are!" The husband went on scolding her, while he counted the cash. . . . "When I accept coupons, I see what is written on them. And you probably looked only at the boys' pretty faces. You had better behave yourself in your old age."

His wife could not stand this, and got into a fury.

"That is just like you men! Blaming everybody around you. But when it is you who lose fifty-four roubles at cards—that is of no consequence in your eyes."

"That is a different matter—"

"I don't want to talk to you," said his wife, and went to her room.
There she began to remind herself that her family was opposed to
her marriage, thinking her present husband far below her in social
rank, and that it was she who insisted on marrying him. Then she
went on thinking of the child she had lost, and how indifferent her
husband had been to their loss. She hated him so intensely at that
moment that she wished for his death. Her wish frightened her,
however, and she hurriedly began to dress and left the house. When
her husband came from the shop to the inner rooms of their flat she
was gone. Without waiting for him she had dressed and gone off to
friends—a teacher of French in the school, a Russified Pole, and his
wife—who had invited her and her husband to a party in their house
that evening.

V

The guests at the party had tea and cakes offered to them, and sat
down after that to play whist at a number of card-tables.

The partners of Eugene Mihailovich's wife were the host himself,
an officer, and an old and very stupid lady in a wig, a widow who
owned a music-shop; she loved playing cards and played remarkably
well. But it was Eugene Mihailovich's wife who was the winner all
the time. The best cards were continually in her hands. At her side
she had a plate with grapes and a pear and was in the best of spirits.

"And Eugene Mihailovich? Why is he so late?" asked the hostess,
who played at another table.

"Probably busy settling accounts," said Eugene Mihailovich's wife.
"He has to pay off the tradesmen, to get in firewood." The quarrel
she had with her husband revived in her memory; she frowned, and
her hands, from which she had not taken off the mittens, shook with
fury against him.

"Oh, there he is.—We have just been speaking of you," said the
hostess to Eugene Mihailovich, who came in at that very moment.
"Why are you so late?"

"I was busy," answered Eugene Mihailovich, in a gay voice, rubbing his hands. And to his wife's surprise he came to her side and
said,—

"You know, I managed to get rid of the coupon."

"No! You don't say so!"

"Yes, I used it to pay for a cart-load of firewood I bought from a peasant."

And Eugene Mihailovich related with great indignation to the company present—his wife adding more details to his narrative—how his wife had been cheated by two unscrupulous schoolboys.

"Well, and now let us sit down to work," he said, taking his place at one of the whist-tables when his turn came, and beginning to shuffle the cards.

VI

Eugene Mihailovich had actually used the coupon to buy firewood from the peasant Ivan Mironov, who had thought of setting up in business on the seventeen roubles he possessed. He hoped in this way to earn another eight roubles, and with the twenty-five roubles thus amassed he intended to buy a good strong horse, which he would want in the spring for work in the fields and for driving on the roads, as his old horse was almost played out.

Ivan Mironov's commercial method consisted in buying from the stores a cord of wood and dividing it into five cartloads, and then driving about the town, selling each of these at the price the stores charged for a quarter of a cord. That unfortunate day Ivan Mironov drove out very early with half a cartload, which he soon sold. He loaded up again with another cartload which he hoped to sell, but he looked in vain for a customer; no one would buy it. It was his bad luck all that day to come across experienced townspeople, who knew all the tricks of the peasants in selling firewood, and would not believe that he had actually brought the wood from the country as he assured them. He got hungry, and felt cold in his ragged woollen coat. It was nearly below zero when evening came on; his horse which he had treated without mercy, hoping soon to sell it to the knacker's yard, refused to move a step. So Ivan Mironov was quite ready to sell his firewood at a loss when he met Eugene Mihailovich, who was on his way home from the tobacconist.

"Buy my cartload of firewood, sir. I will give it to you cheap. My poor horse is tired, and can't go any farther."

"Where do you come from?"

"From the country, sir. This firewood is from our place. Good dry wood, I can assure you."

"Good wood indeed! I know your tricks. Well, what is your price?"

Ivan Mironov began by asking a high price, but reduced it once, and finished by selling the cartload for just what it had cost him.

"I'm giving it to you cheap, just to please you, sir.—Besides, I am glad it is not a long way to your house," he added.

Eugene Mihailovich did not bargain very much. He did not mind paying a little more, because he was delighted to think he could make use of the coupon and get rid of it. With great difficulty Ivan Mironov managed at last, by pulling the shafts himself, to drag his cart into the courtyard, where he was obliged to unload the firewood unaided and pile it up in the shed. The yard-porter was out. Ivan Mironov hesitated at first to accept the coupon, but Eugene Mihailovich insisted, and as he looked a very important person the peasant at last agreed.

He went by the backstairs to the servants' room, crossed himself before the ikon, wiped his beard which was covered with icicles, turned up the skirts of his coat, took out of his pocket a leather purse, and out of the purse eight roubles and fifty kopeks, and handed the change to Eugene Mihailovich. Carefully folding the coupon, he put it in the purse. Then, according to custom, he thanked the gentleman for his kindness, and, using the whip-handle instead of the lash, he belaboured the half-frozen horse that he had doomed to an early death, and betook himself to a public-house.

Arriving there, Ivan Mironov called for vodka and tea for which he paid eight kopeks. Comfortable and warm after the tea, he chatted in the very best of spirits with a yard-porter who was sitting at his table. Soon he grew communicative and told his companion all about the conditions of his life. He told him he came from the village Vassilievsky, twelve miles from town, and also that he had his allotment of land given to him by his family, as he wanted to live apart from his father and his brothers; that he had a wife and two children; the elder boy went to school, and did not yet help him in his work. He also said he lived in lodgings and intended going to the horse-fair the next day to look for a good horse, and, may be, to buy one. He went on to state that he had now nearly twenty-five roubles—only one rouble short—and that half of it was a coupon. He took the coupon out of his purse to show to his new friend. The yard-porter was an illiterate man, but he said he had had such coupons given him by lodgers to change; that they were good; but that one might also chance on forged ones; so he advised the peasant, for the sake of security, to change it at once at the counter. Ivan Mironov gave the coupon to the waiter and asked for change. The waiter, however, did not bring the change, but came back with the manager, a bald-headed man with a shining face, who was holding the coupon in his fat hand.

"Your money is no good," he said, showing the coupon, but apparently determined not to give it back.

"The coupon must be all right. I got it from a gentleman."

"It is bad, I tell you. The coupon is forged."

"Forged? Give it back to me."

"I will not. You fellows have got to be punished for such tricks. Of course, you did it yourself—you and some of your rascally friends."

"Give me the money. What right have you—"

"Sidor! Call a policeman," said the barman to the waiter. Ivan Mironov was rather drunk, and in that condition was hard to manage. He seized the manager by the collar and began to shout.

"Give me back my money, I say. I will go to the gentleman who gave it to me. I know where he lives."

The manager had to struggle with all his force to get loose from Ivan Mironov, and his shirt was torn,—

"Oh, that's the way you behave! Get hold of him."

The waiter took hold of Ivan Mironov; at that moment the policeman arrived. Looking very important, he inquired what had happened, and unhesitatingly gave his orders:

"Take him to the police-station."

As to the coupon, the policeman put it in his pocket; Ivan Mironov, together with his horse, was brought to the nearest station.

VII

Ivan Mironov had to spend the night in the police-station, in the company of drunkards and thieves. It was noon of the next day when he was summoned to the police officer; put through a close examination, and sent in the care of a policeman to Eugene Mihailovich's shop. Ivan Mironov remembered the street and the house. The policeman asked for the shopkeeper, showed him the coupon and confronted him with Ivan Mironov, who declared that he had received the coupon in that very place. Eugene Mihailovich at once assumed a very severe and astonished air.

"You are mad, my good fellow," he said. "I have never seen this man before in my life," he added, addressing the policeman.

"It is a sin, sir," said Ivan Mironov. "Think of the hour when you will die."

"Why, you must be dreaming! You have sold your firewood to some one else," said Eugene Mihailovich. "But wait a minute. I will go and ask my wife whether she bought any firewood yesterday." Eugene Mihailovich left them and immediately called the yard-porter Vassily, a strong, handsome, quick, cheerful, well-dressed man.

He told Vassily that if any one should inquire where the last supply of firewood was bought, he was to say they'd got it from the stores, and not from a peasant in the street.

"A peasant has come," he said to Vassily, "who has declared to the police that I gave him a forged coupon. He is a fool and talks nonsense, but you are a clever man. Mind you say that we always get the firewood from the stores. And, by the way, I've been thinking some time of giving you money to buy a new jacket," added Eugene Mihailovich, and gave the man five roubles. Vassily looking with pleasure first at the five rouble note, then at Eugene Mihailovich's face, shook his head and smiled.

"I know, those peasant folks have no brains. Ignorance, of course. Don't you be uneasy. I know what I have to say."

Ivan Mironov, with tears in his eyes, implored Eugene Mihailovich over and over again to acknowledge the coupon he had given him, and the yard-porter to believe what he said, but it proved quite useless; they both insisted that they had never bought firewood from a peasant in the street. The policeman brought Ivan Mironov back to the police-station, and he was charged with forging the coupon. Only after taking the advice of a drunken office clerk in the same cell with him, and bribing the police officer with five roubles, did Ivan Mironov get out of jail, without the coupon, and with only seven roubles left out of the twenty-five he had the day before.

Of these seven roubles he spent three in the public-house and came home to his wife dead drunk, with a bruised and swollen face.

His wife was expecting a child, and felt very ill. She began to scold her husband; he pushed her away, and she struck him. Without answering a word he lay down on the plank and began to weep bitterly.

Not till the next day did he tell his wife what had actually happened. She believed him at once, and thoroughly cursed the dastardly rich man who had cheated Ivan. He was sobered now, and remembering the advice a workman had given him, with whom he had many a drink the day before, decided to go to a lawyer and tell him of the wrong the owner of the photograph shop had done him.

VIII

The lawyer consented to take proceedings on behalf of Ivan Mironov, not so much for the sake of the fee, as because he believed the peasant, and was revolted by the wrong done to him.

Both parties appeared in the court when the case was tried, and the yard-porter Vassily was summoned as witness. They repeated in the court all they had said before to the police officials. Ivan Mironov again called to his aid the name of the Divinity, and reminded the shopkeeper of the hour of death. Eugene Mihailovich, although quite aware of his wickedness, and the risks he was running, despite the rebukes of his conscience, could not now change his testimony, and went on calmly to deny all the allegations made against him.

The yard-porter Vassily had received another ten roubles from his master, and, quite unperturbed, asserted with a smile that he did not know anything about Ivan Mironov. And when he was called upon to take the oath, he overcame his inner qualms, and repeated with assumed ease the terms of the oath, read to him by the old priest appointed to the court. By the holy Cross and the Gospel, he swore that he spoke the whole truth.

The case was decided against Ivan Mironov, who was sentenced to pay five roubles for expenses. This sum Eugene Mihailovich generously paid for him. Before dismissing Ivan Mironov, the judge severely admonished him, saying he ought to take care in the future not to accuse respectable people, and that he also ought to be thankful that he was not forced to pay the costs, and that he had escaped a prosecution for slander, for which he would have been condemned to three months' imprisonment.

"I offer my humble thanks," said Ivan Mironov; and, shaking his head, left the court with a heavy sigh.

The whole thing seemed to have ended well for Eugene Mihailovich and the yard-porter Vassily. But only in appearance. Something had happened which was not noticed by any one, but which was much more important than all that had been exposed to view.

Vassily had left his village and settled in town over two years ago. As time went on he sent less and less money to his father, and he did not ask his wife, who remained at home, to join him. He was in no need of her; he could in town have as many wives as he wished, and much better ones too than that clumsy, village-bred woman. Vassily, with each recurring year, became more and more familiar with the ways of the town people, forgetting the conventions of a country life. There everything was so vulgar, so grey, so poor and untidy. Here, in town, all seemed on the contrary so refined, nice, clean, and rich; so orderly too. And he became more and more convinced that people in the country live just like wild beasts, having no idea of what life is, and that only life in town is real. He read books written by clever writers, and went to the performances in the Peoples' Palace. In the country, people would not see such wonders even in dreams. In the country old men say: "Obey the law, and live with your wife; work; don't eat too much; don't care for finery," while here, in town, all the clever and learned people—those, of course, who know what in reality the law is—only pursue their own pleasures. And they are the better for it.

Previous to the incident of the forged coupon, Vassily could not actually believe that rich people lived without any moral law. But after that, still more after having perjured himself, and not being the worse for it in spite of his fears—on the contrary, he had gained ten roubles out of it—Vassily became firmly convinced that no moral laws whatever exist, and that the only thing to do is to pursue one's own interests and pleasures. This he now made his rule in life. He accordingly got as much profit as he could out of purchasing goods for lodgers. But this did not pay all his expenses. Then he took to stealing, whenever chance offered—money and all sorts of valuables. One day he stole a purse full of money from Eugene Mihailovich, but was found out. Eugene Mihailovich did not hand him over to the police, but dismissed him on the spot.

Vassily had no wish whatever to return home to his village, and remained in Moscow with his sweetheart, looking out for a new job. He got one as yard-porter at a grocer's, but with only small wages. The next day after he had entered that service he was caught stealing bags. The grocer did not call in the police, but gave him a good thrashing and turned him out. After that he could not find work. The money he had left was soon gone; he had to sell all his clothes and went about nearly in rags. His sweetheart left him. But notwithstanding, he kept up his high spirits, and when the spring came he started to walk home.

IX

Peter Nikolaevich Sventizky, a short man in black spectacles (he had weak eyes, and was threatened with complete blindness), got up, as was his custom, at dawn of day, had a cup of tea, and putting on his short fur coat trimmed with astrachan, went to look after the work on his estate.

Peter Nikolaevich had been an official in the Customs, and had gained eighteen thousand roubles during his service. About twelve years ago he quitted the service—not quite of his own accord: as a matter of fact he had been compelled to leave—and bought an estate from a young land-owner who had dissipated his fortune. Peter Nikolaevich had married at an earlier period, while still an official in the Customs. His wife, who belonged to an old noble family, was an orphan, and was left without money. She was a tall, stoutish, good-looking woman. They had no children. Peter Nikolaevich had considerable practical talents and a strong will. He was the son of a Polish gentleman, and knew nothing about agriculture and land management; but when he acquired an estate of his own, he managed it so well that after fifteen years the waste piece of land, consisting of three hundred acres, became a model estate. All the buildings, from the dwelling-house to the corn stores and the shed for the fire engine were solidly built, had iron roofs, and were painted at the right time. In the tool house carts, ploughs, harrows, stood in perfect order, the harness was well cleaned and oiled. The horses were not very big, but all home-bred, grey, well fed, strong and devoid of blemish.

The threshing machine worked in a roofed barn, the forage was kept in a separate shed, and a paved drain was made from the stables. The cows were home-bred, not very large, but giving plenty of milk; fowls were also kept in the poultry yard, and the hens were of a special kind, laying a great quantity of eggs. In the orchard the fruit trees were well whitewashed and propped on poles to enable them to grow straight. Everything was looked after—solid, clean, and in perfect order. Peter Nikolaevich rejoiced in the perfect condition of his estate, and was proud to have achieved it—not by oppressing the peasants, but, on the contrary, by the extreme fairness of his dealings with them.

Among the nobles of his province he belonged to the advanced party, and was more inclined to liberal than conservative views, always taking the side of the peasants against those who were still in favour of serfdom. "Treat them well, and they will be fair to you," he used to say. Of course, he did not overlook any carelessness on the part of those who worked on his estate, and he urged them on to work if they were lazy; but then he gave them good lodging, with plenty of good food, paid their wages without any delay, and gave them drinks on days of festival.

Walking cautiously on the melting snow—for the time of the year was February—Peter Nikolaevich passed the stables, and made his way to the cottage where his workmen were lodged. It was still dark, the darker because of the dense fog; but the windows of the cottage were lighted. The men had already got up. His intention was to urge them to begin work. He had arranged that they should drive out to the forest and bring back the last supply of firewood he needed before spring.

"What is that?" he thought, seeing the door of the stable wide open. "Hallo, who is there?"

No answer. Peter Nikolaevich stepped into the stable. It was dark; the ground was soft under his feet, and the air smelt of dung; on the right side of the door were two loose boxes for a pair of grey horses. Peter Nikolaevich stretched out his hand in their direction—one box was empty. He put out his foot—the horse might have been lying down. But his foot did not touch anything solid. "Where could they have taken the horse?" he thought. They certainly had not harnessed it; all the sledges stood still outside. Peter Nikolaevich went out of the stable.

"Stepan, come here!" he called.

Stepan was the head of the workmen's gang. He was just stepping out of the cottage.

"Here I am!" he said, in a cheerful voice. "Oh, is that you, Peter Nikolaevich? Our men are coming."

"Why is the stable door open?"

"Is it? I don't know anything about it. I say, Proshka, bring the lantern!"

Proshka came with the lantern. They all went to the stable, and Stepan knew at once what had happened.

"Thieves have been here, Peter Nikolaevich," he said. "The lock is broken."

"No; you don't say so!"

"Yes, the brigands! I don't see 'Mashka.' 'Hawk' is here. But 'Beauty' is not. Nor yet 'Dapple-grey.'"

Three horses had been stolen!

Peter Nikolaevich did not utter a word at first. He only frowned and took deep breaths.

"Oh," he said after a while. "If only I could lay hands on them! Who was on guard?"

"Peter. He evidently fell asleep."

Peter Nikolaevich called in the police, and making an appeal to all the authorities, sent his men to track the thieves. But the horses were not to be found.

"Wicked people," said Peter Nikolaevich. "How could they! I was always so kind to them. Now, wait! Brigands! Brigands the whole lot of them. I will no longer be kind."

X

In the meanwhile the horses, the grey ones, had all been disposed of; Mashka was sold to the gipsies for eighteen roubles; Dapple-grey was exchanged for another horse, and passed over to another peasant who lived forty miles away from the estate; and Beauty died on the way. The man who conducted the whole affair was—Ivan Mironov. He had been employed on the estate, and knew all the whereabouts of Peter Nikolaevich. He wanted to get back the money he had lost, and stole the horses for that reason.

After his misfortune with the forged coupon, Ivan Mironov took to drink; and all he possessed would have gone on drink if it had not been for his wife, who locked up his clothes, the horses' collars, and all the rest of what he would otherwise have squandered in public-houses. In his drunken state Ivan Mironov was continually thinking, not only of the man who had wronged him, but of all the rich people who live on robbing the poor. One day he had a drink with some peasants from the suburbs of Podolsk, and was walking home together with them. On the way the peasants, who were completely drunk, told him they had stolen a horse from a peasant's cottage. Ivan Mironov got angry, and began to abuse the horse-thieves.

"What a shame!" he said. "A horse is like a brother to the peasant. And you robbed him of it? It is a great sin, I tell you. If you go in for stealing horses, steal them from the landowners. They are worse than dogs, and deserve anything."

The talk went on, and the peasants from Podolsk told him that it required a great deal of cunning to steal a horse on an estate.

"You must know all the ins and outs of the place, and must have somebody on the spot to help you."

Then it occurred to Ivan Mironov that he knew a landowner—Sventizky; he had worked on his estate, and Sventizky, when paying him off, had deducted one rouble and a half for a broken tool. He remembered well the grey horses which he used to drive at Sventizky's.

Ivan Mironov called on Peter Nikolaevich pretending to ask for employment, but really in order to get the information he wanted. He took precautions to make sure that the watchman was absent, and that the horses were standing in their boxes in the stable. He brought the thieves to the place, and helped them to carry off the three horses.

They divided their gains, and Ivan Mironov returned to his wife with five roubles in his pocket. He had nothing to do at home, having no horse to work in the field, and therefore continued to steal horses in company with professional horse-thieves and gipsies.

XI

Peter Nikolaevich Sventizky did his best to discover who had stolen his horses. He knew somebody on the estate must have helped the thieves, and began to suspect all his staff. He inquired who had slept out that night, and the gang of the working men told him Proshka had not been in the whole night. Proshka, or Prokofy Nikolaevich, was a young fellow who had just finished his military service, handsome, and skilful in all he did; Peter Nikolaevich employed him at times as coachman. The district constable was a friend of Peter Nikolaevich, as were the provincial head of the police, the marshal of the nobility, and also the rural councillor and the examining magistrate. They all came to his house on his saint's day, drinking the cherry brandy he offered them with pleasure, and eating the nice preserved mushrooms of all kinds to accompany the liqueurs. They all sympathised with him in his trouble and tried to help him.

"You always used to take the side of the peasants," said the district constable, "and there you are! I was right in saying they are worse than wild beasts. Flogging is the only way to keep them in order. Well, you say it is all Proshka's doings. Is it not he who was your coachman sometimes?"

"Yes, that is he."

"Will you kindly call him?"

Proshka was summoned before the constable, who began to examine him.

"Where were you that night?"

Proshka pushed back his hair, and his eyes sparkled.

"At home."

"How so? All the men say you were not in."

"Just as you please, your honour."

"My pleasure has nothing to do with the matter. Tell me where you were that night."

"At home."

"Very well. Policeman, bring him to the police-station."

The reason why Proshka did not say where he had been that night was that he had spent it with his sweetheart, Parasha, and had promised not to give her away. He kept his word. No proofs were discovered against him, and he was soon discharged. But Peter Nikolaevich was convinced that Prokofy had been at the bottom of the whole affair, and began to hate him. One day Proshka bought as usual at the merchant's two measures of oats. One and a half he gave to the horses, and half a measure he gave back to the merchant; the money for it he spent in drink. Peter Nikolaevich found it out, and charged Prokofy with cheating. The judge sentenced the man to three months' imprisonment.

Prokofy had a rather proud nature, and thought himself superior to others. Prison was a great humiliation for him. He came out of it very depressed; there was nothing more to be proud of in life. And more than that, he felt extremely bitter, not only against Peter Nikolaevich, but against the whole world.

On the whole, as all the people around him noticed, Prokofy became another man after his imprisonment, both careless and lazy; he took to drink, and he was soon caught stealing clothes at some woman's house, and found himself again in prison.

All that Peter Nikolaevich discovered about his grey horses was the hide of one of them, Beauty, which had been found somewhere on the estate. The fact that the thieves had got off scot-free irritated Peter Nikolaevich still more. He was unable now to speak of the peasants or to look at them without anger. And whenever he could he tried to oppress them.

XII

After having got rid of the coupon, Eugene Mihailovich forgot all about it; but his wife, Maria Vassilievna, could not forgive herself for having been taken in, nor yet her husband for his cruel words. And most of all she was furious against the two boys who had so skilfully cheated her. From the day she had accepted the forged coupon as payment, she looked closely at all the schoolboys who came in her way in the streets. One day she met Mahin, but did not recognise him, for on seeing her he made a face which quite changed his features. But when, a fortnight after the incident with the coupon, she met Mitia Smokovnikov face to face, she knew him at once.

She let him pass her, then turned back and followed him, and arriving at his house she made inquiries as to whose son he was. The next day she went to the school and met the divinity instructor, the priest Michael Vedensky, in the hall. He asked her what she wanted. She answered that she wished to see the head of the school. "He is not quite well," said the priest. "Can I be of any use to you, or give him your message?"

Maria Vassilievna thought that she might as well tell the priest what was the matter. Michael Vedensky was a widower, and a very ambitious man. A year ago he had met Mitia Smokovnikov's father in society, and had had a discussion with him on religion. Smokovnikov had beaten him decisively on all points; indeed, he had made him appear quite ridiculous. Since that time the priest had decided to pay special attention to Smokovnikov's son; and, finding him as indifferent to religious matters as his father was, he began to persecute him, and even brought about his failure in examinations.

When Maria Vassilievna told him what young Smokovnikov had done to her, Vedensky could not help feeling an inner satisfaction. He saw in the boy's conduct a proof of the utter wickedness of those who are not guided by the rules of the Church. He decided to take advantage of this great opportunity of warning unbelievers of the perils that threatened them. At all events, he wanted to persuade himself that this was the only motive that guided him in the course he had resolved to take. But at the bottom of his heart he was only anxious to get his revenge on the proud atheist.

"Yes, it is very sad indeed," said Father Michael, toying with the cross he was wearing over his priestly robes, and passing his hands over its polished sides. "I am very glad you have given me your confidence. As a servant of the Church I shall admonish the young man—of course with the utmost kindness. I shall certainly do it in the way that befits my holy office," said Father Michael to himself, really thinking that he had forgotten the ill-feeling the boy's father had towards him. He firmly believed the boy's soul to be the only object of his pious care.

The next day, during the divinity lesson which Father Michael was giving to Mitia Smokovnikov's class, he narrated the incident of the forged coupon, adding that the culprit had been one of the pupils of the school. "It was a very wicked thing to do," he said; "but to deny the crime is still worse. If it is true that the sin has been committed by one of you, let the guilty one confess." In saying this, Father Michael looked sharply at Mitia Smokovnikov. All the boys, following his glance, turned also to Mitia, who blushed, and felt extremely ill at ease, with large beads of perspiration on his face. Finally, he burst into tears, and ran out of the classroom. His mother, noticing his trouble, found out the truth, ran at once to the photographer's shop, paid over the twelve roubles and fifty kopeks to Maria Vassilievna, and made her promise to deny the boy's guilt. She further implored Mitia to hide the truth from everybody, and in any case to withhold it from his father.

Accordingly, when Fedor Mihailovich had heard of the incident in the divinity class, and his son, questioned by him, had denied all accusations, he called at once on the head of the school, told him what had happened, expressed his indignation at Father Michael's conduct, and said he would not let matters remain as they were.

Father Michael was sent for, and immediately fell into a hot dispute with Smokovnikov.

"A stupid woman first falsely accused my son, then retracts her accusation, and you of course could not hit on anything more sensible to do than to slander an honest and truthful boy!"

"I did not slander him, and I must beg you not to address me in such a way. You forget what is due to my cloth."

"Your cloth is of no consequence to me."

"Your perversity in matters of religion is known to everybody in the town!" replied Father Michael; and he was so transported with anger that his long thin head quivered.

"Gentlemen! Father Michael!" exclaimed the director of the school, trying to appease their wrath. But they did not listen to him.

"It is my duty as a priest to look after the religious and moral education of our pupils."

"Oh, cease your pretence to be religious! Oh, stop all this hum-bug of religion! As if I did not know that you believe neither in God nor Devil."

"I consider it beneath my dignity to talk to a man like you," said Father Michael, very much hurt by Smokovnikov's last words, the more so because he knew they were true.

Michael Vedensky carried on his studies in the academy for priests, and that is why, for a long time past, he ceased to believe in what he confessed to be his creed and in what he preached from the pulpit; he only knew that men ought to force themselves to believe in what he tried to make himself believe.

Smokovnikov was not shocked by Father Michael's conduct; he only thought it illustrative of the influence the Church was beginning to exercise on society, and he told all his friends how his son had been insulted by the priest.

Seeing not only young minds, but also the elder generation, con-taminated by atheistic tendencies, Father Michael became more and more convinced of the necessity of fighting those tendencies. The more he condemned the unbelief of Smokovnikov, and those like him, the more confident he grew in the firmness of his own faith, and the less he felt the need of making sure of it, or of bringing his life into harmony with it. His faith, acknowledged as such by all the world around him, became Father Michael's very best weapon with which to fight those who denied it.

The thoughts aroused in him by his conflict with Smokovnikov, together with the annoyance of being blamed by his chiefs in the school, made him carry out the purpose he had entertained ever since his wife's death—of taking monastic orders, and of following the course carried out by some of his fellow-pupils in the academy. One of them was already a bishop, another an archimandrite and on the way to become a bishop.

At the end of the term Michael Vedensky gave up his post in the school, took orders under the name of Missael, and very soon got a post as rector in a seminary in a town on the river Volga.

XIII

Meanwhile the yard-porter Vassily was marching on the open road down to the south.

He walked in daytime, and when night came some policeman would get him shelter in a peasant's cottage. He was given bread everywhere, and sometimes he was asked to sit down to the evening meal. In a village in the Orel district, where he had stayed for the night, he heard that a merchant who had hired the landowner's orchard for the season, was looking out for strong and able men to serve as watchmen for the fruit-crops. Vassily was tired of tramping, and as he had also no desire whatever to go back to his native village, he went to the man who owned the orchard, and got engaged as watchman for five roubles a month.

Vassily found it very agreeable to live in his orchard shed, and all the more so when the apples and pears began to grow ripe, and when the men from the barn supplied him every day with large bundles of fresh straw from the threshing machine. He used to lie the whole day long on the fragrant straw, with fresh, delicately smelling apples in heaps at his side, looking out in every direction to prevent the village boys from stealing fruit; and he used to whistle and sing meanwhile, to amuse himself. He knew no end of songs, and had a fine voice. When peasant women and young girls came to ask for apples, and to have a chat with him, Vassily gave them larger or smaller apples according as he liked their looks, and received eggs or money in return. The rest of the time he had nothing to do, but to lie on his back and get up for his meals in the kitchen. He had only one shirt left, one of pink cotton, and that was in holes. But he was strongly built and enjoyed excellent health. When the kettle with black gruel was taken from the stove and served to the working men, Vassily used to eat enough for three, and filled the old watchman on the estate with unceasing wonder. At nights Vassily never slept. He whistled or shouted from time to time to keep off thieves, and his piercing, cat-like eyes saw clearly in the darkness.

One night a company of young lads from the village made their way stealthily to the orchard to shake down apples from the trees. Vassily, coming noiselessly from behind, attacked them; they tried to escape, but he took one of them prisoner to his master.

Vassily's first shed stood at the farthest end of the orchard, but after the pears had been picked he had to remove to another shed only forty paces away from the house of his master. He liked this new place very much. The whole day long he could see the young ladies and gentlemen enjoying themselves; going out for drives in the evenings and quite late at nights, playing the piano or the violin, and singing and dancing. He saw the ladies sitting with the young students on the window sills, engaged in animated conversation, and then going in pairs to walk the dark avenue of lime trees, lit up only by streaks of moonlight. He saw the servants running about with food and drink, he saw the cooks, the stewards, the laundresses, the gardeners, the coachmen, hard at work to supply their masters with food and drink and constant amusement. Sometimes the young people from the master's house came to the shed, and Vassily offered them the choicest apples, juicy and red. The young ladies used to take large bites out of the apples on the spot, praising their taste, and spoke French to one another—Vassily quite understood it was all about him—and asked Vassily to sing for them.

Vassily felt the greatest admiration for his master's mode of living, which reminded him of what he had seen in Moscow; and he became more and more convinced that the only thing that mattered in life was money. He thought and thought how to get hold of a large sum of money. He remembered his former ways of making small profits whenever he could, and came to the conclusion that that was altogether wrong. Occasional stealing is of no use, he thought. He must arrange a well-prepared plan, and after getting all the information he wanted, carry out his purpose so as to avoid detection.

After the feast of Nativity of the Blessed Virgin Mary, the last crop of autumn apples was gathered; the master was content with the results, paid off Vassily, and gave him an extra sum as reward for his faithful service.

Vassily put on his new jacket, and a new hat—both were presents from his master's son—but did not make his way homewards. He hated the very thought of the vulgar peasants' life. He went back to Moscow in company of some drunken soldiers, who had been watchmen in the orchard together with him. On his arrival there he at once resolved, under cover of night, to break into the shop where he had been employed, and beaten, and then turned out by the proprietor without being paid. He knew the place well, and knew where the money was locked up. So he bade the soldiers, who helped him, keep watch outside, and forcing the courtyard door entered the shop and took all the money he could lay his hands on. All this was done very cleverly, and no trace was left of the burglary. The money Vassily had found in the shop amounted to 370 roubles. He gave a hundred roubles to his assistants, and with the rest left for another town where he gave way to dissipation in company of friends of both sexes. The police traced his movements, and when at last he was arrested and put into prison he had hardly anything left out of the money which he had stolen.

XIV

Ivan Mironov had become a very clever, fearless and successful horse-thief. Afimia, his wife, who at first used to abuse him for his evil ways, as she called it, was now quite content and felt proud of her husband, who possessed a new sheepskin coat, while she also had a warm jacket and a new fur cloak.

In the village and throughout the whole district every one knew quite well that Ivan Mironov was at the bottom of all the horse-stealing; but nobody would give him away, being afraid of the consequences. Whenever suspicion fell on him, he managed to clear his character. Once during the night he stole horses from the pasture ground in the village Kolotovka. He generally preferred to steal horses from landowners or tradespeople. But this was a harder job, and when he had no chance of success he did not mind robbing peasants too. In Kolotovka he drove off the horses without making sure whose they were. He did not go himself to the spot, but sent a young and clever fellow, Gerassim, to do the stealing for him. The peasants only got to know of the theft at dawn; they rushed in all directions to hunt for the robbers. The horses, meanwhile, were hidden in a ravine in the forest lands belonging to the state.

Ivan Mironov intended to leave them there till the following night, and then to transport them with the utmost haste a hundred miles away to a man he knew. He visited Gerassim in the forest, to see how he was getting on, brought him a pie and some vodka, and was returning home by a side track in the forest where he hoped to meet nobody. But by ill-luck, he chanced on the keeper of the forest, a retired soldier.

"I say! Have you been looking for mushrooms?" asked the soldier.

"There were none to be found," answered Ivan Mironov, showing the basket of lime bark he had taken with him in case he might want it.

"Yes, mushrooms are scarce this summer," said the soldier. He stood still for a moment, pondered, and then went his way. He clearly saw that something was wrong. Ivan Mironov had no business whatever to take early morning walks in that forest. The soldier went back after a while and looked round. Suddenly he heard the snorting of horses in the ravine. He made his way cautiously to the place whence the sounds came. The grass in the ravine was trodden down, and the marks of horses' hoofs were clearly to be seen. A little further he saw Gerassim, who was sitting and eating his meal, and the horses tied to a tree.

The soldier ran to the village and brought back the bailiff, a police officer, and two witnesses. They surrounded on three sides the spot where Gerassim was sitting and seized the man. He did not deny anything; but, being drunk, told them at once how Ivan Mironov had given him plenty of drink, and induced him to steal the horses; he also said that Ivan Mironov had promised to come that night in order to take the horses away. The peasants left the horses and Gerassim in the ravine, and hiding behind the trees prepared to lie in ambush for Ivan Mironov. When it grew dark, they heard a whistle. Gerassim answered it with a similar sound. The moment Ivan Mironov descended the slope, the peasants surrounded him and brought him back to the village. The next morning a crowd assembled in front of the bailiff's cottage. Ivan Mironov was brought out and subjected to a close examination. Stepan Pelageushkine, a tall, stooping man with long arms, an aquiline nose, and a gloomy face was the first to put questions to him. Stepan had terminated his military service, and was of a solitary turn of mind. When he had separated from his father, and started his own home, he had his first experience of losing a horse. After that he worked for two years in the mines, and made money enough to buy two horses. These two had been stolen by Ivan Mironov.

"Tell me where my horses are!" shouted Stepan, pale with fury, alternately looking at the ground and at Ivan Mironov's face.

Ivan Mironov denied his guilt. Then Stepan aimed so violent a blow at his face that he smashed his nose and the blood spurted out.

"Tell the truth, I say, or I'll kill you!"

Ivan Mironov kept silent, trying to avoid the blows by stooping. Stepan hit him twice more with his long arm. Ivan Mironov remained silent, turning his head backwards and forwards.

"Beat him, all of you!" cried the bailiff, and the whole crowd rushed upon Ivan Mironov. He fell without a word to the ground, and then shouted,—

"Devils, wild beasts, kill me if that's what you want! I am not afraid of you!"

Stepan seized a stone out of those that had been collected for the purpose, and with a heavy blow smashed Ivan Mironov's head.

XV

Ivan Mironov's murderers were brought to trial, Stepan Pelageushkine among them. He had a heavier charge to answer than the others, all the witnesses having stated that it was he who had smashed Ivan Mironov's head with a stone. Stepan concealed nothing when in court. He contented himself with explaining that, having been robbed of his two last horses, he had informed the police. Now it was comparatively easy at that time to trace the horses with the help of professional thieves among the gipsies. But the police officer would not even permit him, and no search had been ordered.

"Nothing else could be done with such a man. He has ruined us all."

"But why did not the others attack him. It was you alone who broke his head open."

"That is false. We all fell upon him. The village agreed to kill him. I only gave the final stroke. What is the use of inflicting unnecessary sufferings on a man?"

The judges were astonished at Stepan's wonderful coolness in narrating the story of his crime—how the peasants fell upon Ivan Mironov, and how he had given the final stroke. Stepan actually did not see anything particularly revolting in this murder. During his military service he had been ordered on one occasion to shoot a soldier, and, now with regard to Ivan Mironov, he saw nothing loathsome in it. "A man shot is a dead man—that's all. It was him to-day, it might be me to-morrow," he thought. Stepan was only sentenced to one year's imprisonment, which was a mild punishment for what he had done. His peasant's dress was taken away from him and put in the prison stores, and he had a prison suit and felt boots given to him instead. Stepan had never had much respect for the authorities, but now he became quite convinced that all the chiefs, all the fine folk, all except the Czar—who alone had pity on the peasants and was just—all were robbers who suck blood out of the people. All he heard from the deported convicts, and those sentenced to hard labour, with whom he had made friends in prisons, confirmed him in his views. One man had been sentenced to hard labour for having convicted his superiors of a theft; another for having struck an official who had unjustly confiscated the property of a peasant; a third because he forged bank notes. The well-to-do-people, the merchants, might do whatever they chose and come to no harm; but a poor peasant, for a trumpery reason or for none at all, was sent to prison to become food for vermin.

He had visits from his wife while in prison. Her life without him was miserable enough, when, to make it worse, her cottage was destroyed by fire. She was completely ruined, and had to take to begging with her children. His wife's misery embittered Stepan still more. He got on very badly with all the people in the prison; was rude to every one; and one day he nearly killed the cook with an axe, and therefore got an additional year in prison. In the course of that year he received the news that his wife was dead, and that he had no longer a home.

When Stepan had finished his time in prison, he was taken to the prison stores, and his own dress was taken down from the shelf and handed to him.

"Where am I to go now?" he asked the prison officer, putting on his old dress.

"Why, home."

"I have no home. I shall have to go on the road. Robbery will not be a pleasant occupation."

"In that case you will soon be back here."

"I am not so sure of that."

And Stepan left the prison. Nevertheless he took the road to his own place. He had nowhere else to turn.

On his way he stopped for a night's rest in an inn that had a public bar attached to it. The inn was kept by a fat man from the town, Vladimir, and he knew Stepan. He knew that Stepan had been put into prison through ill luck, and did not mind giving him shelter for the night. He was a rich man, and had persuaded his neighbour's wife to leave her husband and come to live with him. She lived in his house as his wife, and helped him in his business as well.

Stepan knew all about the innkeeper's affairs—how he had wronged the peasant, and how the woman who was living with him had left her husband. He saw her now sitting at the table in a rich dress, and looking very hot as she drank her tea. With great condescension she asked Stepan to have tea with her. No other travellers were stopping in the inn that night. Stepan was given a place in the kitchen where he might sleep. Matrena—that was the woman's name—cleared the table and went to her room. Stepan went to lie down on the large stove in the kitchen, but he could not sleep, and the wood splinters put on the stove to dry were crackling under him, as he tossed from side to side. He could not help thinking of his host's fat paunch protruding under the belt of his shirt, which had lost its colour from having been washed ever so many times. Would not it be a good thing to make a good clean incision in that paunch. And that woman, too, he thought.

One moment he would say to himself, "I had better go from here to-morrow, bother them all!" But then again Ivan Mironov came back to his mind, and he went on thinking of the innkeeper's paunch and Matrena's white throat bathed in perspiration. "Kill I must, and it must be both!"

He heard the cock crow for the second time. "I must do it at once, or dawn will be here." He had seen in the evening before he went to bed a knife and an axe. He crawled down from the stove, took the knife and axe, and went out of the kitchen door. At that very moment he heard the lock of the entrance door open. The innkeeper was going out of the house to the courtyard. It all turned out contrary to what Stepan desired. He had no opportunity of using the knife; he just swung the axe and split the innkeeper's head in two. The man tumbled down on the threshold of the door, then on the ground.

Stepan stepped into the bedroom. Matrena jumped out of bed, and remained standing by its side. With the same axe Stepan killed her also.

Then he lighted the candle, took the money out of the desk, and left the house.

XVI

In a small district town, some distance away from the other buildings, an old man, a former official, who had taken to drink, lived in his own house with his two daughters and his son-in-law. The married daughter was also addicted to drink and led a bad life, and it was the elder daughter, the widow Maria Semenovna, a wrinkled woman of fifty, who supported the whole family. She had a pension of two hundred and fifty roubles a year, and the family lived on this. Maria Semenovna did all the work in the house, looked after the drunken old father, who was very weak, attended to her sister's child, and managed all the cooking and the washing of the family. And, as is always the case, whatever there was to do, she was expected to do it, and was, moreover, continually scolded by all the three people in the house; her brother-in-law used even to beat her when he was drunk. She bore it all patiently, and as is also always the case, the more work she had to face, the quicker she managed to get through it. She helped the poor, sacrificing her own wants; she gave them her clothes, and was a ministering angel to the sick.

Once the lame, crippled village tailor was working in Maria Semenovna's house. He had to mend her old father's coat, and to mend and repair Maria Semenovna's fur-jacket for her to wear in winter when she went to market.

The lame tailor was a clever man, and a keen observer: he had seen many different people owing to his profession, and was fond of reflection, condemned as he was to a sedentary life.

Having worked a week at Maria Semenovna's, he wondered greatly about her life. One day she came to the kitchen, where he was sitting with his work, to wash a towel, and began to ask him how he was getting on. He told her of the wrong he had suffered from his brother, and how he now lived on his own allotment of land, separated from that of his brother.

"I thought I should have been better off that way," he said. "But I am now just as poor as before."

"It is much better never to change, but to take life as it comes," said Maria Semenovna. "Take life as it comes," she repeated.

"Why, I wonder at you, Maria Semenovna," said the lame tailor. "You alone do the work, and you are so good to everybody. But they don't repay you in kind, I see."

Maria Semenovna did not utter a word in answer.

"I dare say you have found out in books that we are rewarded in heaven for the good we do here."

"We don't know that. But we must try to do the best we can."

"Is it said so in books?"

"In books as well," she said, and read to him the Sermon on the Mount. The tailor was much impressed. When he had been paid for his job and gone home, he did not cease to think about Maria Semenovna, both what she had said and what she had read to him.

XVII

Peter Nikolaevich Sventizky's views of the peasantry had now changed for the worse, and the peasants had an equally bad opinion of him. In the course of a single year they felled twenty-seven oaks in his forest, and burnt a barn which had not been insured. Peter Nikolaevich came to the conclusion that there was no getting on with the people around him.

At that very time the landowner, Liventsov, was trying to find a manager for his estate, and the Marshal of the Nobility recommended Peter Nikolaevich as the ablest man in the district in the management of land. The estate owned by Liventsov was an extremely large one, but there was no revenue to be got out of it, as the peasants appropriated all its wealth to their own profit. Peter Nikolaevich undertook to bring everything into order; rented out his own land to somebody else; and settled with his wife on the Liventsov estate, in a distant province on the river Volga.

Peter Nikolaevich was always fond of order, and wanted things to be regulated by law; and now he felt less able of allowing those raw and rude peasants to take possession, quite illegally too, of property that did not belong to them. He was glad of the opportunity of giving them a good lesson, and set seriously to work at once. One peasant was sent to prison for stealing wood; to another he gave a thrashing for not having made way for him on the road with his cart, and for not having lifted his cap to salute him. As to the pasture ground which was a subject of dispute, and was considered by the peasants as their property, Peter Nikolaevich informed the peasants that any of their cattle grazing on it would be driven away by him.

The spring came and the peasants, just as they had done in previous years, drove their cattle on to the meadows belonging to the landowner. Peter Nikolaevich called some of the men working on the estate and ordered them to drive the cattle into his yard. The peasants were working in the fields, and, disregarding the screaming of the women, Peter Nikolaevich's men succeeded in driving in the cattle. When they came home the peasants went in a crowd to the cattle-yard on the estate, and asked for their cattle. Peter Nikolaevich came out to talk to them with a gun slung on his shoulder; he had just returned from a ride of inspection. He told them that he would not let them have their cattle unless they paid a fine of fifty kopeks for each of the horned cattle, and twenty kopeks for each sheep. The peasants loudly declared that the pasture ground was their property, because their fathers and grandfathers had used it, and protested that he had no right whatever to lay hand on their cattle.

"Give back our cattle, or you will regret it," said an old man coming up to Peter Nikolaevich.

"How shall I regret it?" cried Peter Nikolaevich, turning pale, and coming close to the old man.

"Give them back, you villain, and don't provoke us."

"What?" cried Peter Nikolaevich, and slapped the old man in the face.

"You dare to strike me? Come along, you fellows, let us take back our cattle by force."

The crowd drew close to him. Peter Nikolaevich tried to push his way through them, but the peasants resisted him. Again he tried force.

His gun, accidentally discharged in the *mêlée*, killed one of the peasants. Instantly the fight began. Peter Nikolaevich was trodden down, and five minutes later his mutilated body was dragged into the ravine.

The murderers were tried by martial law, and two of them sentenced to the gallows.

XVIII

In the village where the lame tailor lived, in the Zemliansk district of the Voronesh province, five rich peasants hired from the landowner a hundred and five acres of rich arable land, black as tar, and let it out on lease to the rest of the peasants at fifteen to eighteen roubles an acre. Not one acre was given under twelve roubles. They got a very profitable return, and the five acres which were left to each of their company practically cost them nothing. One of the five peasants died, and the lame tailor received an offer to take his place.

When they began to divide the land, the tailor gave up drinking vodka, and, being consulted as to how much land was to be divided, and to whom it should be given, he proposed to give allotments to all on equal terms, not taking from the tenants more than was due for each piece of land out of the sum paid to the landowner.

"Why so?"

"We are no heathens, I should think," he said. "It is all very well for the masters to be unfair, but we are true Christians. We must do as God bids. Such is the law of Christ."

"Where have you got that law from?"

"It is in the Book, in the Gospels. Just come to me on Sunday. I will read you a few passages, and we will have a talk afterwards."

They did not all come to him on Sunday, but three came, and he began reading to them.

He read five chapters of St. Matthew's Gospel, and they talked. One man only, Ivan Chouev, accepted the lesson and carried it out completely, following the rule of Christ in everything from that day. His family did the same. Out of the arable land he took only what was his due, and refused to take more.

The lame tailor and Ivan had people calling on them, and some of these people began to grasp the meaning of the Gospels, and in consequence gave up smoking, drinking, swearing, and using bad language and tried to help one another. They also ceased to go to church, and took their ikons to the village priest, saying they did not want them any more. The priest was frightened, and reported what had occurred to the bishop. The bishop was at a loss what to do. At last he resolved to send the archimandrite Missael to the village, the one who had formerly been Mitia Smokovnikov's teacher of religion.

XIX

Asking Father Missael on his arrival to take a seat, the bishop told him what had happened in his diocese.

"It all comes from weakness of spirit and from ignorance. You are a learned man, and I rely on you. Go to the village, call the parishioners together, and convince them of their error."

"If your Grace bids me go, and you give me your blessing, I will do my best," said Father Missael. He was very pleased with the task entrusted to him. Every opportunity he could find to demonstrate the firmness of his faith was a boon to him. In trying to convince others he was chiefly intent on persuading himself that he was really a firm believer.

"Do your best. I am greatly distressed about my flock," said the bishop, leisurely taking a cup with his white plump hands from the servant who brought in the tea.

"Why is there only one kind of jam? Bring another," he said to the servant. "I am greatly distressed," he went on, turning to Father Missael.

Missael earnestly desired to prove his zeal; but, being a man of small means, he asked to be paid for the expenses of his journey; and being afraid of the rough people who might be ill-disposed towards him, he also asked the bishop to get him an order from the governor of the province, so that the local police might help him in case of need. The bishop complied with his wishes, and Missael got his things ready with the help of his servant and his cook. They furnished him with a case full of wine, and a basket with the victuals he might need in going to such a lonely place. Fully provided with all he wanted, he started for the village to which he was commissioned. He was pleasantly conscious of the importance of his mission. All his doubts as to his own faith passed away, and he was now fully convinced of its reality.

His thoughts, far from being concerned with the real foundation of his creed—this was accepted as an axiom—were occupied with the arguments used against the forms of worship.

XX

The village priest and his wife received Father Missael with great honours, and the next day after he had arrived the parishioners were invited to assemble in the church. Missael in a new silk cassock, with a large cross on his chest, and his long hair carefully combed, ascended the pulpit; the priest stood at his side, the deacons and the choir at a little distance behind him, and the side entrances were guarded by the police. The dissenters also came in their dirty sheepskin coats.

After the service Missael delivered a sermon, admonishing the dissenters to return to the bosom of their mother, the Church, threatening them with the torments of hell, and promising full forgiveness to those who would repent.

The dissenters kept silent at first. Then, being asked questions, they gave answers. To the question why they dissented, they said that their chief reason was the fact that the Church worshipped gods made of wood, which, far from being ordained, were condemned by the Scriptures.

When asked by Missael whether they actually considered the holy ikons to be mere planks of wood, Chouev answered,—

"Just look at the back of any ikon you choose and you will see what they are made of."

When asked why they turned against the priests, their answer was that the Scripture says: "As you have received it without fee, so you must give it to the others; whereas the priests require payment for the grace they bestow by the sacraments." To all attempts which

Missael made to oppose them by arguments founded on Holy Writ, the tailor and Ivan Chouev gave calm but very firm answers, contradicting his assertions by appeal to the Scriptures, which they knew uncommonly well.

Missael got angry and threatened them with persecution by the authorities. Their answer was: It is said, I have been persecuted and so will you be.

The discussion came to nothing, and all would have ended well if Missael had not preached the next day at mass, denouncing the wicked seducers of the faithful and saying that they deserved the worst punishment. Coming out of the church, the crowd of peasants began to consult whether it would not be well to give the infidels a good lesson for disturbing the minds of the community. The same day, just when Missael was enjoying some salmon and gangfish, dining at the village priest's in company with the inspector, a violent brawl arose in the village. The peasants came in a crowd to Chouev's cottage, and waited for the dissenters to come out in order to give them a thrashing.

The dissenters assembled in the cottage numbered about twenty men and women. Missael's sermon and the attitude of the orthodox peasants, together with their threats, aroused in the mind of the dissenters angry feelings, to which they had before been strangers. It was near evening, the women had to go and milk the cows, and the peasants were still standing and waiting at the door.

A boy who stepped out of the door was beaten and driven back into the house. The people within began consulting what was to be done, and could come to no agreement. The tailor said, "We must bear whatever is done to us, and not resist." Chouev replied that if they decided on that course they would, all of them, be beaten to death. In consequence, he seized a poker and went out of the house. "Come!" he shouted, "let us follow the law of Moses!" And, falling upon the peasants, he knocked out one man's eye, and in the meanwhile all those who had been in his house contrived to get out and make their way home.

Chouev was thrown into prison and charged with sedition and blasphemy.

XXI

Two years previous to those events a strong and handsome young girl of an eastern type, Katia Turchaninova, came from the Don military settlements to St. Petersburg to study in the university college for women. In that town she met a student, Turin, the son of a district governor in the Simbirsk province, and fell in love with him. But her love was not of the ordinary type, and she had no desire to become his wife and the mother of his children. He was a dear comrade to her, and their chief bond of union was a feeling of revolt they had in common, as well as the hatred they bore, not only to the existing forms of government, but to all those who represented that government. They had also in common the sense that they both excelled their enemies in culture, in brains, as well as in morals. Katia Turchaninova was a gifted girl, possessed of a good memory, by means of which she easily mastered the lectures she attended. She was successful in her examinations, and, apart from that, read all the newest books. She was certain that her vocation was not to bear and rear children, and even looked on such a task with disgust and contempt. She thought herself chosen by destiny to destroy the present government, which was fettering the best abilities of the nation, and to reveal to the people a higher standard of life, inculcated by the latest writers of other countries. She was handsome, a little inclined to stoutness: she had a good complexion, shining black eyes, abundant black hair. She inspired the men she knew with feelings she neither wished nor had time to share, busy as she was with propaganda work, which consisted chiefly in mere talking. She was not displeased, however, to inspire these feelings; and, without dressing too smartly, did not neglect her appearance. She liked to be admired, as it gave her opportunities of showing how little she prized what was valued so highly by other women.

In her views concerning the method of fighting the government she went further than the majority of her comrades, and than her friend Turin; all means, she taught, were justified in such a struggle, not excluding murder. And yet, with all her revolutionary ideas, Katia Turchaninova was in her soul a very kind girl, ready to sacrifice herself for the welfare and the happiness of other people, and sincerely pleased when she could do a kindness to anybody, a child, an old person, or an animal.

She went in the summer to stay with a friend, a schoolmistress in a small town on the river Volga. Turin lived near that town, on his father's estate. He often came to see the two girls; they gave each other books to read, and had long discussions, expressing their common indignation with the state of affairs in the country. The district doctor, a friend of theirs, used also to join them on many occasions.

The estate of the Turins was situated in the neighbourhood of the Liventsov estate, the one that was entrusted to the management of Peter Nikolaevich Sventizky. Soon after Peter Nikolaevich had settled there, and begun to enforce order, young Turin, having observed an independent tendency in the peasants on the Liventsov estate, as well as their determination to uphold their rights, became interested in them. He came often to the village to talk with the men, and developed his socialistic theories, insisting particularly on the nationalisation of the land.

After Peter Nikolaevich had been murdered, and the murderers sent to trial, the revolutionary group of the small town boiled over with indignation, and did not shrink from openly expressing it. The fact of Turin's visits to the village and his propaganda work among the students, became known to the authorities during the trial. A search was made in his house; and, as the police found a few revolutionary leaflets among his effects, he was arrested and transferred to prison in St. Petersburg.

Katia Turchaninova followed him to the metropolis, and went to visit him in prison. She was not admitted on the day she came, and was told to come on the day fixed by regulations for visits to the prisoners. When that day arrived, and she was finally allowed to see him, she had to talk to him through two gratings separating the prisoner from his visitor. This visit increased her indignation against the authorities. And her feelings become all the more revolutionary after a visit she paid to the office of a gendarme officer who had to deal with the Turin case. The officer, a handsome man, seemed obviously disposed to grant her exceptional favours in visiting the prisoner, if she would allow him to make love to her. Disgusted with him, she appealed to the chief of police. He pretended—just as the officer did when talking officially to her—to be powerless himself, and to depend entirely on orders coming from the minister of state. She sent a petition to the minister asking for an interview, which was refused.

Then she resolved to do a desperate thing and bought a revolver.

XXII

The minister was receiving petitioners at the usual hour appointed for the reception. He had talked successively to three of them, and now a pretty young woman with black eyes, who was holding a petition in her left hand, approached. The minister's eyes gleamed when he saw how attractive the petitioner was, but recollecting his high position he put on a serious face.

"What do you want?" he asked, coming down to where she stood. Without answering his question the young woman quickly drew a revolver from under her cloak and aiming it at the minister's chest fired—but missed him.

The minister rushed at her, trying to seize her hand, but she escaped, and taking a step back, fired a second time. The minister ran out of the room. The woman was immediately seized. She was trembling violently, and could not utter a single word; after a while she suddenly burst into a hysterical laugh. The minister was not even wounded.

That woman was Katia Turchaninova. She was put into the prison of preliminary detention. The minister received congratulations and marks of sympathy from the highest quarters, and even from the emperor himself, who appointed a commission to investigate the plot that had led to the attempted assassination. As a matter of fact there was no plot whatever, but the police officials and the detectives set to work with the utmost zeal to discover all the threads of the non-existing conspiracy. They did everything to deserve the fees they were paid; they got up in the small hours of the morning, searched one house after another, took copies of papers and of books they found, read diaries, personal letters, made extracts from them on the very best notepaper and in beautiful handwriting, interrogated Katia Turchaninova ever so many times, and confronted her with all those whom they suspected of conspiracy, in order to extort from her the names of her accomplices.

The minister, a good-natured man at heart, was sincerely sorry for the pretty girl. But he said to himself that he was bound to consider his high state duties imposed upon him, even though they did not imply much work and trouble. So, when his former colleague, a chamberlain and a friend of the Turins, met him at a court ball and tried to rouse his pity for Turin and the girl Turchaninova, he shrugged his shoulders, stretching the red ribbon on his white waistcoat, and said: *"Je ne demanderais pas mieux que de relacher cette pauvre fillette, mais vous savez le devoir.*" And in the meantime Katia Turchaninova was kept in prison. She was at times in a quiet mood, communicated with her fellow-prisoners by knocking on the walls, and read the books that were sent to her. But then came days when she had fits of desperate fury, knocking with her fists against the wall, screaming and laughing like a madwoman.

XXIII

One day Maria Semenovna came home from the treasurer's office, where she had received her pension. On her way she met a school-master, a friend of hers.

"Good day, Maria Semenovna! Have you received your money?" the schoolmaster asked, in a loud voice from the other side of the street.

"I have," answered Maria Semenovna. "But it was not much; just enough to fill the holes."

"Oh, there must be some tidy pickings out of such a lot of money," said the schoolmaster, and passed on, after having said good-bye.

"Good-bye," said Maria Semenovna. While she was looking at her friend, she met a tall man face to face, who had very long arms and a stern look in his eyes. Coming to her house, she was very startled on again seeing the same man with the long arms, who had evidently followed her. He remained standing another moment after she had gone in, then turned and walked away.

Maria Semenovna felt somewhat frightened at first. But when she had entered the house, and had given her father and her nephew Fedia the presents she had brought for them, and she had patted the dog Treasure, who whined with joy, she forgot her fears. She gave the money to her father and began to work, as there was always plenty for her to do.

The man she met face to face was Stepan.

After he had killed the innkeeper, he did not return to town. Strange to say, he was not sorry to have committed that murder. His mind went back to the murdered man over and over again during the following day; and he liked the recollection of having done the thing so skilfully, so cleverly, that nobody would ever discover it, and he would not therefore be prevented from murdering other people in the same way. Sitting in the public-house and having his tea, he looked at the people around him with the same thought how he should murder them. In the evening he called at a carter's, a man from his village, to spend the night at his house. The carter was not in. He said he would wait for him, and in the meanwhile began talking to the carter's wife. But when she moved to the stove, with her back turned to him, the idea entered his mind to kill her. He marvelled at himself at first, and shook his head; but the next moment he seized the knife he had hidden in his boot, knocked the woman down on the floor, and cut her throat. When the children began to scream, he killed them also and went away. He did not look out for another place to spend the night, but at once left the town. In a village some distance away he went to the inn and slept there. The next day he returned to the district town, and there he overheard in the street Maria Semenovna's talk with the schoolmaster. Her look frightened him, but yet he made up his mind to creep into her house, and rob her of the money she had received. When the night came he broke the lock and entered the house. The first person who heard his steps was the younger daughter, the married one. She screamed. Stepan stabbed her immediately with his knife. Her husband woke up and fell upon Stepan, seized him by his throat, and struggled with him desperately. But Stepan was the stronger man and overpowered him. After murdering him, Stepan, excited by the long fight, stepped into the next room behind a partition. That was Maria Semenovna's bedroom. She rose in her bed, looked at Stepan with her mild frightened eyes, and crossed herself.

Once more her look scared Stepan. He dropped his eyes.

"Where is your money?" he asked, without raising his face.

She did not answer.

"Where is the money?" asked Stepan again, showing her his knife.

"How can you . . ." she said.

"You will see how."

Stepan came close to her, in order to seize her hands and prevent her struggling with him, but she did not even try to lift her arms or offer any resistance; she pressed her hands to her chest, and sighed heavily.

"Oh, what a great sin!" she cried. "How can you! Have mercy on yourself. To destroy somebody's soul . . . and worse, your own! . . ."

Stepan could not stand her voice any longer, and drew his knife sharply across her throat. "Stop that talk!" he said. She fell back with a hoarse cry, and the pillow was stained with blood. He turned away, and went round the rooms in order to collect all he thought worth taking. Having made a bundle of the most valuable things, he lighted a cigarette, sat down for a while, brushed his clothes, and left the house. He thought this murder would not matter to him more than those he had committed before; but before he got a night's lodging, he felt suddenly so exhausted that he could not walk any farther. He stepped down into the gutter and remained lying there the rest of the night, and the next day and the next night.

PART SECOND

I

The whole time he was lying in the gutter Stepan saw continually before his eyes the thin, kindly, and frightened face of Maria Semenovna, and seemed to hear her voice. "How can you?" she went on saying in his imagination, with her peculiar lisping voice. Stepan saw over again and over again before him all he had done to her. In horror he shut his eyes, and shook his hairy head, to drive away these thoughts and recollections. For a moment he would get rid of them, but in their place horrid black faces with red eyes appeared and frightened him continuously. They grinned at him, and kept repeating, "Now you have done away with her you must do away with yourself, or we will not leave you alone." He opened his eyes, and again he saw *her* and heard her voice; and felt an immense pity for her and a deep horror and disgust with himself. Once more he shut his eyes, and the black faces reappeared. Towards the evening of the next day he rose and went, with hardly any strength left, to a public-house. There he ordered a drink, and repeated his demands over and over again, but no quantity of liquor could make him intoxicated. He was sitting at a table, and swallowed silently one glass after another.

A police officer came in. "Who are you?" he asked Stepan.

"I am the man who murdered all the Dobrotvorov people last night," he answered.

He was arrested, bound with ropes, and brought to the nearest police-station; the next day he was transferred to the prison in the town. The inspector of the prison recognised him as an old inmate, and a very turbulent one; and, hearing that he had now become a real criminal, accosted him very harshly.

"You had better be quiet here," he said in a hoarse voice, frowning, and protruding his lower jaw. "The moment you don't behave, I'll flog you to death! Don't try to escape—I will see to that!"

"I have no desire to escape," said Stepan, dropping his eyes. "I surrendered of my own free will."

"Shut up! You must look straight into your superior's eyes when you talk to him," cried the inspector, and struck Stepan with his fist under the jaw.

At that moment Stepan again saw the murdered woman before him, and heard her voice; he did not pay attention, therefore, to the inspector's words.

"What?" he asked, coming to his senses when he felt the blow on his face.

"Be off! Don't pretend you don't hear."

The inspector expected Stepan to be violent, to talk to the other prisoners, to make attempts to escape from prison. But nothing of the kind ever happened. Whenever the guard or the inspector himself looked into his cell through the hole in the door, they saw Stepan sitting on a bag filled with straw, holding his head with his hands and whispering to himself. On being brought before the examining magistrate charged with the inquiry into his case, he did not behave like an ordinary convict. He was very absent-minded, hardly listening to the questions; but when he heard what was asked, he answered truthfully, causing the utmost perplexity to the magistrate, who, accustomed as he was to the necessity of being very clever and very cunning with convicts, felt a strange sensation just as if he were lifting up his foot to ascend a step and found none. Stepan told him the story of all his murders; and did it frowning, with a set look, in a quiet, businesslike voice, trying to recollect all the circumstances of his crimes. "He stepped out of the house," said Stepan, telling the tale of his first murder, "and stood barefooted at the door; I hit him, and he just groaned; I went to his wife, ..." And so on.

One day the magistrate, visiting the prison cells, asked Stepan whether there was anything he had to complain of, or whether he had any wishes that might be granted him. Stepan said he had no wishes whatever, and had nothing to complain of the way he was treated in prison. The magistrate, on leaving him, took a few steps in the foul passage, then stopped and asked the governor who had accompanied him in his visit how this prisoner was behaving.

"I simply wonder at him," said the governor, who was very pleased with Stepan, and spoke kindly of him. "He has now been with us about two months, and could be held up as a model of good behaviour. But I am afraid he is plotting some mischief. He is a daring man, and exceptionally strong."

II

During the first month in prison Stepan suffered from the same agonising vision. He saw the grey wall of his cell, he heard the sounds of the prison; the noise of the cell below him, where a number of convicts were confined together; the striking of the prison clock; the steps of the sentry in the passage; but at the same time he saw *her* with that kindly face which conquered his heart the very first time he met her in the street, with that thin, strongly-marked neck, and he heard her soft, lisping, pathetic voice: "To destroy somebody's soul . . . and, worst of all, your own. . . . How can you? . . ."

After a while her voice would die away, and then black faces would appear. They would appear whether he had his eyes open or shut. With his closed eyes he saw them more distinctly. When he opened his eyes they vanished for a moment, melting away into the walls and the door; but after a while they reappeared and surrounded him from three sides, grinning at him and saying over and over: "Make an end! Make an end! Hang yourself! Set yourself on fire!" Stepan shook all over when he heard that, and tried to say all the prayers he knew: "Our Lady" or "Our Father." At first this seemed to help. In saying his prayers he began to recollect his whole life; his father, his mother, the village, the dog "Wolf," the old grandfather lying on the stove, the bench on which the children used to play; then the girls in the village with their songs, his horses and how they had been stolen, and how the thief was caught and how he killed him with a stone. He recollected also the first prison he was in and his leaving it, and the fat innkeeper, the carter's wife and the children. Then again *she* came to his mind and again he was terrified. Throwing his prison overcoat off his shoulders, he jumped out of bed, and, like a wild animal in a cage, began pacing up and down his tiny cell, hastily turning round when he had reached the damp walls. Once more he tried to pray, but it was of no use now.

The autumn came with its long nights. One evening when the wind whistled and howled in the pipes, Stepan, after he had paced up and down his cell for a long time, sat down on his bed. He felt he could not struggle any more; the black demons had overpowered him, and he had to submit. For some time he had been looking at the funnel of the oven. If he could fix on the knob of its lid a loop made of thin shreds of narrow linen straps it would hold. . . . But he would have to manage it very cleverly. He set to work, and spent two days in making straps out of the linen bag on which he slept. When the guard came into the cell he covered the bed with his overcoat. He tied the straps with big knots and made them double, in order that they might be strong enough to hold his weight. During these preparations he was free from tormenting visions. When the straps were ready he made a slip-knot out of them, and put it round his neck, stood up in his bed, and hanged himself. But at the very moment that his tongue began to protrude the straps got loose, and he fell down. The guard rushed in at the noise. The doctor was called in, Stepan was brought to the infirmary. The next day he recovered, and was removed from the infirmary, no more to solitary confinement, but to share the common cell with other prisoners.

In the common cell he lived in the company of twenty men, but felt as if he were quite alone. He did not notice the presence of the rest; did not speak *to* anybody, and was tormented by the old agony. He felt it most of all when the men were sleeping and he alone could not get one moment of sleep. Continually he saw *her* before his eyes, heard her voice, and then again the black devils with their horrible eyes came and tortured him in the usual way.

He again tried to say his prayers, but, just as before, it did not help him. One day when, after his prayers, she was again before his eyes, he began to implore her dear soul to forgive him his sin, and release him. Towards morning, when he fell down quite exhausted on his crushed linen bag, he fell asleep at once, and in his dream she came to him with her thin, wrinkled, and severed neck. "Will you forgive me?" he asked. She looked at him with her mild eyes and did not answer. "Will you forgive me?" And so he asked her three times. But she did not say a word, and he awoke. From that time onwards he suffered less, and seemed to come to his senses, looked around him, and began for the first time to talk to the other men in the cell.

III

Stepan's cell was shared among others by the former yard-porter, Vassily, who had been sentenced to deportation for robbery, and by Chouev, sentenced also to deportation. Vassily sang songs the whole day long with his fine voice, or told his adventures to the other men in the cell. Chouev was working at something all day, mending his clothes, or reading the Gospel and the Psalter.

Stepan asked him why he was put into prison, and Chouev answered that he was being persecuted because of his true Christian faith by the priests, who were all of them hypocrites and hated those who followed the law of Christ. Stepan asked what that true law was, and Chouev made clear to him that the true law consists in not worshipping gods made with hands, but worshipping the spirit and the truth. He told him how he had learnt the truth from the lame tailor at the time when they were dividing the land.

"And what will become of those who have done evil?" asked Stepan.

"The Scriptures give an answer to that," said Chouev, and read aloud to him Matthew xxv. 31:—

"When the Son of Man shall come in His glory, and all the holy angels with Him, then shall He sit upon the throne of His glory: and before Him shall be gathered all nations: and He shall separate them one from another, as a shepherd divideth His sheep from the goats: and He shall set the sheep on His right hand, but the goats on the left. Then shall the King say unto them on His right hand, Come, ye blessed of My Father, inherit the kingdom prepared for you from the foundation of the world: for I was an hungred, and ye gave Me meat: I was thirsty, and ye gave Me drink: I was a stranger, and ye took Me in : naked, and ye clothed Me: I was sick, and ye visited Me: I was in prison, and ye came unto Me. Then shall the righteous answer Him, saying, Lord, when saw we Thee an hungred, and fed Thee? or thirsty, and gave Thee drink? When saw we Thee a stranger, and took Thee in? or naked, and clothed Thee? Or when saw we Thee sick, or in prison, and came unto Thee? And the King shall answer and say unto them, Verily I say unto you, inasmuch as ye have done it unto one of the least of these My brethren, ye have done it unto Me. Then shall He say also unto them on the left hand, Depart from Me, ye cursed, into everlasting fire, prepared for the devil and his angels: for I was an hungred, and ye gave Me no meat: I was thirsty, and ye gave Me no drink: I was a stranger and ye took Me not in: naked, and ye clothed Me not; sick, and in prison, and ye visited Me not. Then shall they also answer Him, saying, Lord, when saw we Thee an hungred, or athirst, or a stranger, or naked, or sick, or in prison, and did not minister unto Thee? Then shall He answer them, saying, Verily I say unto you, Inasmuch as ye did it not to one of the least of these, ye did it not to Me. And these shall go away into everlasting punishment: but the righteous into life eternal."

Vassily, who was sitting on the floor at Chouev's side, and was listening to his reading the Gospel, nodded his handsome head in approval. "True," he said in a resolute tone. "Go, you cursed villains, into everlasting punishment, since you did not give food to the hungry, but swallowed it all yourself. Serves them right! I have read the holy Nikodim's writings," he added, showing off his erudition.

"And will they never be pardoned?" asked Stepan, who had listened silently, with his hairy head bent low down.

"Wait a moment, and be silent," said Chouev to Vassily, who went on talking about the rich who had not given meat to the stranger, nor visited him in the prison.

"Wait, I say!" said Chouev, again turning over the leaves of the Gospel. Having found what he was looking for, Chouev smoothed the page with his large and strong hand, which had become exceedingly white in prison:

"And there were also two other malefactors, led with Him"—it means with Christ—"to be put to death. And when they were come to the place, which is called Calvary, there they crucified Him, and the malefactors, one on the right hand, and the other on the left. Then said Jesus,—'Father, forgive them; for they know not what they do.' And the people stood beholding. And the rulers also with them derided Him, saying,—'He saved others; let Him save Himself if He be Christ, the chosen of God.' And the soldiers also mocked Him, coming to Him, and offering Him vinegar, and saying, 'If Thou be the King of the Jews save Thyself.' And a superscription also was written over Him in letters of Greek, and Latin, and Hebrew, 'This is the King of the Jews.' And one of the malefactors which were hanged railed on Him, saying, 'If thou be Christ, save Thyself and us.' But the other answering rebuked Him, saying, 'Dost not thou fear God, seeing thou art in the same condemnation? And we indeed justly, for we receive the due reward of our deeds: but this man hath done nothing amiss.' And he said unto Jesus, 'Lord, remember me when Thou comest into Thy kingdom.' And Jesus said unto him, 'Verily I say unto thee, to-day shalt thou be with Me in paradise.'"

Stepan did not say anything, and was sitting in thought, as if he were listening.

Now he knew what the true faith was. Those only will be saved who have given food and drink to the poor and visited the prisoners; those who have not done it, go to hell. And yet the malefactor had repented on the cross, and went nevertheless to paradise. This did not strike him as being inconsistent. Quite the contrary. The one, confirmed the other: the fact that the merciful will go to Heaven, and the unmerciful to hell, meant that everybody ought to be merciful, and the malefactor having been forgiven by Christ meant that Christ was merciful. This was all new to Stepan, and he wondered why it had been hidden from him so long.

From that day onward he spent all his free time with Chouev, asking him questions and listening to him. He saw but a single truth at the bottom of the teaching of Christ as revealed to him by Chouev: that all men are brethren, and that they ought to love and pity one another in order that all might be happy. And when he listened to Chouev, everything that was consistent with this fundamental truth came to him like a thing he had known before and only forgotten since, while whatever he heard that seemed to contradict it, he would take no notice of, as he thought that he simply had not understood the real meaning. And from that time Stepan was a different man.

IV

Stepan had been very submissive and meek ever since he came to the prison, but now he made the prison authorities and all his fellow-prisoners wonder at the change in him. Without being ordered, and out of his proper turn he would do all the very hardest work in prison, and the dirtiest too. But in spite of his humility, the other prisoners stood in awe of him, and were afraid of him, as they knew he was a resolute man, possessed of great physical strength. Their respect for him increased after the incident of the two tramps who fell upon him; he wrenched himself loose from them and broke the arm of one of them in the fight. These tramps had gambled with a young prisoner of some means and deprived him of all his money. Stepan took his part, and deprived the tramps of their winnings. The tramps poured their abuse on him; but when they attacked him, he got the better of them. When the Governor asked how the fight had come about, the tramps declared that it was Stepan who had begun it. Stepan did not try to exculpate himself, and bore patiently his sentence which was three days in the punishment-cell, and after that solitary confinement.

In his solitary cell he suffered because he could no longer listen to Chouev and his Gospel. He was also afraid that the former visions of *her* and of the black devils would reappear to torment him. But the visions were gone for good. His soul was full of new and happy ideas. He felt glad to be alone if only he could read, and if he had the Gospel. He knew that he might have got hold of the Gospel, but he could not read.

He had started to learn the alphabet in his boyhood, but could not grasp the joining of the syllables, and remained illiterate. He made up his mind to start reading anew, and asked the guard to bring him the Gospels. They were brought to him, and he sat down to work. He contrived to recollect the letters, but could not join them into syllables. He tried as hard as he could to understand how the letters ought to be put together to form words, but with no result whatever. He lost his sleep, had no desire to eat, and a deep sadness came over him, which he was unable to shake off.

"Well, have you not yet mastered it?" asked the guard one day.

"No."

"Do you know 'Our Father'?"

"I do."

"Since you do, read it in the Gospels. Here it is," said the guard, showing him the prayer in the Gospels. Stepan began to read it, comparing the letters he knew with the familiar sounds.

And all of a sudden the mystery of the syllables was revealed to him, and he began to read. This was a great joy. From that moment he could read, and the meaning of the words, spelt out with such great pains, became more significant.

Stepan did not mind any more being alone. He was so full of his work that he did not feel glad when he was transferred back to the common cell, his private cell being needed for a political prisoner who had been just sent to prison.

V

In the meantime Mahin, the schoolboy who had taught his friend Smokovnikov to forge the coupon, had finished his career at school and then at the university, where he had studied law. He had the advantage of being liked by women, and as he had won favour with a vice-minister's former mistress, he was appointed when still young as examining magistrate. He was dishonest, had debts, had gambled, and had seduced many women; but he was clever, sagacious, and a good magistrate. He was appointed to the court of the district where Stepan Pelageushkine had been tried. When Stepan was brought to him the first time to give evidence, his sincere and quiet answers puzzled the magistrate. He somehow unconsciously felt that this man, brought to him in fetters and with a shorn head, guarded by two soldiers who were waiting to take him back to prison, had a free soul and was immeasurably superior to himself. He was in consequence somewhat troubled, and had to summon up all his courage in order to go on with the inquiry and not blunder in his questions. He was amazed that Stepan should narrate the story of his crimes as if they had been things of long ago, and committed not by him but by some different man.

"Had you no pity for them?" asked Mahin.

"No. I did not know then."

"Well, and now?"

Stepan smiled with a sad smile. "Now," he said, "I would not do it even if I were to be burned alive."

"But why?"

"Because I have come to know that all men are brethren."

"What about me? Am I your brother also?"

"Of course you are."

"And how is it that I, your brother, am sending you to hard labour?"

"It is because you don't know."

"What do I not know?"

"Since you judge, it means obviously that you don't know."

"Go on. . . . What next?"

VI

Now it was not Chouev, but Stepan who used to read the gospel in the common cell. Some of the prisoners were singing coarse songs, while others listened to Stepan reading the gospel and talking about what he had read. The most attentive among those who listened were two of the prisoners, Vassily, and a convict called Mahorkin, a murderer who had become a hangman. Twice during his stay in this prison he was called upon to do duty as hangman, and both times in faraway places where nobody could be found to execute the sentences.

Two of the peasants who had killed Peter Nikolaevich Sventizky, had been sentenced to the gallows, and Mahorkin was ordered to go to Pensa to hang them. On all previous occasions he used to write a petition to the governor of the province—he knew well how to read and to write—stating that he had been ordered to fulfil his duty, and asking for money for his expenses. But now, to the greatest astonishment of the prison authorities, he said he did not intend to go, and added that he would not be a hangman any more.

"And what about being flogged?" cried the governor of the prison.

"I will have to bear it, as the law commands us not to kill."

"Did you get that from Pelageushkine? A nice sort of a prison prophet! You just wait and see what this will cost you!"

When Mahin was told of that incident, he was greatly impressed by the fact of Stepan's influence on the hangman, who refused to do his duty, running the risk of being hanged himself for insubordination.

VII

At an evening party at the Eropkins, Mahin, who was paying attentions to the two young daughters of the house—they were rich matches, both of them—having earned great applause for his fine singing and playing the piano, began telling the company about the strange convict who had converted the hangman. Mahin told his story very accurately, as he had a very good memory, which was all the more retentive because of his total indifference to those with whom he had to deal. He never paid the slightest attention to other people's feelings, and was therefore better able to keep all they did or said in his memory. He got interested in Stepan Pelageushkine, and, although he did not thoroughly understand him, yet asked himself involuntarily what was the matter with the man? He could not find an answer, but feeling that there was certainly something remarkable going on in Stepan's soul, he told the company at the Eropkins all about Stepan's conversion of the hangman, and also about his strange behaviour in prison, his reading the Gospels and his great influence on the rest of the prisoners. All this made a special impression on the younger daughter of the family, Lisa, a girl of eighteen, who was just recovering from the artificial life she had been living in a boarding-school; she felt as if she had emerged out of water, and was taking in the fresh air of true life with ecstasy. She asked Mahin to tell her more about the man Pelageushkine, and to explain to her how such a great change had come over him. Mahin told her what he knew from the police official about Stepan's last murder, and also what he had heard from Pelageushkine himself—how he had been conquered by the humility, mildness, and fearlessness of a kind woman, who had been his last victim, and how his eyes had been opened, while the reading of the Gospels had completed the change in him.

Lisa Eropkin was not able to sleep that night. For a couple of months a struggle had gone on in her heart between society life, into which her sister was dragging her, and her infatuation for Mahin, combined with a desire to reform him. This second desire now became the stronger. She had already heard about poor Maria Semenovna. But, after that kind woman had been murdered in such a ghastly way, and after Mahin, who learnt it from Stepan, had communicated to her all the facts concerning Maria Semenovna's life, Lisa herself passionately desired to become like her. She was a rich girl, and was afraid that Mahin had been courting her because of her money. So she resolved to give all she possessed to the poor, and told Mahin about it.

Mahin was very glad to prove his disinterestedness, and told Lisa that he loved her and not her money. Such proof of his innate nobility made him admire himself greatly. Mahin helped Lisa to carry out her decision. And the more he did so, the more he came to realise the new world of Lisa's spiritual ambitions, quite unknown to him heretofore.

VIII

All were silent in the common cell. Stepan was lying in his bed, but was not yet asleep. Vassily approached him, and, pulling him by his leg, asked him in a whisper to get up and to come to him. Stepan stepped out of his bed, and came up to Vassily.

"Do me a kindness, brother," said Vassily. "Help me!"

"In what?"

"I am going to fly from the prison."

Vassily told Stepan that he had everything ready for his flight.

"To-morrow I shall stir them up—" He pointed to the prisoners asleep in their beds. "They will give me away, and I shall be transferred to the cell in the upper floor. I know my way from there. What I want you for is to unscrew the prop in the door of the mortuary."

"I can do that. But where will you go?"

"I don't care where. Are not there plenty of wicked people in every place?"

"Quite so, brother. But it is not our business to judge them."

"I am not a murderer, to be sure. I have not destroyed a living soul in my life. As for stealing, I don't see any harm in that. As if they have not robbed us!"

"Let them answer for it themselves, if they do."

"Bother them all! Suppose I rob a church, who will be hurt? This time I will take care not to break into a small shop, but will get hold of a lot of money, and then I will help people with it. I will give it to all good people."

One of the prisoners rose in his bed and listened. Stepan and Vassily broke off their conversation. The next day Vassily carried out his idea. He began complaining of the bread in prison, saying it was moist, and induced the prisoners to call the governor and to tell him of their discontent. The governor came, abused them all, and when he heard it was Vassily who had stirred up the men, he ordered him to be transferred into solitary confinement in the cell on the upper floor. This was all Vassily wanted.

IX

Vassily knew well that cell on the upper floor. He knew its floor, and began at once to take out bits of it. When he had managed to get under the floor he took out pieces of the ceiling beneath, and jumped down into the mortuary a floor below. That day only one corpse was lying on the table. There in the corner of the room were stored bags to make hay mattresses for the prisoners. Vassily knew about the bags, and that was why the mortuary served his purposes. The prop in the door had been unscrewed and put in again. He took it out, opened the door, and went out into the passage to the lavatory which was being built. In the lavatory was a large hole connecting the third floor with the basement floor. After having found the door of the lavatory he went back to the mortuary, stripped the sheet off the dead body which was as cold as ice (in taking off the sheet Vassily touched his hand), took the bags, tied them together to make a rope, and carried the rope to the lavatory. Then he attached it to the cross-beam, and climbed down along it. The rope did not reach the ground, but he did not know how much was wanting. Anyhow, he had to take the risk. He remained hanging in the air, and then jumped down. His legs were badly hurt, but he could still walk on. The basement had two windows; he could have climbed out of one of them but for the grating protecting them. He had to break the grating, but there was no tool to do it with. Vassily began to look around him, and chanced on a piece of plank with a sharp edge; armed with that weapon he tried to loosen the bricks which held the grating. He worked a long time at that task. The cock crowed for the second time, but the grating still held. At last he had loosened one side; and then he pushed the plank under the loosened end and pressed with all his force. The grating gave way completely, but at that moment one of the bricks fell down heavily. The noise could have been heard by the sentry. Vassily stood motionless. But silence reigned. He climbed out of the window. His way of escape was to climb the wall. An outhouse stood in the corner of the courtyard. He had to reach its roof, and pass thence to the top of the wall. But he would not be able to reach the roof without the help of the plank; so he had to go back through the basement window to fetch it. A moment later he came out of the window with the plank in his hands; he stood still for a while listening to the steps of the sentry. His expectations were justified. The sentry was walking up and down on the other side of the courtyard. Vassily came up to the outhouse, leaned the plank against it, and began climbing. The plank slipped and fell on the ground. Vassily had his stockings on; he took them off so that he could cling with his bare feet in coming down. Then he leaned the plank again against the house, and seized the water-pipe with his hands. If only this time the plank would hold! A quick movement up the water-pipe, and his knee rested on the roof. The sentry was approaching. Vassily lay motionless. The sentry did not notice him, and passed on. Vassily leaped to his feet; the iron roof cracked under him. Another step or two, and he would reach the wall. He could touch it with his hand now. He leaned forward with one hand, then with the other, stretched out his body as far as he could, and found himself on the wall. Only, not to break his legs in jumping down, Vassily turned round, remained hanging in the air by his hands, stretched himself out, loosened the grip of one hand, then the other. "Help me, God!" He was on the ground. And the ground was soft. His legs were not hurt, and he ran at the top of his speed. In a suburb, Malania opened her door, and he crept under her warm coverlet, made of small pieces of different colours stitched together.

X

The wife of Peter Nikolaevich Sventizky, a tall and handsome woman, as quiet and sleek as a well-fed heifer, had seen from her window how her husband had been murdered and dragged away into the fields. The horror of such a sight to Natalia Ivanovna was so intense—how could it be otherwise?—that all her other feelings vanished. No sooner had the crowd disappeared from view behind the garden fence, and the voices had become still; no sooner had the bare-footed Malania, their servant, run in with her eyes starting out of her head, calling out in a voice more suited to the proclamation of glad tidings the news that Peter Nikolaevich had been murdered and thrown into the ravine, than Natalia Ivanovna felt that behind her first sensation of horror, there was another sensation; a feeling of joy at her deliverance from the tyrant, who through all the nineteen years of their married life had made her work without a moment's rest. Her joy made her aghast; she did not confess it to herself, but hid it the more from those around. When his mutilated, yellow and hairy body was being washed and put into the coffin, she cried with horror, and wept and sobbed. When the coroner—a special coroner for serious cases—came and was taking her evidence, she noticed in the room, where the inquest was taking place, two peasants in irons, who had been charged as the principal culprits. One of them was an old man with a curly white beard, and a calm and severe countenance. The other was rather young, of a gipsy type, with bright eyes and curly dishevelled hair. She declared that they were the two men who had first seized hold of Peter Nikolaevich's hands. In spite of the gipsy-like peasant looking at her with his eyes glistening from under his moving eyebrows, and saying reproachfully: "A great sin, lady, it is. Remember your death hour!"—in spite of that, she did not feel at all sorry for them. On the contrary, she began to hate them during the inquest, and wished desperately to take revenge on her husband's murderers.

A month later, after the case, which was committed for trial by court-martial, had ended in eight men being sentenced to hard labour, and in two—the old man with the white beard, and the gipsy boy, as she called the other—being condemned to be hanged, Natalia felt vaguely uneasy. But unpleasant doubts soon pass away under the solemnity of a trial. Since such high authorities considered that this was the right thing to do, it must be right.

The execution was to take place in the village itself. One Sunday Malania came home from church in her new dress and her new boots, and announced to her mistress that the gallows were being erected, and that the hangman was expected from Moscow on Wednesday. She also announced that the families of the convicts were raging, and that their cries could be heard all over the village.

Natalia Ivanovna did not go out of her house; she did not wish to see the gallows and the people in the village; she only wanted what had to happen to be over quickly. She only considered her own feelings, and did not care for the convicts and their families.

On Tuesday the village constable called on Natalia Ivanovna. He was a friend, and she offered him vodka and preserved mushrooms of her own making. The constable, after eating a little, told her that the execution was not to take place the next day.

"Why?"

"A very strange thing has happened. There is no hangman to be found. They had one in Moscow, my son told me, but he has been reading the Gospels a good deal and says: 'I will not commit a murder.' He had himself been sentenced to hard labour for having committed a murder, and now he objects to hang when the law orders him. He was threatened with flogging. 'You may flog me,' he said, 'but I won't do it.'"

Natalia Ivanovna grew red and hot at the thought which suddenly came into her head.

"Could not the death sentence be commuted now?"

"How so, since the judges have passed it? The Czar alone has the right of amnesty."

"But how would he know?"

"They have the right of appealing to him."

"But it is on my account they are to die," said that stupid woman, Natalia Ivanovna. "And I forgive them."

The constable laughed. "Well—send a petition to the Czar."

"May I do it?"

"Of course you may."

"But is it not too late?"

"Send it by telegram."

"To the Czar himself?"

"To the Czar, if you like."

The story of the hangman having refused to do his duty, and preferring to take the flogging instead, suddenly changed the soul of Natalia Ivanovna. The pity and the horror she felt the moment she heard that the peasants were sentenced to death, could not be stifled now, but filled her whole soul.

"Filip Vassilievich, my friend. Write that telegram for me. I want to appeal to the Czar to pardon them."

The constable shook his head. "I wonder whether that would not involve us in trouble?"

"I do it upon my own responsibility. I will not mention your name."

"Is not she a kind woman," thought the constable. "Very kind-hearted, to be sure. If my wife had such a heart, our life would be a paradise, instead of what it is now." And he wrote the telegram,—

"To his Imperial Majesty, the Emperor. Your Majesty's loyal subject, the widow of Peter Nikolaevich Sventizky, murdered by the peasants, throws herself at the sacred feet (this sentence, when he wrote it down, pleased the constable himself most of all) of your Imperial Majesty, and implores you to grant an amnesty to the peasants so and so, from such a province, district, and village, who have been sentenced to death."

The telegram was sent by the constable himself, and Natalia Ivanovna felt relieved and happy. She had a feeling that since she, the widow of the murdered man, had forgiven the murderers, and was applying for an amnesty, the Czar could not possibly refuse it.

XI

Lisa Eropkin lived in a state of continual excitement. The longer she lived a true Christian life as it had been revealed to her, the more convinced she became that it was the right way, and her heart was full of joy.

She had two immediate aims before her. The one was to convert Mahin; or, as she put it to herself, to arouse his true nature, which

was good and kind. She loved him, and the light of her love revealed
the divine element in his soul which is at the bottom of all souls.
But, further, she saw in him an exceptionally kind and tender heart,
as well as a noble mind. Her other aim was to abandon her riches.
She had first thought of giving away what she possessed in order to
test Mahin; but afterwards she wanted to do so for her own sake, for
the sake of her own soul. She began by simply giving money to any
one who wanted it. But her father stopped that; besides which, she
felt disgusted at the crowd of supplicants who personally, and by
letters, besieged her with demands for money. Then she resolved to
apply to an old man, known to be a saint by his life, and to give him
her money to dispose of in the way he thought best. Her father got
angry with her when he heard about it. During a violent altercation
he called her mad, a raving lunatic, and said he would take measures
to prevent her from doing injury to herself.

Her father's irritation proved contagious. Losing all control over
herself, and sobbing with rage, she behaved with the greatest imper-
tinence to her father, calling him a tyrant and a miser.

Then she asked his forgiveness. He said he did not mind what she
said; but she saw plainly that he was offended, and in his heart did
not forgive her. She did not feel inclined to tell Mahin about her
quarrel with her father; as to her sister, she was very cold to Lisa,
being jealous of Mahin's love for her.

"I ought to confess to God," she said to herself. As all this happened in Lent, she made up her mind to fast in preparation for the
communion, and to reveal all her thoughts to the father confessor,
asking his advice as to what she ought to decide for the future.

At a small distance from her town a monastery was situated, where
an old monk lived who had gained a great reputation by his holy
life, by his sermons and prophecies, as well as by the marvellous cures
ascribed to him.

The monk had received a letter from Lisa's father announcing the
visit of his daughter, and telling him in what a state of excitement
the young girl was. He also expressed the hope in that letter that the
monk would influence her in the right way, urging her not to depart
from the golden mean, and to live like a good Christian without
trying to upset the present conditions of her life.

The monk received Lisa after he had seen many other people, and
being very tired, began by quietly recommending her to be modest
and to submit to her present conditions of life and to her parents.
Lisa listened silently, blushing and flushed with excitement. When

he had finished admonishing her, she began saying with tears in her eyes, timidly at first, that Christ bade us leave father and mother to follow Him. Getting more and more excited, she told him her conception of Christ. The monk smiled slightly, and replied as he generally did when admonishing his penitents; but after a while he remained silent, repeating with heavy sighs, "O God!" Then he said, "Well, come to confession tomorrow," and blessed her with his wrinkled hands.

The next day Lisa came to confession, and without renewing their interrupted conversation, he absolved her and refused to dispose of her fortune, giving no reasons for doing so.

Lisa's purity, her devotion to God and her ardent soul, impressed the monk deeply. He had desired long ago to renounce the world entirely; but the brotherhood, which drew a large income from his work as a preacher, insisted on his continuing his activity. He gave way, although he had a vague feeling that he was in a false position. It was rumoured that he was a miracle-working saint, whereas in reality he was a weak man, proud of his success in the world. When the soul of Lisa was revealed to him, he saw clearly into his own soul. He discovered how different he was to what he wanted to be, and realised the desire of his heart.

Soon after Lisa's visit he went to live in a separate cell as a hermit, and for three weeks did not officiate again in the church of the friary. After the celebration of the mass, he preached a sermon denouncing his own sins and those of the world, and urging all to repent.

From that day he preached every fortnight, and his sermons attracted increasing audiences. His fame as a preacher spread abroad. His sermons were extraordinarily fearless and sincere, and deeply impressed all who listened to him.

XII

Vassily was actually carrying out the object he had in leaving the prison. With the help of a few friends he broke into the house of the rich merchant Krasnopuzov, whom he knew to be a miser and a debauchee. Vassily took out of his writing-desk thirty thousand roubles, and began disposing of them as he thought right. He even gave up drink, so as not to spend that money on himself, but to distribute it to the poor; helping poor girls to get married; paying off people's debts, and doing this all without ever revealing himself to those he helped; his only desire was to distribute his money in the right way. As he also gave bribes to the police, he was left in peace for a long time.

His heart was singing for joy. When at last he was arrested and put to trial, he confessed with pride that he had robbed the fat merchant. "The money," he said, "was lying idle in that fool's desk, and he did not even know how much he had, whereas I have put it into circulation and helped a lot of good people."

The counsel for the defence spoke with such good humour and kindness that the jury felt inclined to discharge Vassily, but sentenced him nevertheless to confinement in prison. He thanked the jury, and assured them that he would find his way out of prison before long.

XIII

Natalia Ivanovna Sventizky's telegram proved useless. The committee appointed to deal with the petitions in the Emperor's name, decided not even to make a report to the Czar. But one day when the Sventizky case was discussed at the Emperor's luncheon-table, the chairman of the committee, who was present, mentioned the telegram which had been received from Sventizky's widow.

"*C'est très gentil de sa part,*" said one of the ladies of the imperial family.

The Emperor sighed, shrugged his shoulders, adorned with epaulettes. "The law," he said; and raised his glass for the groom of the chamber to pour out some Moselle.

All those present pretended to admire the wisdom of the sovereign's words. There was no further question about the telegram. The two peasants, the old man and the young boy, were hanged by a Tartar hangman from Kazan, a cruel convict and a murderer.

The old man's wife wanted to dress the body of her husband in a white shirt, with white bands which serve as stockings, and new boots, but she was not allowed to do so. The two men were buried together in the same pit outside the churchyard wall.

"Princess Sofia Vladimirovna tells me he is a very remarkable preacher," remarked the old Empress, the Emperor's mother, one day to her son: "*Faites le venir. Il peut precher à la cathédrale.*"

"No, it would be better in the palace church," said the Emperor, and ordered the hermit Isidor to be invited.

All the generals, and other high officials, assembled in the church of the imperial palace; it was an event to hear the famous preacher.

A thin and grey old man appeared, looked at those present, and said: "In the name of God, the Son, and the Holy Ghost," and began to speak.

At first all went well, but the longer he spoke the worse it became. *"Il devient de plus en plus aggressif,"* as the Empress put it afterwards. He fulminated against every one. He spoke about the executions and charged the government with having made so many necessary. How can the government of a Christian country kill men?

Everybody looked at everybody else, thinking of the bad taste of the sermon, and how unpleasant it must be for the Emperor to listen to it; but nobody expressed these thoughts aloud.

When Isidor had said Amen, the metropolitan approached, and asked him to call on him.

After Isidor had had a talk with the metropolitan and with the attorney-general, he was immediately sent away to a friary, not his own, but one at Suzdal, which had a prison attached to it; the prior of that friary was now Father Missael.

XIV

Every one tried to look as if Isidor's sermon contained nothing unpleasant, and nobody mentioned it. It seemed to the Czar that the hermit's words had not made any impression on himself; but once or twice during that day he caught himself thinking of the two peasants who had been hanged, and the widow of Sventizky who had asked an amnesty for them. That day the Emperor had to be present at a parade; after which he went out for a drive; a reception of ministers came next, then dinner, after dinner the theatre. As usual, the Czar fell asleep the moment his head touched the pillow. In the night an awful dream awoke him: he saw gallows in a large field and corpses dangling on them; the tongues of the corpses were protruding, and their bodies moved and shook. And somebody shouted, "It is you— you who have done it." The Czar woke up bathed in perspiration and began to think. It was the first time that he had ever thought of the responsibilities which weighed on him, and the words of old Isidor came back to his mind. . . .

But only dimly could he see himself as a mere human being, and he could not consider his mere human wants and duties, because of all that was required of him as Czar. As to acknowledging that human

duties were more obligatory than those of a Czar—he had not strength
for that.

XV

Having served his second term in the prison, Prokofy, who had
formerly worked on the Sventizky estate, was no longer the brisk,
ambitious, smartly dressed fellow he had been. He seemed, on the
contrary, a complete wreck. When sober he would sit idle and
would refuse to do any work, however much his father scolded
him; moreover, he was continually seeking to get hold of something
secretly, and take it to the public-house for a drink. When he came
home he would continue to sit idle, coughing and spitting all the
time. The doctor on whom he called, examined his chest and shook
his head.

"You, my man, ought to have many things which you have not
got."

"That is usually the case, isn't it?"

"Take plenty of milk, and don't smoke."

"These are days of fasting, and besides we have no cow."

Once in spring he could not get any sleep; he was longing to have
a drink. There was nothing in the house he could lay his hand on to
take to the public-house. He put on his cap and went out. He walked
along the street up to the house where the priest and the deacon
lived together. The deacon's harrow stood outside leaning against
the hedge. Prokofy approached, took the harrow upon his shoulder,
and walked to an inn kept by a woman, Petrovna. She might give
him a small bottle of vodka for it. But he had hardly gone a few steps
when the deacon came out of his house. It was already dawn, and
he saw that Prokofy was carrying away his harrow.

"Hey, what's that?" cried the deacon.

The neighbours rushed out from their houses. Prokofy was seized,
brought to the police station, and then sentenced to eleven months'
imprisonment. It was autumn, and Prokofy had to be transferred to
the prison hospital. He was coughing badly; his chest was heaving
from the exertion; and he could not get warm. Those who were
stronger contrived not to shiver; Prokofy on the contrary shivered
day and night, as the superintendent would not light the fires in the
hospital till November, to save expense.

Prokofy suffered greatly in body, and still more in soul. He was
disgusted with his surroundings, and hated every one—the deacon,

the superintendent who would not light the fires, the guard, and the man who was lying in the bed next to his, and who had a swollen red lip. He began also to hate the new convict who was brought into hospital. This convict was Stepan. He was suffering from some disease on his head, and was transferred to the hospital and put in a bed at Prokofy's side. After a time that hatred to Stepan changed, and Prokofy became, on the contrary, extremely fond of him; he delighted in talking to him. It was only after a talk with Stepan that his anguish would cease for a while. Stepan always told every one he met about his last murder, and how it had impressed him.

"Far from shrieking, or anything of that kind," he said to Prokofy, "she did not move. 'Kill me! There I am,' she said. 'But it is not my soul you destroy, it is your own.'"

"Well, of course, it is very dreadful to kill. I had one day to slaughter a sheep, and even that made me half mad. I have not destroyed any living soul; why then do those villains kill me? I have done no harm to anybody . . ."

"That will be taken into consideration."

"By whom?"

"By God, to be sure."

"I have not seen anything yet showing that God exists, and I don't believe in Him, brother. I think when a man dies, grass will grow over the spot, and that is the end of it."

"You are wrong to think like that. I have murdered so many people, whereas she, poor soul, was helping everybody. And you think she and I are to have the same lot? Oh no! Only wait."

"Then you believe the soul lives on after a man is dead?"

"To be sure; it truly lives."

Prokofy suffered greatly when death drew near. He could hardly breathe. But in the very last hour he felt suddenly relieved from all pain. He called Stepan to him. "Farewell, brother," he said. "Death has come, I see. I was so afraid of it before. And now I don't mind. I only wish it to come quicker."

XVI

In the meanwhile, the affairs of Eugene Mihailovich had grown worse and worse. Business was very slack. There was a new shop in the town; he was losing his customers, and the interest had to be paid. He borrowed again on interest. At last his shop and his goods were to be sold up. Eugene Mihailovich and his wife applied to every one they knew, but they could not raise the four hundred roubles they needed to save the shop anywhere.

They had some hope of the merchant Krasnopuzov, Eugene Mihailovich's wife being on good terms with his mistress. But news came that Krasnopuzov had been robbed of a huge sum of money. Some said of half a million roubles. "And do you know who is said to be the thief?" said Eugene Mihailovich to his wife. "Vassily, our former yard-porter. They say he is squandering the money, and the police are bribed by him."

"I knew he was a villain. You remember how he did not mind perjuring himself? But I did not expect it would go so far."

"I hear he has recently been in the courtyard of our house. Cook says she is sure it was he. She told me he helps poor girls to get married."

"They always invent tales. I don't believe it."

At that moment a strange man, shabbily dressed, entered the shop.

"What is it you want?"

"Here is a letter for you."

"From whom?"

"You will see yourself."

"Don't you require an answer? Wait a moment."

"I cannot." The strange man handed the letter and disappeared.

"How extraordinary!" said Eugene Mihailovich, and tore open the envelope. To his great amazement several hundred rouble notes fell out. "Four hundred roubles!" he exclaimed, hardly believing his eyes. "What does it mean?"

The envelope also contained a badly-spelt letter, addressed to Eugene Mihailovich. "It is said in the Gospels," ran the letter, "do good for evil. You have done me much harm; and in the coupon case you made me wrong the peasants greatly. But I have pity for you. Here are four hundred notes. Take them, and remember your porter Vassily."

"Very extraordinary!" said Eugene Mihailovich to his wife and to himself. And each time He remembered that incident, or spoke about it to his wife, tears would come to his eyes.

XVII

Fourteen priests were kept in the Suzdal friary prison, chiefly for having been untrue to the orthodox faith. Isidor had been sent to that place also. Father Missael received him according to the instructions he had been given, and without talking to him ordered him to be put into a separate cell as a serious criminal. After a fortnight Father Missael, making a round of the prison, entered Isidor's cell, and asked him whether there was anything he wished for.

"There is a great deal I wish for," answered Isidor; "but I cannot tell you what it is in the presence of anybody else. Let me talk to you privately."

They looked at each other, and Missael saw he had nothing to be afraid of in remaining alone with Isidor. He ordered Isidor to be brought into his own room, and when they were alone, he said,—

"Well, now you can speak."

Isidor fell on his knees.

"Brother," said Isidor. "What are you doing to yourself! Have mercy on your own soul. You are the worst villain in the world. You have offended against all that is sacred . . ."

A month after Missael sent a report, asking that Isidor should be released as he had repented, and he also asked for the release of the rest of the prisoners. After which he resigned his post.

XVIII

Ten years passed. Mitia Smokovnikov had finished his studies in the Technical College; he was now an engineer in the gold mines in Siberia, and was very highly paid. One day he was about to make a round in the district. The governor offered him a convict, Stepan Pelageushkine, to accompany him on his journey.

"A convict, you say? But is not that dangerous?"

"Not if it is this one. He is a holy man. You may ask anybody, they will all tell you so."

"Why has he been sent here?"

The governor smiled. "He had committed six murders, and yet he is a holy man. I go bail for him."

Mitia Smokovnikov took Stepan, now a baldheaded, lean, tanned man, with him on his journey. On their way Stepan took care of Smokovnikov like his own child, and told him his story; told him why he had been sent here, and what now filled his life.

And, strange to say, Mitia Smokovnikov, who up to that time used to spend his time drinking, eating, and gambling, began for the first time to meditate on life. These thoughts never left him now, and produced a complete change in his habits. After a time he was offered a very advantageous position. He refused it, and made up his mind to buy an estate with the money he had, to marry, and to devote himself to the peasantry, helping them as much as he could.

XIX

He carried out his intentions. But before retiring to his estate he called on his father, with whom he had been on bad terms, and who had settled apart with his new family. Mitia Smokovnikov wanted to make it up. The old man wondered at first, and laughed at the change he noticed in his son; but after a while he ceased to find fault with him, and thought of the many times when it was he who was the guilty one.

AFTER THE DANCE

"—AND YOU SAY that a man cannot, of himself, understand what is good and evil; that it is all environment, that the environment swamps the man. But I believe it is all chance. Take my own case . . ."

Thus spoke our excellent friend, Ivan Vasilievich, after a conversation between us on the impossibility of improving individual character without a change of the conditions under which men live. Nobody had actually said that one could not of oneself understand good and evil; but it was a habit of Ivan Vasilievich to answer in this way the thoughts aroused in his own mind by conversation, and to illustrate those thoughts by relating incidents in his own life. He often quite forgot the reason for his story in telling it; but he always told it with great sincerity and feeling.

He did so now.

"Take my own case. My whole life was moulded, not by environment, but by something quite different."

"By what, then?" we asked.

"Oh, that is a long story. I should have to tell you about a great many things to make you understand."

"Well, tell us then."

Ivan Vasilievich thought a little, and shook his head.

"My whole life," he said, "was changed in one night, or, rather, morning."

"Why, what happened?" one of us asked.

"What happened was that I was very much in love. I have been in love many times, but this was the most serious of all. It is a thing of the past; she has married daughters now. It was Varinka B——." Ivan Vasilievich mentioned her surname. "Even at fifty she is remarkably handsome; but in her youth, at eighteen, she was exquisite—tall, slender, graceful, and stately. Yes, stately is the word; she held herself very erect, by instinct as it were; and carried her head high, and that together with her beauty and height gave her a queenly air in spite of being thin, even bony one might say. It might indeed have been deterring had it not been for her smile, which was always gay and cordial, and for the charming light in her eyes and for her youthful sweetness."

"What an entrancing description you give, Ivan Vasilievich!"

"Description, indeed! I could not possibly describe her so that you could appreciate her. But that does not matter; what I am going to tell you happened in the forties. I was at that time a student in a provincial university. I don't know whether it was a good thing or no, but we had no political clubs, no theories in our universities then. We were simply young and spent our time as young men do, studying and amusing ourselves. I was a very gay, lively, careless fellow, and had plenty of money too. I had a fine horse, and used to go tobogganing with the young ladies. Skating had not yet come into fashion. I went to drinking parties with my comrades—in those days we drank nothing but champagne—if we had no champagne we drank nothing at all. We never drank vodka, as they do now. Evening parties and balls were my favourite amusements. I danced well, and was not an ugly fellow."

"Come, there is no need to be modest," interrupted a lady near him. "We have seen your photograph. Not ugly, indeed! You were a handsome fellow."

"Handsome, if you like. That does not matter. When my love for her was at its strongest, on the last day of the carnival, I was at a ball at the provincial marshal's, a good-natured old man, rich and hospitable, and a court chamberlain. The guests were welcomed by his wife, who was as good-natured as himself. She was dressed in puce-coloured velvet, and had a diamond diadem on her forehead, and her plump, old white shoulders and bosom were bare like the portraits of Empress Elizabeth, the daughter of Peter the Great.

"It was a delightful ball. It was a splendid room, with a gallery for the orchestra, which was famous at the time, and consisted of serfs belonging to a musical landowner. The refreshments were magnificent, and the champagne flowed in rivers. Though I was fond of champagne I did not drink that night, because without it I was drunk with love. But I made up for it by dancing waltzes and polkas till I was ready to drop—of course, whenever possible, with Varinka. She wore a white dress with a pink sash, white shoes, and white kid gloves, which did not quite reach to her thin pointed elbows. A disgusting engineer named Anisimov robbed me of the mazurka with her—to this day I cannot forgive him. He asked her for the dance the minute she arrived, while I had driven to the hairdresser's to get a pair of gloves, and was late. So I did not dance the mazurka with her, but with a German girl to whom I had previously paid a little attention; but I am afraid I did not behave very politely to her that evening. I hardly spoke or looked at her, and saw nothing but the tall, slender figure in a white dress, with a pink sash, a flushed, beaming, dimpled face, and sweet, kind eyes. I was not alone; they were all looking at her with admiration, the men and women alike, although she outshone all of them. They could not help admiring her.

"Although I was not nominally her partner for the mazurka, I did as a matter of fact dance nearly the whole time with her. She always came forward boldly the whole length of the room to pick me out I flew to meet her without waiting to be chosen, and she thanked me with a smile for my intuition. When I was brought up to her with somebody else, and she guessed wrongly, she took the other man's hand with a shrug of her slim shoulders, and smiled at me regretfully.

"Whenever there was a waltz figure in the mazurka, I waltzed with her for a long time, and breathing fast and smiling, she would say, *'Encore';* and I went on waltzing and waltzing, as though unconscious of any bodily existence."

"Come now, how could you be unconscious of it with your arm round her waist? You must have been conscious, not only of your own existence, but of hers," said one of the party.

Ivan Vasilievich cried out, almost shouting in anger: "There you are, moderns all over! Nowadays you think of nothing but the body. It was different in our day. The more I was in love the less corporeal was she in my eyes. Nowadays you think of nothing but the body. It was different in our day. The more I was in love the less corporeal was she in my eyes. Nowadays you see legs, ankles, and I don't know what. You undress the women you are in love with. In my eyes, as Alphonse Karr said—and he was a good writer—'the one I loved was always draped in robes of bronze.' We never thought of doing so; we tried to veil her nakedness, like Noah's good-natured son. Oh, well, you can't understand."

"Don't pay any attention to him. Go on," said one of them.

"Well, I danced for the most part with her, and did not notice how time was passing. The musicians kept playing the same mazurka tunes over and over again in desperate exhaustion—you know what it is towards the end of a ball. Papas and mammas were already getting up from the card-tables in the drawing-room in expectation of supper, the men-servants were running to and fro bringing in things. It was nearly three o'clock. I had to make the most of the last minutes. I chose her again for the mazurka, and for the hundredth time we danced across the room.

"'The quadrille after supper is mine,' I said, taking her to her place.

"'Of course, if I am not carried off home,' she said, with a smile.

"'I won't give you up,' I said.

"'Give me my fan, anyhow,' she answered.

"'I am so sorry to part with it,' I said, handing her a cheap white fan.

"'Well, here's something to console you,' she said, plucking a feather out of the fan, and giving it to me.

"I took the feather, and could only express my rapture and gratitude with my eyes. I was not only pleased and gay, I was happy, delighted; I was good, I was not myself but some being not of this earth, knowing nothing of evil. I hid the feather in my glove, and stood there unable to tear myself away from her.

"'Look, they are urging father to dance,' she said to me, pointing to the tall, stately figure of her father, a colonel with silver epaulettes, who was standing in the doorway with some ladies.

"'Varinka, come here!' exclaimed our hostess, the lady with the diamond *ferronnière* and with shoulders like Elizabeth, in a loud voice.

"Varinka went to the door, and I followed her.

"'Persuade your father to dance the mazurka with you, *ma chère*.—Do, please, Peter Valdislavovich,' she said, turning to the colonel.

"Varinka's father was a very handsome, well-preserved old man. He had a good colour, moustaches curled in the style of Nicolas I., and white whiskers which met the moustaches. His hair was combed on to his forehead, and a bright smile, like his daughter's, was on his lips and in his eyes. He was splendidly set up, with a broad military chest, on which he wore some decorations, and he had powerful shoulders and long slim legs. He was that ultra-military type produced by the discipline of Emperor Nicolas I.

"When we approached the door the colonel was just refusing to dance, saying that he had quite forgotten how; but at that instant he smiled, swung his arm gracefully around to the left, drew his sword from its sheath, handed it to an obliging young man who stood near, and smoothed his suède glove on his right hand.

"'Everything must be done according to rule,' he said with a smile. He took the hand of his daughter, and stood one-quarter turned, waiting for the music.

"At the first sound of the mazurka, he stamped one foot smartly, threw the other forward, and, at first slowly and smoothly, then buoyantly and impetuously, with stamping of feet and clicking of boots, his tall, imposing figure moved the length of the room. Varinka swayed gracefully beside him, rhythmically and easily, making her steps short or long, with her little feet in their white satin slippers.

"All the people in the room followed every movement of the couple. As for me I not only admired, I regarded them with enraptured sympathy. I was particularly impressed with the old gentleman's boots. They were not the modern pointed affairs, but were made of cheap leather, squared-toed, and evidently built by the regimental cobbler. In order that his daughter might dress and go out in society, he did not buy fashionable boots, but wore home-made ones, I thought, and his square toes seemed to me most touching. It was obvious that in his time he had been a good dancer; but now he was too heavy, and his legs had not spring enough for all the beautiful steps he tried to take. Still, he contrived to go twice round the room. When at the end, standing with legs apart, he suddenly clicked his feet together and fell on one knee, a bit heavily, and she danced gracefully around him, smiling and adjusting her skirt, the whole room applauded.

"Rising with an effort, he tenderly took his daughter's face between his hands. He kissed her on the forehead, and brought her to me, under the impression that I was her partner for the mazurka. I said I was not. 'Well, never mind. Just go around the room once with her,' he said, smiling kindly, as he replaced his sword in the sheath.

"As the contents of a bottle flow readily when the first drop has been poured, so my love for Varinka seemed to set free the whole force of loving within me. In surrounding her it embraced the world. I loved the hostess with her diadem and her shoulders like Elizabeth, and her husband and her guests and her footmen, and even the engineer Anisimov who felt peevish towards me. As for Varinka's father, with his home-made boots and his kind smile, so like her own, I felt a sort of tenderness for him that was almost rapture.

"After supper I danced the promised quadrille with her, and though I had been infinitely happy before, I grew still happier every moment.

"We did not speak of love. I neither asked myself nor her whether she loved me. It was quite enough to know that I loved her. And I had only one fear—that something might come to interfere with my great joy.

"When I went home, and began to undress for the night, I found it quite out of the question. I held the little feather out of her fan in my hand, and one of her gloves which she gave me when I helped her into the carriage after her mother. Looking at these things, and without closing my eyes I could see her before me as she was for an instant when she had to choose between two partners. She tried to guess what kind of person was represented in me, and I could hear her sweet voice as she said, 'Pride—am I right?' and merrily gave me her hand. At supper she took the first sip from my glass of champagne, looking at me over the rim with her caressing glance. But, plainest of all, I could see her as she danced with her father, gliding along beside him, and looking at the admiring observers with pride and happiness.

"He and she were united in my mind in one rush of pathetic tenderness.

"I was living then with my brother, who has since died. He disliked going out, and never went to dances; and besides, he was busy preparing for his last university examinations, and was leading a very regular life. He was asleep. I looked at him, his head buried in the pillow and half covered with the quilt; and I affectionately pitied him—pitied him for his ignorance of the bliss I was experiencing. Our serf Petrusha had met me with a candle, ready to undress me, but I sent him away. His sleepy face and tousled hair seemed to me so touching. Trying not to make a noise, I went to my room on tiptoe and sat down on my bed. No, I was too happy; I could not sleep. Besides, it was too hot in the rooms. Without taking off my uniform, I went quietly into the hall, put on my overcoat, opened the front door and stepped out into the street.

"It was after four when I had left the ball; going home and stopping there a while had occupied two hours, so by the time I went out it was dawn. It was regular carnival weather—foggy, and the road full of water-soaked snow just melting, and water dripping from the eaves. Varinka's family lived on the edge of town near a large field, one end of which was a parade ground: at the other end was a boarding-school for young ladies. I passed through our empty little street and came to the main thoroughfare, where I met pedestrians and sledges laden with wood, the runners grating the road. The horses swung with regular paces beneath their shining yokes, their backs covered with straw mats and their heads wet with rain;

while the drivers, in enormous boots, splashed through the mud beside the sledges. All this, the very horses themselves, seemed to me stimulating and fascinating, full of suggestion.

"When I approached the field near their house, I saw at one end of it, in the direction of the parade ground, something very huge and black, and I heard sounds of fife and drum proceeding from it. My heart had been full of song, and I had heard in imagination the tune of the mazurka, but this was very harsh music. It was not pleasant.

"'What can that be?' I thought, and went towards the sound by a slippery path through the centre of the field. Walking about a hundred paces, I began to distinguish many black objects through the mist. They were evidently soldiers. 'It is probably a drill,' I thought.

"So I went along in that direction in company with a blacksmith, who wore a dirty coat and an apron, and was carrying something. He walked ahead of me as we approached the place. The soldiers in black uniforms stood in two rows, facing each other motionless, their guns at rest. Behind them stood the fifes and drums, incessantly repeating the same unpleasant tune.

"'What are they doing?' I asked the blacksmith, who halted at my side.

"'A Tartar is being beaten through the ranks for his attempt to desert,' said the blacksmith in an angry tone, as he looked intently at the far end of the line.

"I looked in the same direction, and saw between the files something horrid approaching me. The thing that approached was a man, stripped to the waist, fastened with cords to the guns of two soldiers who were leading him. At his side an officer in overcoat and cap was walking, whose figure had a familiar look. The victim advanced under the blows that rained upon him from both sides, his whole body plunging, his feet dragging through the snow. Now he threw himself backward, and the subalterns who led him thrust him forward. Now he fell forward, and they pulled him up short; while ever at his side marched the tall officer, with firm and nervous pace. It was Varinka's father, with his rosy face and white moustache.

"At each stroke the man, as if amazed, turned his face, grimacing with pain, towards the side whence the blow came, and showing his white teeth repeated the same words over and over. But I could only hear what the words were when he came quite near. He did not speak them, he sobbed them out,—

"'Brothers, have mercy on me! Brothers, have mercy on me!' But the brothers had no mercy, and when the procession came close to me, I saw how a soldier who stood opposite me took a firm step forward and lifting his stick with a whirr, brought it down upon the man's back. The man plunged forward, but the subalterns pulled him back, and another blow came down from the other side, then from this side and then from the other. The colonel marched beside him, and looking now at his feet and now at the man, inhaled the air, puffed out his cheeks, and breathed it out between his protruded lips. When they passed the place where I stood, I caught a glimpse between the two files of the back of the man that was being punished. It was something so many-coloured, wet, red, unnatural, that I could hardly believe it was a human body.

"'My God!' muttered the blacksmith.

"The procession moved farther away. The blows continued to rain upon the writhing, falling creature; the fifes shrilled and the drums beat, and the tall imposing figure of the colonel moved alongside the man, just as before. Then, suddenly, the colonel stopped, and rapidly approached a man in the ranks.

"'I'll teach you to hit him gently,' I heard his furious voice say. 'Will you pat him like that? Will you?' and I saw how his strong hand in the suede glove struck the weak, bloodless, terrified soldier for not bringing down his stick with sufficient strength on the red neck of the Tartar.

"'Bring new sticks!' he cried, and looking round, he saw me. Assuming an air of not knowing me, and with a ferocious, angry frown, he hastily turned away. I felt so utterly ashamed that I didn't know where to look. It was as if I had been detected in a disgraceful act. I dropped my eyes, and quickly hurried home. All the way I had the drums beating and the fifes whistling in my ears. And I heard the words, 'Brothers, have mercy on me!' or 'Will you pat him? Will you?' My heart was full of physical disgust that was almost sickness. So much so that I halted several times on my way, for I had the feeling that I was going to be really sick from all the horrors that possessed me at that sight. I do not remember how I got home and got to bed. But the moment I was about to fall asleep I heard and saw again all that had happened, and I sprang up.

"'Evidently he knows something I do not know,' I thought about the colonel. 'If I knew what he knows I should certainly grasp—understand—what I have just seen, and it would not cause me such suffering.'

"But however much I thought about it, I could not understand the thing that the colonel knew. It was evening before I could get to sleep, and then only after calling on a friend and drinking till I was quite drunk.

"Do you think I had come to the conclusion that the deed I had witnessed was wicked? Oh, no. Since it was done with such assurance, and was recognised by every one as indispensable, they doubtless knew something which I did not know. So I thought, and tried to understand. But no matter, I could never understand it, then or afterwards. And not being able to grasp it, I could not enter the service as I had intended. I don't mean only the military service: I did not enter the Civil Service either. And so I have been of no use whatever, as you can see."

"Yes, we know how useless you've been," said one of us. "Tell us, rather, how many people would be of any use at all if it hadn't been for you."

"Oh, that's utter nonsense," said Ivan Vasilievich, with genuine annoyance.

"Well; and what about the love affair?"

"My love? It decreased from that day. When, as often happened, she looked dreamy and meditative, I instantly recollected the colonel on the parade ground, and I felt so awkward and uncomfortable that I began to see her less frequently. So my love came to naught. Yes; such chances arise, and they alter and direct a man's whole life," he said in summing up. "And you say . . ."

ALYOSHA THE POT

ALYOSHA WAS THE younger brother. He was called the Pot, because his mother had once sent him with a pot of milk to the deacon's wife, and he had stumbled against something and broken it. His mother had beaten him, and the children had teased him. Since then he was nicknamed the Pot. Alyosha was a tiny, thin little fellow, with ears like wings, and a huge nose. "Alyosha has a nose that looks like a dog on a hill!" the children used to call after him. Alyosha went to the village school, but was not good at lessons; besides, there was so little time to learn. His elder brother was in town, working for a merchant, so Alyosha had to help his father from a very early age. When he was no more than six he used to go out with the girls to watch the cows and sheep in the pasture, and a little later he looked after the horses by day and by night. And at twelve years of age he had already begun to plough and to drive the cart. The skill was there though the strength was not. He was always cheerful. Whenever the children made fun of him, he would either laugh or be silent When his father scolded him he would stand mute and listen attentively, and as soon as the scolding was over would smile and go on with his work. Alyosha was nineteen when his brother was taken as a soldier. So his father placed him with the merchant as a yard-porter. He was given his brother's old boots, his father's old coat and cap, and was taken to town. Alyosha was delighted with his clothes, but the merchant was not impressed by his appearance.

"I thought you would bring me a man in Simeon's place," he said, scanning Alyosha; "and you've brought me *this!* What's the good of him?"

"He can do everything; look after horses and drive. He's a good one to work. He looks rather thin, but he's tough enough. And he's very willing."

"He looks it. All right; we'll see what we can do with him."

So Alyosha remained at the merchant's.

The family was not a large one. It consisted of the merchant's wife: her old mother: a married son poorly educated who was in his father's business: another son, a learned one who had finished school and entered the University, but having been expelled, was living at home: and a daughter who still went to school.

They did not take to Alyosha at first. He was uncouth, badly dressed, and had no manner, but they soon got used to him. Alyosha worked even better than his brother had done; he was really very willing. They sent him on all sorts of errands, but he did everything quickly and readily, going from one task to another without stopping. And so here, just as at home, all the work was put upon his shoulders. The more he did, the more he was given to do. His mistress, her old mother, the son, the daughter, the clerk, and the cook—all ordered him about, and sent him from one place to another.

"Alyosha, do this! Alyosha, do that! What! have you forgotten, Alyosha? Mind you don't forget, Alyosha!" was heard from morning till night. And Alyosha ran here, looked after this and that, forgot nothing, found time for everything, and was always cheerful.

His brother's old boots were soon worn out, and his master scolded him for going about in tatters with his toes sticking out. He ordered another pair to be bought for him in the market. Alyosha was delighted with his new boots, but was angry with his feet when they ached at the end of the day after so much running about. And then he was afraid that his father would be annoyed when he came to town for his wages, to find that his master had deducted the cost of the boots.

In the winter Alyosha used to get up before daybreak. He would chop the wood, sweep the yard, feed the cows and horses, light the stoves, clean the boots, prepare the samovars and polish them afterwards; or the clerk would get him to bring up the goods; or the cook would set him to knead the bread and clean the saucepans. Then he was sent to town on various errands, to bring the daughter home from school, or to get some olive oil for the old mother. "Why the devil have you been so long?" first one, then another, would say to him. Why should they go? Alyosha can go. "Alyosha! Alyosha!" And Alyosha ran here and there. He breakfasted in snatches while he was working, and rarely managed to get his dinner at the proper hour. The cook used to scold him for being late, but she was sorry for him all the same, and would keep something hot for his dinner and supper.

At holiday times there was more work than ever, but Alyosha liked holidays because everybody gave him a tip. Not much certainly, but it would amount up to about sixty kopeks [1s 2d]—his very own money. For Alyosha never set eyes on his wages. His father used to come and take them from the merchant, and only scold Alyosha for wearing out his boots.

When he had saved up two roubles [4s], by the advice of the cook he bought himself a red knitted jacket, and was so happy when he put it on, that he couldn't close his mouth for joy. Alyosha was not talkative; when he spoke at all, he spoke abruptly, with his head turned away. When told to do anything, or asked if he could do it, he would say yes without the smallest hesitation, and set to work at once.

Alyosha did not know any prayer; and had forgotten what his mother had taught him. But he prayed just the same, every morning and every evening, prayed with his hands, crossing himself.

He lived like this for about a year and a half, and towards the end of the second year a most startling thing happened to him. He discovered one day, to his great surprise, that, in addition to the relation of usefulness existing between people, there was also another, a peculiar relation of quite a different character. Instead of a man being wanted to clean boots, and go on errands and harness horses, he is not wanted to be of any service at all, but another human being wants to serve him and pet him. Suddenly Alyosha felt he was such a man.

He made this discovery through the cook Ustinia. She was young, had no parents, and worked as hard as Alyosha. He felt for the first time in his life that he—not his services, but he himself—was necessary to another human being. When his mother used to be sorry for him, he had taken no notice of her. It had seemed to him quite natural, as though he were feeling sorry for himself. But here was Ustinia, a perfect stranger, and sorry for him. She would save him some hot porridge, and sit watching him, her chin propped on her bare arm, with the sleeve rolled up, while he was eating it. When he looked at her she would begin to laugh, and he would laugh too.

This was such a new, strange thing to him that it frightened Alyosha. He feared that it might interfere with his work. But he was pleased, nevertheless, and when he glanced at the trousers that Ustinia had mended for him, he would shake his head and smile. He would often think of her while at work, or when running on errands. "A fine girl, Ustinia!" he sometimes exclaimed.

Ustinia used to help him whenever she could, and he helped her. She told him all about her life; how she had lost her parents; how her aunt had taken her in and found a place for her in the town; how the merchant's son had tried to take liberties with her, and how she had rebuffed him. She liked to talk, and Alyosha liked to listen to her. He had heard that peasants who came up to work in the towns frequently got married to servant girls. On one occasion she asked him if his parents intended marrying him soon. He said that he did not know; that he did not want to marry any of the village girls.

"Have you taken a fancy to some one, then?"

"I would marry you, if you'd be willing."

"Get along with you, Alyosha the Pot; but you've found your tongue, haven't you?" she exclaimed, slapping him on the back with a towel she held in her hand. "Why shouldn't I?"

At Shrovetide Alyosha's father came to town for his wages. It had come to the ears of the merchant's wife that Alyosha wanted to marry Ustinia, and she disapproved of it. "What will be the use of her with a baby?" she thought, and informed her husband.

The merchant gave the old man Alyosha's wages.

"How is my lad getting on?" he asked. "I told you he was willing."

"That's all right, as far as it goes, but he's taken some sort of nonsense into his head. He wants to marry our cook. Now I don't approve of married servants. We won't have them in the house."

"Well, now, who would have thought the fool would think of such a thing?" the old man exclaimed. "But don't you worry. I'll soon settle that."

He went into the kitchen, and sat down at the table waiting for his son. Alyosha was out on an errand, and came back breathless.

"I thought you had some sense in you; but what's this you've taken into your head?" his father began.

"I? Nothing."

"How, nothing? They tell me you want to get married. You shall get married when the time comes. I'll find you a decent wife, not some town hussy."

His father talked and talked, while Alyosha stood still and sighed. When his father had quite finished, Alyosha smiled.

"All right. I'll drop it,"

"Now that's what I call sense."

When he was left alone with Ustinia he told her what his father had said. (She had listened at the door.)

"It's no good; it can't come off. Did you hear? He was angry—won't have it at any price."

Ustinia cried into her apron.

Alyosha shook his head.

"What's to be done? We must do as we're told."

"Well, are you going to give up that nonsense, as your father told you?" his mistress asked, as he was putting up the shutters in the evening.

"To be sure we are," Alyosha replied with a smile, and then burst into tears.

From that day Alyosha went about his work as usual, and no longer talked to Ustinia about their getting married. One day in Lent the clerk told him to clear the snow from the roof. Alyosha climbed on to the roof and swept away all the snow; and, while he was still raking out some frozen lumps from the gutter, his foot slipped and he fell over. Unfortunately he did not fall on the snow, but on a piece of iron over the door. Ustinia came running up, together with the merchant's daughter.

"Have you hurt yourself, Alyosha?"

"Ah! no, it's nothing."

But he could not raise himself when he tried to, and began to smile.

He was taken into the lodge. The doctor arrived, examined him, and asked where he felt the pain.

"I feel it all over," he said. "But it doesn't matter. I'm only afraid master will be annoyed. Father ought to be told."

Alyosha lay in bed for two days, and on the third day they sent for the priest.

"Are you really going to die?" Ustinia asked.

"Of course I am. You can't go on living for ever. You must go when the time comes." Alyosha spoke rapidly as usual. "Thank you, Ustina. You've been very good to me. What a lucky thing they didn't let us marry! Where should we have been now? It's much better as it is."

When the priest came, he prayed with his hands and with his heart. "As it is good here when you obey and do no harm to others, so it will be there," was the thought within it.

He spoke very little; he only said he was thirsty, and he seemed full of wonder at something.

He lay in wonderment, then stretched himself, and died.